ALIEN
PERFECT
ORGANISMS

THE COMPLETE ALIEN™ LIBRARY FROM TITAN BOOKS

The Official Movie Novelizations
by Alan Dean Foster
Alien, Aliens™, Alien 3, Alien: Covenant,
Alien: Covenant Origins
Alien: Resurrection by A.C. Crispin
Alien 3: The Unproduced Screenplay
by William Gibson & Pat Cadigan

Alien
Out of the Shadows by Tim Lebbon
Sea of Sorrows by James A. Moore
River of Pain by Christopher Golden
The Cold Forge by Alex White
Isolation by Keith R.A. DeCandido
Prototype by Tim Waggoner
Into Charybdis by Alex White
Colony War by David Barnett
Inferno's Fall by Philippa Ballantine
Enemy of My Enemy by Mary SanGiovanni
Uncivil War by Brendan Deneen
Seventh Circle by Philippa Ballantine
and Clara Carija
Perfect Organisms by Shaun Hamill
Cult by Gavin G. Smith

The Complete Alien Collection
The Shadow Archive
Symphony of Death

The Rage War
by Tim Lebbon
Predator™: Incursion, Alien: Invasion
Alien vs. Predator™: Armageddon

Aliens
Bug Hunt edited by Jonathan Maberry
Phalanx by Scott Sigler
Infiltrator by Weston Ochse
Vasquez by V. Castro
Bishop by T. R. Napper

The Complete Aliens Collection
Living Nightmares

The Complete Aliens Omnibus
Volumes 1–7

Predator
If It Bleeds edited by Bryan Thomas Schmidt
The Predator by Christopher Golden
& Mark Morris
The Predator: Hunters and Hunted
by James A. Moore
Stalking Shadows by James A. Moore
& Mark Morris
Eyes of the Demon edited by
Bryan Thomas Schmidt
The Complete Predator Omnibus
by Nathan Archer & Sandy Scofield

Non-Fiction
AVP: Alien vs. Predator
by Alec Gillis & Tom Woodruff, Jr.
Aliens vs. Predator Requiem:
Inside The Monster Shop
by Alec Gillis & Tom Woodruff, Jr.
Alien: The Illustrated Story
by Archie Goodwin & Walter Simonson
The Art of Alien: Isolation by Andy McVittie
Alien: The Archive
Alien: The Weyland-Yutani Report
by S.D. Perry
Aliens: The Set Photography by Simon Ward
Alien: The Coloring Book
The Art and Making of Alien: Covenant
by Simon Ward
Alien Covenant: David's Drawings
by Dane Hallett & Matt Hatton
The Predator: The Art and Making
of the Film by James Nolan
The Making of Alien by J.W. Rinzler
Alien: The Blueprints by Graham Langridge
Alien: 40 Years 40 Artists
Alien: The Official Cookbook
by Chris-Rachael Oseland
Aliens: Artbook by Printed In Blood

Aliens vs. Predators
Ultimate Prey edited by Jonathan Maberry
& Bryan Thomas Schmidt
Rift War by Weston Ochse & Yvonne Navarro
The Complete Aliens vs. Predator Omnibus by Steve Perry & S.D. Perry

ALIEN™
PERFECT ORGANISMS

A NOVEL BY SHAUN HAMILL

TITAN BOOKS

ALIEN™: PERFECT ORGANISMS
Print edition ISBN: 9781803360973
E-book edition ISBN: 9781803361895

Published by Titan Books
A division of Titan Publishing Group Ltd
144 Southwark Street, London SE1 0UP
www.titanbooks.com

First edition: October 2025
10 9 8 7 6 5 4 3 2 1

This is a work of fiction. All of the characters, organizations, and events portrayed in this novel are either products of the author's imagination or are used fictitiously. Any resemblance to actual persons, living or dead (except for satirical purposes), is entirely coincidental.

TM & © 2025 20th Century Studios

Shaun Hamill asserts the moral right to be identified as the author of this work.

No part of this publication may be reproduced, stored in a retrieval system, or transmitted, in any form or by any means without the prior written permission of the publisher, nor be otherwise circulated in any form of binding or cover other than that in which it is published and without a similar condition being imposed on the subsequent purchaser.

A CIP catalogue record for this title is available from the British Library.

EU RP (for authorities only)
eucomply OÜ, Pärnu mnt. 139b-14, 11317 Tallinn, Estonia
hello@eucompliancepartner.com, +3375690241

Printed and bound by CPI Group (UK) Ltd, Croydon CR0 4YY.

Dedicated, with love,
to The Jeckylloafs Fun Club: Chris, Brian, Rodie,
Darrel, Jessica, Andy, Cleveland, Sam, and Kurt

Our regular barkeeps at Dr. Jeckyll's Beer Lab:
Nathan, Natalie, and John

You all make Wednesday the best night of the week.

"No one understands the lonely perfection of my dreams."

DAVID, *ALIEN: COVENANT*

1

FRATTO

Another night meant another graveyard shift aboard the USS *Fratto*, watching the sensors on the mostly empty bridge, and that was fine with Corporal Jared Briscoe. Ever since boyhood, he'd preferred the late hours, and the quiet that came with them. During the day, you had officers and enlisted personnel filling the corridors with their chatter and nervous energy. At night, though, you could hear the ship's systems humming along. You could hear yourself think.

Unless you got a hard ass on the con, which Briscoe's CO, Lieutenant Diaz, definitely was *not*. At night nobody cared if you slouched at your station or stared into the middle distance for a while. Nobody noticed if you chewed your nails while you pondered the infinite.

Of course, 'night' and 'day' were relative terms in the vacuum of space. For Briscoe, this was part of the appeal, why he'd enlisted with the Colonial Marines. Sure, the military kept time, put on a façade of circadian rhythms—breakfast at this hour, dinner at this hour, day shift, night shift—but unless you were planetside, it was all pretend. All you had to do was look out any of the *Fratto*'s viewports and you'd find yourself face-to-face with endless night as far as you could see.

Fresh from the commissary with the night's second cup of coffee, Briscoe now re-settled into his station on the bridge, steaming mug in hand. He raised it to his lips and blew on its contents, sending tendrils of steam wafting through the air before him. He gave his monitors a cursory glance, saw nothing of note, then looked up, out the main viewport, at the spill of stars ahead, and, to his left, the planet hogging most of the view.

The planet appeared mostly gray from space. According to the data packets Briscoe had reviewed before deployment, there were large bodies of water down there, and mountains, and even verdant forests, but the view was usually obscured by frequent thunderstorms that raged across the surface.

This world was the *Fratto*'s assignment. Its alphanumeric designation was DSJ-1020, but most of the enlisted personnel (and a few officers, when they thought their superiors weren't listening) colloquially referred to it by the name of its one colony: 'New Providence.'

Briscoe pondered the mottled gray planet. He (and the *Fratto*) had been stationed here for six months, but he still wasn't sure why. The orders from above had been vague: *Fratto* was to orbit DSJ-1020 and prevent any other vessels from landing on or departing from the world. That was it. No explanations or reasoning had been offered, other than that the world was "under quarantine." Quarantine for what? Nobody seemed to know.

In the time since the *Fratto*'s arrival, not a single ship had appeared on the sensors, and there'd been no transmissions from below. Briscoe wasn't stupid. He knew *something* must have happened down there. Something that caused the colony to go radio silent. But when, in his off-time, he'd searched newsfeeds for keywords "DSJ-1020" and "New Providence," he'd found nothing. Nothing about a crisis, or an SOS, or an evacuation. Not even puff pieces about the founding of the colony.

That in itself didn't necessarily mean anything. After all, Briscoe had used the ship's systems to access the feeds; it would've been a simple matter for command to have blocked certain articles, or sites. For all he knew, there was a wealth of info out there on New Providence. He doubted it, though. After all, if New Providence were a mystery that the news orgs had presented for public consumption, there would've been visitors. Reporters looking to make their name, or looky-loos with nothing better to do. The *Fratto* would've been turning them away around the clock. No, whatever had happened down on New Providence, it had been kept quiet.

Command discouraged the crew from discussing the assignment, and reiterated this wish at least once every four weeks. At the last bridge crew meeting, Lieutenant Diaz had said, *Remember, you already know everything you need to know to do your job. If more information becomes necessary, I'll tell you. Until then, keep your head down and stay out of trouble.*

This hadn't stopped the enlisted grunts from running their mouths, of course. Even working the graveyard shift, Briscoe had heard a few rumors. The prevalent theories seemed to be a reactor meltdown, or some form of plague. Briscoe could understand and almost believe the former; a reactor failure would have wiped out all life on the colony in milliseconds. But then why send *Fratto* to guard the planet? That didn't make sense. The United Americas could just post a 'do not travel' warning for the planet and leave it at that. Was Weyland-Yutani that paranoid about people finding out the reactor had failed? Were they worried about bad public relations?

Still, the reactor made more sense to Briscoe than a plague. A contagious virus would have caused a panic on New Providence. There would be radio signals from the surface, begging for help. People would have tried to leave, to save themselves. The *Fratto* would've been tasked with shooting escaping ships out of the sky to prevent sickness from spreading across the galaxy. But the last six months, DSJ-1020 had been quiet as a tomb.

Maybe someone did that part before you got here, reasoned a little voice in the back of Briscoe's head.

Before he was able to pursue this particular line of thought, a chirping noise sounded from his station. He was so startled that he nearly dropped his coffee. It was a sound he hadn't heard once in the last six months: the *Fratto*'s sensors had just picked up another ship in the area.

Briscoe was so taken aback by this unexpected arrival that it took him a moment to remember the protocol. He hadn't been called upon to do more than drink coffee and stare into space for half a year. He set down his coffee now, glanced at the monitors, and frowned. The sensors were picking up the presence of another ship, but no additional data. That meant the new arrival was traveling with its transponder switched off, which could mean trouble.

Briscoe put on his headset and opened a comm channel.

"Unidentified craft," he said, "this is the USS *Fratto*. You have entered restricted space. Please identify yourself at once."

He sat and listened to the crackle of the open channel, waiting for the other ship to respond. The sensors reported the craft growing closer, but no one answered the hail.

Briscoe swallowed hard and sat forward in his seat. "Unidentified craft, this is the USS *Fratto*. Failure to identify yourself will result in an assumption of hostile intentions. We are authorized to use lethal force. Do you understand?"

Another long moment of crackling silence passed on the channel. Briscoe swallowed hard, worried. But he had been trained for this. He turned to his left, to the monitor hooked up to the ship's automatic targeting system. During the day shift, the weapons would have had their own operator, but during graveyard shift, Briscoe was basically a one-man crew. He started to type in a command to arm the targeting system when a chirp sounded to his right. He glanced back at the main monitor. The other craft had apparently activated its transponder.

Briscoe skimmed the info as it was received, and almost snorted with relief. It was a small ship, called *Gnosis*. It had no onboard weapons systems, no FTL drive, and was only capable of 13 parsecs of travel with a full fuel tank. Shit, this thing was probably older than his grandfather. Not exactly a threat, but still—what the hell was it doing out here?

A voice broke the static of the comm channel. Despite the radio distortion, it was calm and clear, and sounded to Briscoe like a man. "I'd like to speak to Lieutenant Diaz."

Diaz wasn't on the bridge at the moment. She was still on meal break. But how did this stranger have her name? With each passing moment, this encounter grew more confusing.

"*Gnosis*, you can either change course now or we will open fire. This is your last warning."

"Lieutenant Diaz. Please." The voice sounded perfectly calm, and at its ease.

Briscoe turned back to the weapons system. He started to type, but his fingers were shaking. He stopped and took a breath. He wasn't like some of the people he served with. People who'd joined up because they wanted a chance to hurt, to kill, and get paid for it. Briscoe didn't relish the thought of killing anyone. But that little voice in the back of his head—the one he tried to listen to, when it spoke—was shouting at him that something was *definitely wrong here*. He needed to act, or something bad would happen.

He put his fingers back on the keys, calmer now, ready to activate the targeting system. A hand landed on his shoulder, startling him for the second time in as many minutes. He jumped in his chair, stifled a shout, and turned to see Lieutenant Diaz.

The lieutenant was usually pretty cool and collected, but looked almost comical now, her cheeks distended with a mouthful of food she was still chewing, her shoulders rising and falling as she took deep breaths. She looked like she'd run here.

She put a hand in front of her mouth as she spoke. "I've got this, Corporal."

"Yes, ma'am," Briscoe said, confused. "But—"

She snapped her fingers and jerked a thumb over one shoulder in the universal *get up out of that chair* gesture. Briscoe took off his headset and stood. The short woman sat down at his station and pulled on the headset.

"*Gnosis*," she said. "This is Lieutenant Diaz, of the USS *Fratto*. You are cleared to proceed."

She sat at Briscoe's station for another few seconds, then took off the headset and stood up again.

"Ma'am?" Briscoe said, completely confused.

She seemed to consider her next words for a moment before she spoke. Or maybe she was just finishing chewing the rest of her mouthful of food.

"You want to forget everything you saw and heard in the last few minutes, Corporal," she said at last.

"I don't understand," Briscoe said.

"Keep it that way," Diaz said. She shook his shoulder lightly. "It's above your pay grade. There are a few things I do need you to understand, though: if you try to tell anyone about what just happened, I'll deny it. If you try to tell anyone about this conversation, I'll deny that, too. By the time the next shift comes on, there will no longer be any record in the ship's logs of what's just transpired. Do you understand?"

Briscoe didn't—not entirely. But he understood what

she was ordering him to do, at least, so he nodded. "Yes, ma'am," he said.

Diaz studied him a moment, leaving her hand on his shoulder, as though trying to assess whether or not he was telling her the truth. Eventually, she must have decided that he was, because she nodded and let him go.

"Carry on, Corporal," she said.

"Yes, ma'am," Briscoe said.

Diaz turned and left the bridge again, likely to return to her aborted meal in the commissary. Briscoe watched her until she was out of sight, then took his seat at his station again. He lifted his headset to put it back on, but paused when he realized his hands were still shaking.

He set the headset down and looked out the viewport again, in time to see the *Gnosis* pass by, a tiny arrowhead shape against the gray of the planet below.

The sight filled him with discomfort. It wasn't just that he'd watched a superior officer break protocol. It wasn't just that said officer had also involved him in her misconduct, and threatened him. No. He wasn't thrilled about those things, but they weren't what was really bothering him.

It was that little voice in the back of his head. He could hear it again, but this time, it wasn't saying anything specific. Right now, it was screaming.

2

CHARIOT

Cynthia Goodwin woke with a sharp intake of breath, only vaguely aware of the lurch in her stomach. She squinted against the bright lights. There was a figure standing over her. Somehow, something had followed her out of her bad dreams and into the real world.

Still more asleep than awake, she scrambled backward, kicking with weak legs and pulling with enervated arms—and bumped the top of her head against something hard. Her arms went to her sides, and they also bumped against hard barriers. She was in a narrow space. A coffin with an open lid.

"Easy," the figure above her said. His voice was soft and soothing. "Easy, Captain."

Something about the impact to her head and the tone of the voice brought her most of the way awake, and reality reasserted itself. She wasn't in a coffin. She was in her cryo pod aboard her ship, the *Chariot*. The figure standing over her was the ship's artificial person, Compton.

He was unusual looking, for an android. Whereas most were designed to look young and clean-cut, Compton had been designed to appear as if he was in his early forties. He was bald, with a thick blonde beard, and looked more like a Viking than a caretaker. His unusual appearance had been a bold experiment by Weyland-Yutani, and not a particularly successful one. He'd been one of the less-popular models on the market, and Goodwin had been able to purchase him at a steep discount. It was the only reason she'd been able to afford him.

The *Chariot*'s crew—particularly Goodwin's pilot, Sam Kurzel—hadn't been thrilled when Goodwin had first brought Compton aboard, but his gentle manner and easy smile had quickly won them over, and now it was difficult for Goodwin to imagine life without him.

Compton offered her a hand now, which she accepted. He pulled her up to a sitting position and offered her a glass of water.

"Another nightmare?" he said.

She nodded before chugging the water. It helped settle her stomach.

"What was it this time?" Compton asked.

Goodwin turned to see her pilot, Sam Kurzel, sitting up in the pod to her left. Now, here was someone good-looking enough to be a typical android. He was clean-shaven, with a strong jaw and bright blue eyes beneath an unruly mop of brown hair. He blinked a few times, and rubbed his eyes with balled fists, like a little kid. Goodwin's heart broke a little at the mix of rugged definition and boyishness. It was almost more than she could take.

"I don't remember," she said to him. "I never do."

Compton gave Goodwin a robe, which she wore to the showers, along with the rest of the crew. Under the spray of hot water, she came the rest of the way awake, and as usual, she felt a little guilty for lying to Compton.

In her thirty years, Goodwin had met plenty of people who claimed not to remember their dreams. Part of her envied these people. Another part flatly disbelieved them.

Goodwin always remembered her dreams. They made indelible marks on her, as vivid and lasting as anything that had ever happened to her in her waking life. The problem wasn't remembering them; the problem was describing them. There was never a story. No characters. Goodwin couldn't describe herself as being 'there' in these dreams, except maybe as a disembodied consciousness, a helpless observer. But what she observed was hard to put into words, less a series of events than a collection of images and sensations: roiling, slimy textures, interspersed with vast, dark voids; inexplicable flesh-like substances stretched and distorted; sharp, stabbing pains; hard, black carapaces that reflected harsh lights; all coupled with a sense of complete hopelessness and dread.

None of it made any sense. The few times Goodwin had tried to explain it to doctors and therapists, she'd felt confounded and stupid. She'd been at a loss to make them understand why the dreams felt so terrible. The doctors always offered the same response: serious head nods, murmurs of sympathy, and prescriptions for sleeping pills.

Goodwin had tried the medication. She'd tried several varieties of pill, at several varying doses. None of it had helped. The dreams persisted, and the medication left her feeling hungover during her waking hours. And anyway, what good was a sleeping pill when you were in technologically-enforced hypersleep? So she'd ditched them, and tried to make peace with her nightmares.

She basked in the shower spray now. She could've contentedly stayed in that warm, steamy stall for an hour, but the hot water only lasted a few minutes, since the whole crew was showering at once. Like almost everything on the *Chariot*, the hot water heater was old. It was something Goodwin meant to replace someday, if she ever managed to whittle down the list of more important fixes the ship needed. So she hurried through the ritual of scrubbing her body and hair clean, then shuffled up to the bridge, to check the nav systems and make sure that they were on course.

If the *Chariot* had had an onboard AI, a MUTH/UR or Apollo, she would've had the info as soon as she'd woken up. As it was, this verification was technically Sam's responsibility, but Goodwin wouldn't be able to fully relax until she'd verified the ship's location for herself. Too many things could go wrong out here in space. Better to know before breakfast if you were fucked or not.

The nav systems showed that the ship was on course, about an hour out from Knapik Station.

Satisfied, she doubled back to the ship's mess, as Sam and the rest of the crew came trickling in. Sam took a seat to Goodwin's right, while the cargo handlers, Danielle Cardona and Loewen White, sat to her right. Harris, the ship's tech, entered last and sat opposite Goodwin. Everyone was quiet at first, looking as beat-up as Goodwin felt, but as Compton served them a breakfast of stale-tasting coffee and dry cereal with milk, they revived enough to start the customary complaints.

"Doesn't matter how I feel when we go into the freezers," Harris grumbled into his coffee. "Whether I'm tired or wide awake when I lay down. Doesn't matter how long we're frozen. Could be a week, could be a month. I always wake up feeling like I went on a bender the night before."

Cardona nodded her sympathy, but Sam just smiled into his mug. It seemed too soon after defrosting for smiles, but that was Sam. Nothing ever kept him down for long.

"Sounds like you need a different career, Harris," Sam said. "Something that doesn't require so much cryo."

Harris grunted, a sound that might charitably have been interpreted as a laugh. "If I were good at anything other than keeping this rust bucket in the sky, I might consider it. But seriously—you'd think that, after all these years of FTL travel, they'd have found a way to make cryo more palatable."

"Believe me," White said. "They have. You think corporate execs at Seegson and Weyland-Yutani are waking up feeling like this when they travel? I guarantee you they've figured out first-class cryo. The tech just hasn't filtered down to us poor people yet."

"Maybe if we gave the pods a tune-up?" Cardona suggested. The youngest member of the crew, only nineteen years old, she always spoke quietly, as though afraid to jar anyone's nerves. She was good at her job, but timid to a fault.

"I'm a starship technician, not a miracle worker," Harris said. "We'd need a new set of pods altogether." The remark was met with small chuckles and wan smiles, but no one would meet Goodwin's eye to see if she shared their amusement. This was the common complaint: the *Chariot* was old. She'd been old when

Goodwin's mother had bought her twenty years ago, and the old girl was showing her age. Two years ago, Harris had started keeping a list of upgrades and repairs the ship needed, but no matter how much money Goodwin poured into the project, the list never seemed to get shorter. Every time they fixed one thing, something else broke.

Sam picked that moment to flee the tension, getting up to check the nav systems on the bridge. He returned a moment later to confirm what Goodwin already knew: they were on course, approaching Knapik Station. The *Chariot* had been contracted to deliver a shipment of food—six months of rations for the crew and civilians onboard. Once the *Chariot* had unloaded its cargo, the crew was supposed to get three days of leave before they departed for their next job.

"Three days off," Harris said now. "I hardly know what to do with myself."

"Is there anything to do on-station?" Cardona asked.

"There's a bar," White said. "Or there was, last time I was out this way."

"It'll still be there," Harris said. "I've yet to see a bar go out of business on the frontier."

"Is that it?" Cardona said. "No other entertainment? No arcades or theaters?"

"No brothels?" Harris said.

Cardona winced. She was a bit prudish, in addition to being timid.

"Let's keep the conversation breakfast-table appropriate," Goodwin said. She always felt a need to protect Cardona. She'd been with the crew for about six months now, and Goodwin couldn't help thinking of her as a little sister.

Harris set down his mug and help up both hands in a gesture of surrender. "No offense intended," he said to Cardona.

Cardona nodded at the table, acknowledging the semi-apology without making eye contact.

Goodwin considered pushing the matter further, but let it lie. She was tired. Harris was tired. Everyone was tired—and worse, they were tired of one another. A few days' rest—seeing some new faces on-station— would do them all some good.

After breakfast, the crew finished getting dressed and presentable, then split. Harris retreated to the engine room, grumbling about a shaky rear stabilizer, while Goodwin and Sam headed for the bridge, joined by White and Cardona, who had nothing to do until landing.

As Goodwin and the others entered the bridge and she took her seat, Knapik Station had already come into view out the main viewport.

Knapik Station hadn't originally been designed as a space station. It had started life as a Cygnus ore refinery—four individual towers in a square formation, rising above a main platform structure—before being repurposed fifteen years previous, to serve as the administrative hub for the Knapik Belt, a series of frontier mining planets. It floated in orbit around the world closest to the solar system's sun, CS-1225, but provided food and other supplies to all five worlds in the belt, as well as arranging transport for the worlds' harvested ore.

The food in Goodwin's cargo hold wasn't fancy. There was no steak, or wine, or even purified water. No, it was all bug juice and WY rations. Nothing you'd rush to the dinner table to consume, but stuff that would keep you alive from one day to the next. It was low-margin cargo, which meant a meager payday for Goodwin and her crew.

Normally, Goodwin wouldn't have taken the assignment, but she had done so for a couple of reasons. First (and most painful to admit), the *Chariot*'s towing clamps had been damaged during the ship's last major haul, and Goodwin couldn't afford to get them fixed yet, so the types of jobs she could take on right now were limited.

The second reason was far more pleasant to contemplate: this job might lead to better work. Maybe even a contract hauling ore for the Knapik Belt. Most ore hauling jobs went to corporation ships, but Goodwin had reason to hope. She'd heard through the grapevine that admin on-station were unhappy with Weyland-Yutani's hauling services of late, and might be open to trying out an independent contractor. Goodwin had a contact in station admin, a friend of a friend who'd agreed to meet her for drinks tonight. If Goodwin could sweet-talk her way into an ore-hauling contract, the signing bonus would be enough to handle the most pressing repairs on the *Chariot* (including the clamps) and keep Goodwin and her crew paid and flying for the foreseeable future.

She contemplated the view of Knapik Station now, its black metal architecture standing in sharp contrast to the gray planet below, almost a silhouette.

"Not much to look at, is it?" White said.

"Oh, I don't know," Goodwin said. Not beautiful, maybe, but functional. In fact, its history as an ore refinery was a good omen, she decided. A promise of better days ahead.

3

KNAPIK STATION

As Sam brought the *Chariot* into one of Knapik Station's landing bays, the ship began to shudder so hard that Goodwin worried she'd shake herself apart.

From somewhere aft, Harris swore loud enough to be heard even over the groan of the ship settling back into stillness. Sam and Goodwin exchanged a look. Sam grimaced sympathetically, then looked back at his instruments.

Goodwin unbuckled her crash harness and ran back to the engine room. She found Harris crouched over an open panel, swearing at it as though it had personally wronged him.

"What is it?" she said. "What's wrong?"

"Aft starboard stabilizer's fucked," he said. "Blew out right as we landed."

Goodwin tried to ignore the sinking feeling in her stomach.

"How fucked are we talking?" she said. "Can you fix it?"

Harris gave her a look. "I can fix almost anything, with enough time, parts, and tools. But I don't know about this, kiddo. I think we may just need a new one."

"I see," Goodwin said.

Harris sighed. He was the longest-serving crew member on the *Chariot*. He'd been with the ship since Goodwin's mother still ran things. He was the closest thing Goodwin had ever had to a father. It was hard for her to keep anything from him.

"Can we afford a new one?" he asked. "After we get paid, I mean."

Goodwin considered how to answer. Losing a stabilizer was bad, but not insurmountable. It was just another repair to add to the list. Once she'd secured the ore-hauling contract with administration, they'd be able to afford it.

"Probably," she said at last.

Harris nodded and wiped his hands with a dirty rag. "I'll take a look around the shops while we're here. See what our options are."

"Sounds good," she said. "Just—do me a favor?"

He raised his eyebrows.

"Don't mention this to the crew. I'll tell them, when the time comes. But for now, I don't want anything putting a damper on their leave."

"Aye-aye, kiddo," Harris said.

***

Goodwin returned to the bridge and flopped into her chair. Sam was running through his post-landing checklist, but paused to look at her.

"Cardona and White went down to cargo to get ready for unloading," he said. "Harris had bad news, I take it?"

She nodded.

"Do I want to know?"

"I'll tell you later," she said. "Once I have some good news to couple it with."

Sam went back to work. He didn't push or prod. Didn't try to weasel the information out of her. She liked this about him. He seemed to exist on a permanent even keel, which made him a perfect foil for her own constant anxiety. Another reason they made a good team.

Before she could tell him so, the comm crackled as a channel opened. "Captain?" Cardona said.

"I'm here," Goodwin said.

"You might want to come down here," Cardona said.

"What is it?"

"It's better if you see for yourself," White piped in.

Goodwin suppressed a groan of frustration as she stood up. "On my way."

She crossed the ship and descended the ladder into the cargo bay. A sickly-sweet, almost nauseating smell hit her before she'd even finished climbing down, and she cursed, knowing what she was about to see: spilled bug juice.

She approached Cardona and White, who stood with their backs to her, peering at a mess of broken boxes and shattered bottles, all soaked dark red with spilled bug juice.

"What happened?" she said.

"A couple of security straps broke," White said. They pointed up at the nearest wall, where formerly taut belts hung torn and limp. "It must've happened during the landing, because I did a visual inspection after we woke up and everything looked okay."

"How bad is it?" Goodwin asked.

"Not as bad as it looks from here," White said. "I checked the rest of the hold, and everything else seems to be secure."

"This is bad enough," Goodwin said. At a glance, she guessed that they'd lost about ten percent of the shipment. Ten percent that would come out of the *Chariot*'s paycheck.

Cardona put a comforting hand on Goodwin's shoulder. "Insurance will cover what we lost, right?"

Goodwin doubted it. She carried insurance on her cargo—she wasn't *that* broke yet—but in her experience, insurance companies didn't part with a single dollar if they didn't have to. She could just see an adjuster looking at those straps, or finding out about the stabilizer, or any number of other problems on the ship, and declaring Goodwin at-fault. Granting her a settlement of 'Go fuck yourself.'

"Probably," Goodwin said to Cardona. No sense letting the kid know they were a little more fucked now than they had been ten minutes ago.

Sam joined Goodwin, Cardona, and White in the hold, and they cleaned up the mess as best they could before they started the unloading process. This part went as well as could have been expected. The rep from station admin, a small man with receding hair and dark bags under his eyes, reviewed the surviving cargo, typed some numbers into a calculator, and determined that they'd lost approximately fifteen percent of the shipment (his exact figure was "fourteen-point-eight-five percent"). He said that, when he returned to the office, he'd authorize a credit for eighty-five-point-fifteen percent of the original agreed-upon price.

Goodwin shook the man's hand and thanked him for his time. Once he was gone, she turned to her crew.

"Get out of here," she said. "I don't want to see any of you again for three days."

Cardona, White, and Harris said their goodbyes and took off, but Sam lingered. When everyone else had left, he said, "Check-in's at three. Want to head over together?"

Sam had booked them a room at the Bowers. Although Knapik Station had a few 'hotels', most were little more than stacks of sleeping tubes for transient workers. The Bowers, by contrast, had actual rooms with beds in them, and bathrooms with full-sized bathtubs. Sam had paid for the whole thing himself, and Goodwin was looking forward to a few days of privacy and decadence with her pilot. But not yet.

"I have a couple of things to do first," she said. "I'll catch up with you."

Once he was gone, she returned to the now-empty cargo hold and stared at the wine-red stain on the floor. Despite their best efforts, the crew had been unable to remove it, and it was still sticky to step on. She wondered how long the stickiness would last. It seemed likely that the stain itself would endure the rest of the ship's days.

Assuming this ship has any days left, she thought.

She shook her head, trying to physically remove the thought from her body. She wasn't licked. Not yet.

Goodwin had a little bit of time to kill before her meeting with the admin rep, and wasn't quite ready to head to the Bowers—once she was checked in there, she didn't want to leave the hotel room until it was time to depart the station. She wanted a chance to truly forget about the whole galaxy for a few days.

So instead she took a lift to the commercial district.

She wandered the vendor stalls and shops for a while, stopping occasionally to examine an interesting item, or ask for a price. She didn't see much worth buying—the wares in the Outer Veil were sparse. The books and movies on offer were years old, content that even Goodwin, with her limited disposable income, had consumed years ago.

But at least it helped kill the time until her meeting. Checking her watch, she headed for the bar. Despite Harris's earlier statements to the contrary, this bar *did* have a name: Ore's Pours. Not very appetizing, but at least it rhymed with the theme of mining.

Despite the dim lighting and relatively upscale location in the commercial district, Ore's Pours had a grubby look, as if everything was covered in dust. Every object in sight, from the décor to the seating, looked like it had been repurposed from mining equipment.

Like every bar on every station she'd ever visited, this one was popular, and Goodwin had to squeeze between groups of people to find an open, sticky table near the back wall, next to the restroom. It took a server several minutes to stop by and take her order, and several more minutes for Goodwin's bottle of Aspen to arrive. It did so in tandem with Goodwin's contact from station admin.

His name was Aldous Hemphill, and Goodwin would've recognized him even if she hadn't seen his photo before now. He stuck out in this dingy little watering hole. Whereas most people here were in dun-colored jumpsuits, this man wore a tailored suit. He was clean-shaven, with a stylish haircut, and a briefcase in his right hand. He frowned as he entered the bar, a look of clear distaste on his handsome face. The expression sent a stab of dislike through Goodwin. He was the one who'd wanted to meet in public. They could've met at his office instead.

Still, she smiled, waved, and called his name. His eyebrows went up when he saw her, and he waved back. He made his way through the crowd, clearly uncomfortable, and she enjoyed watching his discomfort. She ran through what she knew about him—mostly gossip from a mutual friend named Bulloch. Hemphill had grown up in the Knapik Belt, came from a family of miners, but had somehow managed to wriggle out of manual labor and into administration. He was young—still in his mid-twenties—and looking to make a name for himself out here in the Outer Veil. Hoping to get noticed by a bigger company, and get out of the Knapik Belt for good.

When he arrived at the table, he seemed to debate where to set his briefcase. Neither the table nor the floor seemed to meet with his satisfaction, so as he sat across from Goodwin, he cradled the briefcase in his lap. Goodwin was honestly a little surprised he deigned to sit. Surely the chair would dirty up the hindquarters of that expensive suit.

"You're late," Goodwin said. She said it lightly, to let him know it was no big deal.

"I had a meeting that ran over," Hemphill said. It wasn't an apology, but rather a statement of fact. He looked around the bar, caught a server's eye, and summoned her over to order a whiskey neat. Then he sat with both hands on his briefcase, as though someone might try to snatch it.

This all felt wrong so far. Goodwin already disliked the man. However, she would set that aside. She would do whatever it took to walk out of here with a contract.

She tried a smile. "Thank you for taking the time to meet with me," she said.

"I owed your friend Bulloch a favor from way back," Hemphill said. "Thank him."

Goodwin clamped down on her instinctive response—to throw her beer in this smarmy asshole's face—and took a sip from her bottle instead. "I'll do that."

Hemphill's drink arrived. He took one hand off his briefcase to pick it up and sip from it. He made a face, but not the usual face people made when drinking whiskey. This was an expression of distaste. Clearly the drink wasn't up to his usual standards.

"Look, I know you're a busy man," Goodwin said. "I don't want to waste your time. Bulloch tells me that Knapik administration is unhappy with Weyland-Yutani's ore-hauling services."

She paused there to give Hemphill a chance to respond. He just stared back at her, waiting for her to continue.

"Bulloch also indicated that administration might be into the idea of trying out some smaller, different ore-haulers. Maybe an independent contractor, like the *Chariot*. We're a mid-size cargo hauler," she said. "Been in service for a while now." She deliberately left out the model number and age of her ship. No need to tell him exactly how long they'd been flying. "And we have a strong history of reliable service. I sent you some customer testimonials along with the rest of our information a few weeks back."

Hemphill took another sip of his whiskey and made that irritating face again. "'A strong history of reliable service,'" he said, echoing her.

"That's right," Goodwin said.

"Reliable," he said again, as he set the glass down on the table. "Have you updated your records to include the mishap you had in our docking bay a few hours ago?"

Goodwin stopped herself from physically moving in reaction to what he'd said, but couldn't entirely mask her surprise. He'd already heard about that?

"Just a stabilizer malfunction," she said. "Already fixed." A lie, but he didn't need to know that.

"A malfunction that eliminated nearly fifteen percent of our planned rations for the next six months," Hemphill said.

"We took a pay cut for that," Goodwin said, keeping her voice even and reasonable.

"That pay cut for you means stricter rationing for half a year in the Knapik Belt," Hemphill said.

"I didn't realize you were so concerned with the plight of the common worker," Goodwin said.

"I'm not, personally," Hemphill said. "But it's a hard life out here, especially for people at the bottom of the ladder. If things get harder, those people tend to become..." he waved a hand through the air, as though wafting a smell away from himself. "...unproductive," he finished. "When they become unproductive, we start to miss quotas. Once we start missing quotas, my life gets harder. So you might say I have a vested interest in keeping people happy—or at least, maintaining a baseline level of misery. Your little accident today means that my life is about to get harder."

"I'm sorry," Goodwin said. The words were out before she had time to calculate their effect, and she was immediately unhappy with herself for saying them. But they were out, so she had to follow them where they led. "Truly, I am. But accidents *do* happen."

"They seem to happen to the *Chariot* more than the average cargo hauler," Hemphill said. "I did a little independent research on you before you arrived. Learned some information you conveniently left out of your own materials. Like your accident out on Gorham's Folly."

Again, Goodwin struggled to keep her expression neutral. It was getting harder.

"Honestly?" Hemphill said. "I'm surprised that your ship is even capable of hauling ore after the damage you must've sustained. That would've been an expensive repair, getting your cargo clamps replaced."

"It was," Goodwin lied. "But if you'll just give us a chance—give us a probationary job, even—"

He cut her off with a sharp hand gesture. "Look. You heard correctly when Bulloch said we're unhappy with Weyland-Yutani right now. They're screwing us on costs, hurting our margins. We're looking at alternatives. But we're looking at other corporations, like Seegson. Large operations that can handle all over our business and provide consistent results."

"Independent contractors are less expensive," Goodwin said. She knew this. She's known this for years. It was the major selling point for her ship. She had a number in mind, the absolute rock bottom she could accept and keep flying, and it was far lower than the rates a corporation would charge.

"True," Hemphill said, "but hiring lots of independent contractors creates more busywork for admin—and typically provides inconsistent results." He shrugged and drank the rest of his whiskey in a single gulp.

"So there was no point in us meeting at all," Goodwin said. "You never meant to give me the contract."

"I owed Bulloch a favor," Hemphill said, after a swallow and a grimace. "A face-to-face meeting fulfilled my obligation to him. I'm sorry that I didn't say anything you wanted to hear, but that's not my problem." He gave her a little sympathetic shrug. She wanted to punch him in the face.

"Here's some free advice," he said. "You still look relatively young, but that ship of yours isn't. It has a reputation—one that dropped several notches today in the hangar bay. That stink won't come off. So do yourself a favor and get out of the shipping business. Find something else to do. Or sign on with one of the corporate ships. Someplace you can start fresh, and build a new rep. Because this?" He gestured at himself, and then at her. "This is a dead end for you, Captain Goodwin." He pulled a wallet from his jacket, dropped a few bills on the table, and stood. "I'd say 'See you around,' but I hope this is the last time we ever speak." He gave her a gesture somewhere between a nod and a salute, and left the bar.

Goodwin waited until he was gone to count the money on the table. There was enough here for the drinks, several times over. She pocketed most of it, mentally apologizing to their server for the theft.

She'd need the cash.

4

THE BOWERS

The Bowers hotel was in a different tower of the station, so Goodwin had to take the tram. Like the bar, the tram was crowded, although its clientele was a bit more white-collar than that of Ore's Pours. She was the only person in her crowded car wearing a jumpsuit and sneakers. Everyone else wore suits and dress shoes. Most of the other passengers were men. None of them offered her his seat, so she stood, gripping one of the poles that lined the tram car, and swaying gently with the rhythm of travel.

She tried not to think about what had just happened. She was feeling numb, and wanted to stay that way as long as possible.

The tram arrived at the 'rich' part of the station, and Goodwin shuffled off with all the suited men. She followed her station map to the Bowers hotel. It didn't look like much from the outside—just another gray metal entryway, albeit with a fancy sign—but once she passed through the front doors, she found herself in a vast lobby with a marble floor and a working stone fountain in the center.

Goodwin approached the desk, gave the clerk her name, and received a keycard, which she took up to her room on the fourth floor. She stepped out of the elevator into a long hallway with plush carpet on the floor and oil paintings on the walls. The light was dim, but soothing. She paused to look at the painting closest to the elevator. It was a mess of reds and pinks. For some reason, she thought of her nightmares, and had the first stirrings of an emotion. She turned away, determined to stay numb. She made her way to the room, and slid the card through the lock.

As she opened the door, Sam came out of the suite's bathroom. He'd already showered and changed out of his jumpsuit into a fluffy white bathrobe. His hair was still wet and stuck to his forehead in dark curls.

"How'd your meeting go?" he said.

Instead of answering, she pulled him into a kiss. He entered the embrace with gusto, put his hands on her waist as she ran her own through his damp hair. She breathed in the smell of him. Usually this scent was mixed with the smells of the *Chariot*—old oil and lubricants and metal. She wasn't used to him smelling so clean. It was intoxicating. She pushed him toward the bed. He fell backwards and she landed atop him. Their foreheads bumped together.

"Ow," he said.

"Oh hush, you big baby," she said, and kissed him again.

But he wasn't quiet after that. Neither was she. The room was soundproofed—one of the luxuries of such a fancy hotel—but even if it hadn't been, neither Goodwin nor Sam would've worried about bothering the neighbors. There were no personal cabins on the *Chariot*. Just bunks in the common area, with curtains for privacy. Because of this, Goodwin and Sam always had to sneak around when they made love. They had to whisper their exclamations, bite down on their cries of pleasure. But here at the Bowers? They had space. They could be loud. They could be messy. They could fully disappear into one another. And for the next hour, that was exactly what they did.

After, Goodwin drew a bath in the tub while Sam lit candles he'd found somewhere on-station. In the dark bathroom, they luxuriated in the large tub of hot water, Goodwin leaning back against Sam's chest as he rubbed her shoulders, her arms, her neck. She let her head loll against him, content for the first time in forever.

"You are tense," he said, as he tried to massage out some of the knots in her back.

"Surprising no one," Goodwin said.

"It's hard being captain, huh?"

She grunted in agreement.

"I did a little shopping this afternoon," he said. "Didn't actually buy anything, but I saw something I wanted to talk to you about."

"Oh yeah? What's that?"

"It turns out White was right," Sam said. "There's loads of high-end cryo stuff out there. Weyland-Yutani makes dream monitoring equipment that will attach to most hypersleep chambers, and these things called Neuro Visors, that will allow someone to enter a sleeper's dream and communicate with them. The fucked-up thing is that this stuff isn't even new. It's been around for decades. But I guess it's stayed sort of a specialty item, because how often does anyone need to communicate with someone in cryo? And how much does the average company care if their employees are having bad dreams?

"Anyway, I was thinking we might get one of these visors for the *Chariot*," he went on, before she could respond. "So Compton could check in on you during the long hauls. Maybe pull you out of nightmares when necessary?"

Goodwin laid her head flat against Sam's collarbone and turned his face to her own. "Sweet, thoughtful boy," she said, and kissed him. She hoped that would be enough to stop this line of conversation.

Sam paused in his ministrations, and she felt the spell of the last hour—the thin veil of contentment that had settled over them—break. Sam and Goodwin had only been a couple for six standard months, but she could already read him. Even his silences, his hesitations. This pause meant he was about to ask a serious question.

"Are we going to talk about your meeting?" he said.

She sat up and leaned away from him. She drew her legs to her chest and wrapped her arms around her knees.

"I'm guessing it didn't go well," he ventured.

"Can we not talk about it tonight?" she said. "I promise to tell you everything in the morning, but for tonight, I want a break."

"Sure," he said. "Sure thing. You bet."

She leaned back against him then, allowed herself to be held, stroked, and kissed. She felt him let go of his curiosity, and sink back into the here and now, the warmth of the water and the softness of their bodies together.

Unfortunately, she was unable to re-conjure the peace that Sam had broken. Even after the bath, even after making love again and falling back into the bed, exhausted, her anxieties clung to her. She laid awake as Sam drifted off, softly snoring on his side of the king-size bed.

When she could no longer make herself lie still, she

got out of the bed, pulled on one of the complimentary robes, and went to the room's window. It wasn't actually a window—a real window would've looked out on the station walkways below. It was a video screen, projecting recorded images. She flipped through a few nature scenes—forests, snowy windows next to crackling fires, aerial shots of cities on Earth—before she came to a field of stars. This was, and always had been, her favorite sight. She settled into the room's big, comfy chair, and stared at the stars now.

This—her life—wasn't supposed to be like this. Cynthia Goodwin was supposed to be master of her own destiny, just like her mother, Alice. Alice Goodwin had been a tough-as-nails trader, who'd learned the shipping trade crewing independent ships while saving up to buy her own: the *Chariot*. Over the course of twenty years, Alice had built a reputation for herself, traveling from the core to the frontier, with her daughter at her side. Cynthia had grown up learning by watching her mother. Alice had been a good teacher. She made sure that Cynthia understood the day-to-day of running a ship, as well as the economics, and the art of managing a crew. The old woman had prepared her daughter for an independent life among the stars. Alice had done her job well; even when she died of lung cancer at age forty-seven, the *Chariot* had continued to fly and do business, with Cynthia at the helm.

For a few years after Alice's death, everything had

run smoothly. Cynthia had overseen the gradual change of her crew (everyone except Harris), and the upkeep of the ship. She'd expected to go on living just as her mother had. Maybe have a child of her own, to pass the business along to someday. Someone to whom she could teach the star charts, the art of negotiation. Someone to share her sense of wonder at the spill of light beyond a viewport window.

But about five years ago, things had started to go wrong. The jobs for independent contractors grew less plentiful, and the ones that remained didn't pay as well. Goodwin found herself dipping into her savings more and more often to keep the crew paid and the ship maintained.

Then there was the matter of the ship herself. The *Chariot* had been old when Alice had bought her. She was almost an antique now, and in the past three years, she'd really started to show her age.

Today, with the loss of the stabilizer, and the pay cut from the destroyed cargo, Goodwin was teetering perilously close to bankruptcy. And the Ace up her sleeve—the possibility of a Knapik contract, the magical cure-all that would bail her out—had turned out to be a Joker instead. She was fucked. Her ship was fucked. Her crew was fucked. She had no idea what she was going to do.

She looked away from the 'window' and toward the bed, where Sam lay curled beneath a blanket. His snoring had tapered off. His face was beautiful in the glow of the video screen.

She got back into the bed and snuggled up to Sam. He came partially awake.

"Sgoing on?" he mumbled.

"Nothing. Go back to sleep," she said.

He did as he was told. And eventually, she joined him.

5

AN OFFER

As always, Goodwin had nightmares. She was trapped in wet, mucky darkness. She couldn't move. The harder she tried to free herself, the surer she became that she would never move again. She couldn't breathe. Panic bloomed in her chest. She could feel something nearby. Something coming for her. Something too terrible to be contemplated. It was close. Getting closer.

She was yanked awake by a pounding, at the hotel room door. Confused and still mostly asleep, she stumbled out of the bed to answer it.

"Are you expecting someone?" Sam said behind her.

She opened the door just wide enough to peer out. Compton stood in the hallway, looking as placid as ever, belying the urgency of his knocks a moment before.

"Compton?" she said. "What is it?" Immediately her mind began to supply possibilities. Something else wrong with the ship. Something had happened to one the crew. Station administration wanted to dock their pay even further.

"I apologize for bothering you on your leave, Captain," Compton said. "I know you didn't want to be disturbed. But we've received an interesting transmission on the *Chariot*. It's time-sensitive, and I thought you'd want to know."

"What is it?" Sam said. He'd gotten out of bed, too, and stood behind Goodwin.

Goodwin almost interrupted, to order Compton back to the ship, to relay that she'd be available two days from now. This was the closest thing she'd had to a vacation in years. Maybe the last vacation she'd ever get.

But she was still half asleep, and not atop her prickly game, and Compton managed to answer Sam before she could say anything.

"It's from a man named Roman Fade," Compton said. "He's apparently on-station and he's requested a meeting."

"*The* Roman Fade?" Sam said.

"I checked the signature on the transmission," Compton said. "Either it's real, or a very convincing fake."

"Roman Fade," Sam said again.

He was right to sound incredulous. Roman Fade was one of the richest men in the galaxy, an entrepreneur and industrialist who'd made his fortune contracting for the big corporations. He was famous for that—and infamous for his intense privacy. No one knew much about him—there weren't even many photos of him in circulation. What the hell would he be doing on Knapik Station? And moreover, what would he want with Goodwin? There were too many interesting questions here to ignore.

"Give it to me," she said.

Compton handed her a tablet with the message. She read it right there in the doorway:

> Dear Capt. Goodwin,
> I hope this message finds you well (although I imagine it comes as a bit of a surprise). I'm on Knapik Station for the next few days and I'm hoping you'll have time to meet with me. I have a proposition of employment for you—one that's very important to me, and potentially very lucrative for you. Please respond to this message if you're interested.
>
> Best,
> Roman Fade

"Pretty straightforward," Sam said, after they'd both read it through a couple of times.

"Vague as hell," Goodwin said.

"True," Sam said. "What are you going to do?"

Her gut told her there was something off about this. Something weird. It didn't make any sense. Why would Fade, a man with hundreds of employees, reach out to her himself? Wouldn't he have an assistant do it for him? And even putting that aside, why would Fade, someone with considerable resources, reach out to a ship with the *Chariot*'s increasingly dubious reputation? Surely he had ships of his own to carry out his slightest whims. On the other hand, he seemed to be offering work. He was currently the only person offering Goodwin work.

"I guess I'm going to take the meeting," she said, although she didn't feel great about it.

"Can I come this time?" Sam said.

"We'll see," she said, as she began typing out her response.

Goodwin and Fade set up a meeting over the course of several messages, sent and received intermittently as Goodwin rushed through a morning toilet, pulling her hair into a loose ponytail, brushing her teeth, and throwing on her jumpsuit, jacket, and boots. As it turned out, Fade was also staying at the Bowers, in the top-floor penthouse, so Goodwin, Compton, and Sam only needed to take the elevator up to the penthouse to meet Fade.

It was in the elevator that Sam, who had been silent most of the morning, finally spoke up:

"What do you think he wants?"

Nothing good, she thought. "I don't know," she said.

The elevator let them off on the top floor, directly before the penthouse door. Goodwin knocked, and, after a few seconds, the door opened to reveal a handsome middle-aged man in an expensive suit. She recognized him from the few pictures she'd seen: Roman Fade. He had a strong jaw, a full head of graying blonde hair, and bright blue eyes.

He smiled as he opened the door, but the expression faltered when he saw Sam and Compton flanking Goodwin. It only faltered for a second, but Goodwin noted the change. She also noted that Fade had answered his own door, instead of having an assistant do it. Whatever was going on here, he wanted it kept private.

"Captain Goodwin, I presume?" he said. "And company, it seems."

"Yes. I hope that's okay," Goodwin said.

"Of course, of course," he said. He shook hands with all three of his visitors as she introduced them. She was surprised that he shook Compton's hand. It was an unusual gesture for a human, particularly a rich man, and it made Goodwin like Fade a little more, despite her reservations.

He ushered them into the penthouse, and Goodwin

had to stop herself from whistling in appreciation. She'd thought her own room on the fourth floor luxurious, but this suite was something else entirely. It was basically a high-end apartment, with multiple rooms, a full kitchen, and a dining area off a central living area, which was stocked with plush furniture. A table in the middle of the room held a bowl of what appeared to be real fruit. The 'window' on the far wall projected data readouts, rather than images. Financial information, she guessed. Up-to-the-minute updates on how Fade's money was faring in the galactic economy.

"Please, have a seat, make yourselves comfortable," Fade said, gesturing to the furniture in the living room. "Can I offer you anything? Coffee, maybe?"

Sam raised a hand like a kid in school. "I wouldn't say no to coffee. Black, please."

"Nothing for me, thanks," Goodwin said, as she settled onto the couch. She wished she'd talked to Sam on the way over, told him to play things closer to his chest. She didn't want to get too chummy too fast.

Fade entered the kitchen, and returned a moment later with two mugs. He handed one to Sam, who had taken a seat next to her on the couch. Compton stood near the bar between the kitchen and the living room, rather than sitting.

"I can't speak to the quality," Fade said, "but at least it's hot."

He settled in one of the chairs diagonal to the couch.

His knee was only a few inches from Goodwin's. He took a sip of his coffee and set the mug on the table before him.

"I appreciate you hurrying over here to meet me on such short notice," he said. "I'm sure you have better things to do this early in the morning."

Goodwin shrugged. "It's not every day that we receive a mysterious summons from one of the richest men in the galaxy."

Fade smiled, seemed genuinely amused rather than annoyed, and again, Goodwin found herself liking the man a little more.

"Indeed," he said. "It's all very cloak and dagger, isn't it? And I apologize for that. But I have a request—one that's rather delicate, and time-sensitive, and this was the only way I could see going about it."

He sat back and took another sip of his coffee, clearly making space for Goodwin to ask questions. She held her tongue, waited for him to continue.

"I'll get right to it," he said. "Are any of you familiar with Corinth Bloch?"

The name meant nothing to Goodwin. She shook her head and looked at Sam, who appeared equally nonplussed.

"Corinth Bloch," Compton said, from his spot at the bar. "A painter and sculptor, famed in the art world. He's mostly known for intricate, fantastical illustrations of colonization narratives. Was once called 'the Bosch of the Middle Heavens' by the Sol system art critics' association. He's grown less prolific over time. He reached the peak of his fame about five years ago, and hasn't had an exhibition of his work since then."

"I don't know that he's necessarily less prolific," Fade said. "But he's more selective about who he shows his work to."

"You know him, then," Goodwin said.

"Quite well," Fade said. "For the past ten years he's been my… partner. My companion. My person."

"I was unaware of that," Compton said.

"We're both private people," Fade said. "We've paid a great deal to keep our relationship out of the press."

"This is all very interesting," Goodwin said. "But what does it have to do with me?"

Fade leaned forward in his chair, resting his elbows on his knees. "Corinth is brilliant. A once-in-a-generation talent. When people use the word 'genius,' they mean someone like him. But, as unpopular as it is to admit these days, genius often walks hand-in-hand with madness, and Corinth has always been a bit wild. And that unpredictability has grown more pronounced in the last couple of years. I could waste your time giving you a full chronicle, but suffice it to say, Corinth recently stole some information from me, and disappeared. I have reason to suspect he's fled to the colony world of DSJ-ten-twenty. I would like to hire your ship and crew to go there and retrieve him."

"What makes you think he's on DSJ-ten-twenty?" Goodwin said.

"He'd recently become fixated on the world," Fade said. "And specifically, the colony there. New Providence."

Goodwin glanced at Compton. Compton frowned. "I've never heard of it," he said. "It's not in my databanks."

"It's a relatively new colony on the frontier," Fade said. "Only ten years old. An Earthlike planet that required no terraforming. Intended as an agricultural center. It was recently quarantined. There's been a Colonial Marine ship in orbit around the world for months now, to make sure no traffic comes in or out. It's not surprising you haven't heard of it, Compton. Weyland-Yutani would've had it wiped from the public record."

"I don't understand," Goodwin said. "If Weyland-Yutani has wiped the world from the public record, how would Corinth know about it?"

"I do a lot of contract work with Weyland-Yutani," Fade said, studying his own hands. "The record of that world—and the colony—are part of the information that he stole."

"Okay, but even allowing that, the world is quarantined, and the marines have an active checkpoint there," Goodwin said. "They would've turned Bloch away as soon as he arrived."

"Do you know how much the average marine makes?" Fade said. "They're more than susceptible to bribes."

"So assume Bloch bribed someone," Goodwin said. "Why would he want to go there to begin with? It's a plague, right?"

"He'd long been fixated on the peculiar nature of this contagion," Fade said. "I can't tell you more until you take the job and sign an NDA."

"Alright, even setting his desires aside," Goodwin said, "let's say he made it to the planet. He's probably already infected, or dead, right?"

Fade grimaced and Goodwin felt a small twinge of regret. They *were* talking about the love of this man's life. He might be a rich son of a bitch, but he still had human feelings. The words were out, however, and she couldn't take them back. Nor would apologizing make them less true.

"He might be," Fade said. "I'm prepared to pay you quite handsomely to go find out for me."

How handsomely? she wondered. But she kept that question to herself for the moment.

"Why us?" she said. "Why the *Chariot*?"

"Did you mother ever tell you about Source Falls?" Fade said.

Goodwin shook her head. "Mom wasn't much given to storytelling."

"I'm not surprised," Fade said. "She would've wanted to keep this secret. You see, about thirty years ago, Source Falls, a colony world on the Outer Veil, was overrun by deadly parasites. The population was wiped out. Your mother and the *Chariot* happened to be on-world at the onset of the crisis. They managed to escape with a single colonist—Corinth Bloch. Your mother saved his life. He never forgot her, or the *Chariot*, and that's why I've invited you here. It's why I'm on-station today. I have no other business here. It's why I'm asking *you* to rescue him now. Corinth is brilliant, but given to fanatical tendencies. He sees signs and omens everywhere. Assuming he's still alive on DSJ-ten-twenty, I'm hoping he'll see the *Chariot*'s arrival as, well… providence, and be willing to return with you."

Goodwin took all this in. So Bloch had escaped one plague world as a boy, rescued by Alice Goodwin. Now he'd returned to another plague world, as a man, and Alice's daughter, Cynthia, was being asked for an encore performance.

"What's the nature of this contagion?" she asked.

"I can't tell you until you agree to the job," Fade said.

"You're asking me and my crew to take a terrible risk here."

"That's why I'm offering so much money."

"How much money?"

Fade named a number so high that Goodwin was sure she'd misheard him at first. Only Sam's startled expression confirmed that she had, in fact, heard Fade correctly. It was enough money to repair the ship and keep the crew paid for years to come. It would float them through any financial difficulties.

"Of course, I'm only offering a fraction of that amount in advance," Fade said. "Say, ten percent. Enough to pay your expenses for the job, but not enough so that you could run off with my money and not do the actual work. You only receive full payment when you return Corinth to me—or provide proof of his death."

That took some of the wind out of Goodwin's sails. Ten percent was an okay payday, but it would barely be enough to fix the stabilizer, let alone the cargo clamps. They'd still be flying on a wing and a prayer.

"Twenty percent up front," Goodwin said.

Fade shook his head. "Ten."

"Fifteen," Goodwin said.

"Ten," Fade repeated. "I've looked at your financial records. I know how desperately you need this. I need you to remain desperate while you complete this mission. You understand."

Goodwin's hands clenched into fists in her lap. "Then I'm afraid my answer is no. I'm not going to risk my crew's health and wellbeing on something illegal, something we might not survive. Not without more financial incentive."

Fade nodded. "I understand you're on station today and tomorrow. Why don't you take that time and think it over? And," he stood up, crossed to the dining room area, and returned holding a magnetic tape, "take this with you. It has some additional info about Corinth that you may find interesting. The offer of employment stands, for as long as I remain on station. But you should know that the price drops every six hours."

6

DEBATE

After the meeting with Fade, Goodwin would've preferred to return to their room on the fourth floor, with Sam. To forget about Fade and Corinth Bloch, and all her money troubles for another couple of days. But Fade had put a ticking clock on his offer, which meant that decisions needed to be made sooner rather than later. She, Sam, and Compton went back to the *Chariot*, and sent messages to the rest of the crew, ordering them back.

While they waited, Goodwin fixed a pot of coffee, and took a mug up to the cockpit, where she settled into the captain's chair. She set the mug down on the counter, pulled the magnetic tape she'd gotten from Fade from her jacket pocket, and inserted it into her console. The monitor flickered as it retrieved the contents of the tape, and then displayed a list. It was organized as a series of numbered folders.

She opened the folder marked '1' and found a cache of files. The first was entitled '1-1: General Overview.' She opened the file. At the top was a photo of a man. Even on the low-resolution, black-and-white monitor, Goodwin could tell he was handsome, with a mop of unruly, light-colored hair, heavy eyebrows that would have looked excessive on another man, and a strong chin. Goodwin could see how someone might fall in love with Corinth Bloch.

The text below read:

Corinth Bloch (born 9 July 2159) is a United-American painter and sculptor. He is one of the most notable examples of the Modern Colonial school of art. Although he began exhibiting and selling his work in the late 2170s, he came to prominence in the Sol system art world in the early 2180s with his religious-flavored depictions of colonial life.

Goodwin skimmed forward. The article was rather short. There were a few facts about Bloch's working methods (for paintings, he usually worked with oil paints on oak wood surfaces, rather than traditional stretched canvases, and he sculpted with clay), and a few remarks about his intense privacy and increasing reclusiveness over the last few years. It ended by restating what Fade had already told Goodwin: Bloch hadn't exhibited any new work in five years.

Beneath the text were some low-res images depicting

some of Bloch's work. The first image was a painting called 'Supplies.' It depicted an exterior landscape of a rocky, barren world, beneath an ominous, stormy sky. An atmosphere processor loomed in the background, and in the foreground, workers moved crates from a parked starship to a domed colony. The people were tiny against the ship, the colony, and the processor. Almost like ants.

Dissatisfied with the image quality on her console screen, Goodwin threw it up on the cockpit's main monitor, which descended in front of the main viewport. She stood and carried her coffee over for a better look. The resolution still wasn't great, but it was better. She could make out the little people in the foreground now. They didn't look super realistic. Rather, they were stylized, with blank expressions and thousand-yard stares. They weren't posed like people doing hard manual labor, but rather, each figure appeared to be frozen in the middle of a leaping, spinning dance.

Goodwin had never spent much time looking at art. It was an extravagance, a luxury. Something to be contemplated by the rich, while everyone else worked for a living. She had no frame of reference, no context for this painting in front of her. She couldn't honestly say if she liked or disliked it.

She scrolled to the next image file. This one was a photo of a sculpture, entitled 'Transfiguration.' It was from Bloch's last public showing. It depicted a figure basically human in shape, which seemed to be bent forward with its hands on its thighs. Unlike the humans in 'Supplies,' this figure was drawn in sharp, lifelike detail. Goodwin could see the creases in pants, the worn-down soles of the figure's boots. Everything about it looked normal except the head, which was distended and misshapen—too big, asymmetrical, bulging in strange spots. The face was twisted into a mask of agony, the mouth too wide, as if something was fighting to emerge.

Goodwin knew for a fact that she didn't like this second piece. It was ugly. It was upsetting. And yet, she couldn't look away from it.

It's true, she thought. This piece is telling the truth. The truth about what, she couldn't say, exactly. But it was honest.

She was still staring at it when Sam paged her on the ship's intercom, to let her know that the rest of the crew had arrived.

She returned to the galley to find Sam, Cardona, Harris, and White all gathered around the dining table. Compton leaned against a nearby counter, his arms crossed. Cardona and Harris looked curious, but White was obviously pissed at having their mini vacation interrupted. Goodwin sympathized, and the first thing out of her mouth was an apology.

"I'm sorry to call you back like this," she said. "You've all been working hard for months, and deserve a break. I wouldn't do this unless it was important."

From there, she recounted the meeting with Fade, and the mission they'd been offered—to find a madman on a quarantined world—and finished with the money on offer, and the caveat about the price dropping every six hours they delayed their answer.

When she finished, she looked around the table, to gauge her audience's reactions.

"That's a hell of a lot of money," Harris said. "Why didn't you say 'yes' on the spot?"

"How about because it's illegal?" White said. "And dangerous? This man is asking us to break the law and risk our lives, and is offering very little money in advance." They turned to Compton. "Do we even know what this plague is? What we're risking?"

Compton shook his head. "We'll get more information if we accept the job."

White waved their arms at Compton in a See what I mean? gesture. "Captain, this whole thing stinks."

"It does," Goodwin agreed. She leaned forward, putting her elbows on the table and clasping her hands. "But I'll level with you. We—the *Chariot*—are in deep trouble, and I don't know how much longer we'll be able to keep flying. The ship is deep in debt. Taking these light cargo jobs isn't going to pay for the repairs we need and keep all five of us on a steady paycheck. It's a truth I've been avoiding for a while now—one I was hoping to change into another, better truth while we were here on station. But that's not how it turned out. The original, ugly truth is still in play, and it's this: if we want to stay together as a crew, this job is what makes that happen."

She looked around the table, making eye contact with everyone. "I'm going to take the job," she said, surprising herself. She hadn't realized she'd made up her mind until she said so. She'd walked into the galley ready to let the crew hash it out and come to a decision together. What had changed during the course of the conversation?

The image of Bloch's sculpture popped into her mind's eye. Transfiguration. It had put down roots in her head.

"Assuming Harris can get the stabilizer working, that is," she amended.

"I'll see what I can do," Harris said.

"Now each of you has a decision to make," Goodwin said. "Whether to come along or not. You can take until tomorrow to think it over. If you're in, we'll depart then. If not, I'll do my best to arrange transport for you, get you someplace where you can find a new posting. I owe you that much and more."

She leaned back in her chair and waited. Silence hung heavy in the galley as everyone considered what she'd said.

"I don't need to think it over," Sam said. "Where you go, I go too."

Goodwin nodded. She'd expected as much.

Harris sighed. "I'm too old to go looking for a new job. And shit, I doubt you'd be able to get off-station without me to pummel the engine into submission. Guess I'm in, too."

"Me too," Cardona said. "You lot are the closest thing I've ever had to a family. If my family needs me, I'm there."

Everyone turned to look at White. They stared at their lap, frowning.

"I don't like this," they said at last, still staring down. "I really don't. I'll have to think it over."

Goodwin nodded. "Fair enough."

7

DEPARTURE

For the second time in as many days, Goodwin dismissed her crew. She sent Sam ahead to the Bowers, and asked Compton for some privacy on the bridge. He retreated to the far end of the ship while she returned to her station. Her coffee mug was still there, mostly full. She took a sip and grimaced. It had grown cold.

She took Fade's card from her breast pocket and inserted it into the console. After a moment, Fade's image appeared on the screen before her. He smiled.

"Captain Goodwin," he said.

"We're in," she said. "My crew is on leave for the rest of today. We'll leave tomorrow. Is that acceptable?"

"It's not ideal," he said. "Every second we wait is another second Corinth might be killed. But if that's how it is, so be it. I'll have my people deliver everything you'll need later today. Will there be someone at the ship to take delivery?"

Goodwin assured him that there would be. She wondered what he planned to send—supplies? Rations? Weapons? But she didn't ask.

"You have my gratitude, Captain," Fade said.

"I'm sure," Goodwin said, and cut the transmission.

She returned to the Bowers. She and Sam made love, ordered food to their room, and made love again before turning in for the night. As they lay in the vast bed, holding fast to one another, Sam said: "Fade is rich. There's probably no shortage of companionship available to someone with that much money. Fade must really love this Corinth Bloch, to go to so much trouble to rescue him."

"I guess so," Goodwin said.

"Would you try to rescue me?" Sam said. "If I went crazy and headed for a plague world?"

"I don't know," Goodwin said, and as soon as she said it, she knew she'd said the wrong thing. The correct answer—the thing Sam had been hoping to hear—was Yes. I would cross an ocean of stars and fight through hell itself to get to you. But they'd only been together six months, and most of that time had been spent in cryo. It wasn't like they'd had time for their relationship to get serious.

"Oh?" Sam said. He said it lightly, but his entire body stiffened beside her.

"I mean," she said. "You're a big boy. It's not like you were kidnapped or something. You made a choice to go to a plague world."

"Right, but in this scenario I'm not in my right mind."

"Mm," Goodwin said. She traced a fingertip down his narrow chest, between his pecs and down to his belly button. She wondered if he'd be up for more sex. He was a few years younger than she was. He probably could go one more time before they slept.

"For the record, I would come rescue you," he said.

"I know you would," she said. She almost added, You're stupid like that, but stopped herself. No need to hurt his feelings when she was trying to get laid again. She let her hand drift further south, beneath the blankets.

"Because I love you," he said.

Her exploring hand froze, and she sat up to look him in the eye. It was the first time either of them had ever said the words. She'd been expecting them for a while now, had tried to brace herself, but their arrival still hit her hard.

"Oh wow," she said, and swallowed hard. "I uh… That's very sweet of you to say." She knew he wanted her to say it back, but she just didn't have it in her. Not yet, anyway.

"Look, I'm not gonna freak out that you didn't say it back," he said. "I know what you're like. But I thought it was important to say before we head out on a life-and-death mission." He was doing his best to put on a brave face, but he looked hurt, and a little embarrassed.

"Well, thank you for saying it," Goodwin said. "Still want to come along for the dangerous mission, even if I don't say it back?"

"Where you go, I follow," he said. "For better or worse."

"Cheeseball," she said.

"I'm shipping out tomorrow and I don't know if I'll ever make it back," he said. "Wanna fuck?"

As it turned out, she did.

She had nightmares after that. But for the first time in her life, they were more than textures and emotions. There was more than that slicky, slimy feeling, like handling raw chicken, and loneliness and dread. There was a *shape* to the nightmares now, as if a camera were pulling into focus. There were figures lingering nearby. Watching and waiting for... something. She wasn't sure what. And when she woke the following morning, sweaty and gasping, there was an acidic pain in her chest, like the world's worst case of heartburn.

She got out of bed, pulled a roll of antacids from her coat pocket, and ate three of them at once. She nearly choked on the chalky texture and went to the bathroom to put her mouth under the faucet and wash them down.

What was happening with her dreams? It felt like they were progressing, moving from vagueness toward specificity. But what did that mean? Was that a good or bad thing?

She checked her watch. It wasn't even 6 a.m. They didn't have to be out of the hotel until 10. She came out of the bathroom, ready to try and get a little more sleep—or at least lie beside Sam while he slept in—only to find him stirring.

For once, he didn't ask her about her dreams. She found herself wishing he would. It would give her an excuse to talk about this shift she was experiencing.

Instead, he asked if she wanted to order breakfast.

She shook her head. Sure, they still had another four hours, but now that she was awake, all she wanted to do was get moving. She wanted to get back to the ship and see how Harris was doing with the stabilizer.

Sam, as always, was agreeable. He rolled with her desires. They both took quick showers, got dressed, and grabbed food at a stall in the commercial district before heading over to the *Chariot*.

When they arrived in the hangar bay, they found the ship's entry ramp already open. They came aboard to find Compton and Harris in the engine room, both covered in oil and grease, hunkered over the faulty stabilizer.

"Good morning," Harris said, not looking up from his work. "Nice of you to join us."

"Oh my God," Goodwin said. "You fixed it, didn't you?"

Harris gave her a skeptical look. "There's 'fixed' and then there's 'fixed,'" he said. "This isn't a long-term repair. It's temporary. But yeah, it should get us through at least this job. After that, you and I are going parts shopping."

Goodwin would've hugged him, if he weren't so filthy.

"Good work," she said, instead. "And thank you."

"Thank me once we're actually flying again," he said. But he gave her a half-smile and a nod before he returned to work.

Sam and Goodwin got the ship ready for takeoff. It felt good to slide into the routine, cal-checking the systems, cleaning the galley, prepping the pods for cryo.

Roman Fade's courier arrived about an hour after Goodwin. The man didn't come bearing crates of food or other supplies, but rather a single box. Mildly disappointed (but still curious), Goodwin took the box to the galley and opened it at the dining table.

It contained two disks. A small one, that came on a chain, had a note, "For Corinth's eyes only." This one she draped around her neck. It fit neatly inside her shirt. The other was a long data-disk, which she plugged into the galley computer. It appeared to contain information for the journey, including coordinates for DSJ-1020, advice on where to jump in and out of

FTL, topographical maps of the terrain, blueprints for the colony, New Providence, and instructions for getting past the Marine ship in orbit around the planet. Goodwin uploaded all this to the ship's main computer at once.

Per the data on the disk, DSJ-1020 was located on a frontier star system designated MJ-419, which was out past the Solomons. The system had a yellow-white main sequence star, and four planets in orbit. DSJ-1020 was the second-closest of those planets to the star, a mid-sized world about 8000km in diameter. The atmosphere was breathable, although a little cold and stormy by Earth standards, with average surface temperatures ranging from -15 to 15 degrees Celsius, and a geosphere about 70 percent covered with ocean. The remaining 30 percent was land, with large swaths of forest, as well as sweeping plains of grasslands and fertile soil.

Goodwin could see why Weyland-Yutani had been eager to colonize the world. Most surveyed planets, you would be lucky to find useful minerals under the surface. But to find a world with a breathable atmosphere and fertile soil? No terraforming required? That was like winning the interstellar lottery.

Given the Eden-like conditions of the world, what could have gone so terribly wrong that the company had erased it from the official record? Early survey data didn't seem to indicate any particularly dangerous flora or fauna.

Frustratingly, none of Bloch's provided info seemed to indicate the nature of the catastrophe, either. No records, no transmissions. There was a series of encrypted files on the disk, and a note explaining that they would unlock once the *Chariot* landed on DSJ-1020. Again, Goodwin's inner alarm went off. Something about this was wrong. Why so secretive? How was she supposed to prepare for a contagion when all information had been locked away?

More interesting than the info about the world (and less frustrating than the locked files), Fade's disc contained more of Corinth Bloch's work, in higher-resolution files. She immediately went to the image files for 'Transfiguration.' It wasn't that she was eager to look at the sculpture again. She felt compelled.

The galley computer was not an ideal display, but she still managed to pick out some new details she hadn't seen on the magnetic tape version. There was a granularity to the sculpture, a porousness that made it look almost like poured concrete, rather than clay. And the figure's legs—the knees seemed to bend in the wrong direction. The arms, seemed almost *too* long. And there was something about the figure's chest. In the magnetic tape file, it had looked flat, but on the long-disc version, it appeared distended. As though something were trying to get out from inside.

What was it about this sculpture that spoke to her? It triggered an itch in her mind—the sense of something right on the tip of her tongue. Something she ought to know and recognize. But what was she recognizing? She could confidently say she'd never seen anything like this. Not even her nightmares had provided something shaped like this.

Goodwin was so focused on the image that she forgot the world around her, and was startled by the sound of the galley door sliding open behind her. She gasped and took a step away from the computer, feeling both frightened and guilty, as though she'd been caught looking at something she shouldn't have.

It was Cardona, who seemed alarmed by Goodwin's reaction. She put up both hands and took a step back toward the door.

"Sorry," she said. "Didn't mean to interrupt."

"You're not," Goodwin said. "I was just deep in my own head and got startled. Come in, please."

Cardona entered, and fixed herself a mug of coffee. Goodwin took the opportunity to eject the long-disk, and get back to work on departure prep.

About ten minutes before their scheduled departure, Harris paged Goodwin, who was now on the bridge.

"White just arrived," he said. "They're back in the cargo hold with Cardona."

Goodwin stopped what she was doing and headed after. She found Cardona with White in the hold, making a fresh attempt at cleaning the bug juice stains off the floor. Both were on their hands and knees, scrubbing the floor with sponges. A bucket full of some sharp and abrasive-smelling liquid stood between them.

White looked up when she entered, then went back to work.

"Good to see you, White," Goodwin said.

"Wish I could say it was good to be here," White said.

"I'm glad you're here, anyway," Goodwin said.

They shrugged. "I still don't approve of this job. If I had a good idea of somewhere else to go, I would go there. But it's like Cardona said. You assholes are the closest thing I have to family."

"I didn't call anyone an asshole," Cardona said.

"You're too nice to say it out loud," White said. "But I felt it was implied."

"Don't trust that feeling," Cardona said.

Goodwin headed back for the bridge, retracting the boarding ramp along the way. She felt uncharacteristically warm and fuzzy. She imagined parents must feel this way, tucking their children into bed at night. Everyone was home, safe and sound. She didn't know what she'd done to deserve such a loyal crew, but she was lucky to have them.

***

The *Chariot* departed Knapik Station a few minutes later. The whole crew gathered on the bridge for the event, just in case the stabilizer wasn't as repaired as Harris hoped.

The worry was for nothing. It was a smooth takeoff. You'd never have guessed that they had basically crash-landed here two days before. As they slipped through the hangar bay's magnetic seal and back into the monochrome vastness of space, Goodwin made a mental note to increase Harris's pay, as soon as she could afford to.

Sam watched the station recede on the aft sensors, and when they were far enough out, he plugged in their course for DSJ-1020.

"It's a good thing Fade gave us the coordinates," he said, as he punched numbers into his console. "I think the planet's been wiped from all official star maps."

"Guess that's one way to make sure nobody comes poking around," Goodwin said.

"Makes you wonder how many other worlds have been lost out there," White said. "Erased from existence at some company or government whim."

"I don't want to think about that," Cardona said.

"And they don't want you to think about it," White said. "That's how they get away with it."

Sam's work didn't take long. Once the course was plotted, there was nothing left to do but head for the freezers. The crew stripped down to their underwear in the galley, hung their clothes in their lockers, and headed for the cryo chamber, which contained seven hypersleep pods arranged in a circle around a central terminal. As they laid down, Compton tucked each of them in, closing the pods over them. His gentle, smiling, beaded face was the last thing Goodwin saw as the pod's glass top sealed atop her, and then she was gone, drifting away to weeks of dreaming.

8

ARRIVAL

People who couldn't remember their dreams reported their time in cryo as almost instantaneous—one second, their pod was getting colder, and the next, they were waking up, feeling hungover. But for Goodwin, who remembered her nightmares, the weeks left a footprint. They helped her mark time, even while her body was frozen. And so when Compton finally opened her pod, she felt like she was coming to the end of a long journey.

He stood over her, a robe draped over one arm, his free hand extended to help her up.

"How are we doing?" she croaked, as she allowed herself to be pulled up into a sitting position.

"We just dropped out of FTL in the MJ-419 system," Compton said. "Diagnostics report everything is fine. As soon as we arrived, however, we started receiving hails from the USS *Fratto*."

Goodwin came all the way awake at that. She stood, took the robe from Compton, and yanked it on. "Is there coffee?"

"Not yet. The *Fratto* is a Conestoga-class frigate with enough firepower to atomize us," Compton said. His voice was steady and reasonable, despite the urgency of his message. "I thought it prudent to wake you first so you can talk to them. Then I planned to deal with the coffee."

"Fair," Goodwin said.

She put on her slippers and jogged to the bridge. Her console was blinking with the incoming communication light. She flipped a switch and opened the channel, pulling on her headset as she did so.

The channel crackled to life, and she heard a voice. "Repeat, this is the USS *Fratto*. You have entered restricted airspace. *Chariot*, you will either change course now, or we will open fire. This is your last warning."

Goodwin said, "USS *Fratto*, this is Captain Goodwin of the USCSS *Chariot*," Goodwin said. "May I speak to—" She fumbled through Roman Fade's information file, looking for the name. "Lieutenant Diaz?" she finished. "Repeat, I would like to speak to Lieutenant Diaz."

There was a pause on the channel—long enough for Goodwin to wonder if the ship was arming its weapons. But then another voice came on the line.

"*Chariot*, this is Lieutenant Diaz," the voice said. It was a woman. Her voice was light—almost friendly. Some of Goodwin's panic receded.

"Lieutenant Diaz," she said. She had the appropriate file on her monitor and read from it now. "I'm here with humanitarian aid for the people of New Providence. Authorization code one-eight-oh-nine-two-four-six-oh-niner."

"Roger that," Diaz said. "You are cleared for approach."

"Thank you, Lieutenant," Goodwin said.

"Just so you know, Captain. Once you're down there, you're on your own. There will be no record of your arrival. No one will come looking for you. Whether or not you ever leave the planet will be entirely up to you."

"Understood," Goodwin said. "Thanks again."

"Good luck," Diaz said, and closed the channel.

Goodwin headed for the showers after that. She wanted a long shower, so she had Compton wait half an hour to wake the rest of the crew. It was a dick move, using up so much of the ship's hot water while everyone else was still in cryo, but fuck it. Captain's privilege. To make it up to the others, she set the galley table for breakfast and prepared coffee for everyone, just the way they liked it, so that, by the time they emerged from their own lukewarm showers, everything was ready.

Goodwin gave the crew some time to eat and drink before she started talking logistics. She relayed the information she had about the planet, as well as the encrypted files set to unlock once they landed on DSJ-1020.

"What are you getting from the scanners?" Harris said. "Anything strange in the atmosphere?"

"Not much of anything," Compton said. "There seems to be a planetwide storm happening at the moment, and it's blocking our instruments from anything but the most preliminary data. There don't appear to be any airborne contagions—at least nothing the ship's sensors recognize—but that's about it."

"After we get paid, we should invest in a new scanner package," Harris said.

"Add it to the list," Goodwin said. "In the meantime, here's the plan: we'll take the ship in closer to the surface and start scanning for life forms. If this world has been decimated by plague, there shouldn't be a lot living down there. Hopefully we'll locate this Bloch pretty quickly. At that point, we land near his location and head out. I'm going to proceed under the assumption that there's something airborne, no matter what the sensors say, so we'll put on EVA suits when we head out. We'll go to his location, retrieve him, and take off again as soon as the storm clears up. In and out."

"No muss, no fuss," Harris said. "I like it."

"Who's actually going out of the ship?" White asked.

"I'm taking volunteers," Goodwin said. "We only have five EVA suits, and I want to save one for Bloch."

"What's the point of that?" White said. "If he's down there, he's sick, right? He'll have whatever killed everyone else."

"We don't know that," Goodwin replied. "He might be fine. He might be immune. We have no idea. So we put him in a suit until we can get him into cryo, and minimize our chances of spreading something."

"But you'll have to take him out of the suit to put him in the pod," White said. "So you're still putting everyone at risk."

"It's an imperfect solution," Goodwin said. "But it's what we have. Now let's talk ground mission. Compton and I will be going, so that's two of the four suits accounted for. I'd like to bring two more bodies, just in case. Do I have any volunteers?"

"I'll go," Sam said.

Goodwin nodded. She'd expected as much.

"If he's going, I'm staying," Harris said. "We'll need someone who can fly the ship if something happens out there."

"Anyone else?" Goodwin said.

White stared at the dregs in their coffee mug.

Cardona cleared her throat. "I'll go." She was hugging herself, as though cold, and didn't look happy.

"Are you sure?" White said. "You don't have to. It's a volunteer situation."

"I know," she said. "But I'm going."

"Thank you," Goodwin said.

"No muss, no fuss," Cardona said, and gave a small smile.

They all crowded onto the bridge and strapped in for approach. DSJ-1020 grew large outside the viewport. From space, its Earthlike attributes were obscured beneath vast storm clouds, giving the whole planet a mottled, gray appearance, interrupted only occasionally by flashes of lightning.

"Everyone hold on," Sam said. "This may get bumpy."

Soon, space was obscured altogether, and the *Chariot* was lost in a world of gray. The ship began to shake around them. The floor of Goodwin's stomach seemed to open as they dropped into the atmosphere. She gripped her armrests and gritted her teeth, which rattled against one another.

"Harris, I thought you fixed the stabilizers," White shouted over the noise.

"I did," Harris shouted back. "This is the stabilized version of this landing!"

"Can everyone please be quiet?" Sam said. "I'm trying to concentr—"

The end of his sentence was lost in a flash of light out the viewport, and a *boom* that reverberated through the ship. Suddenly the dropping sensation in Goodwin's stomach doubled. There was a new sound atop the rumbling, a harsh blare. An alarm of some kind. Out the viewport, the world remained impenetrable and gray. It was impossible to tell what was happening, but Goodwin's body insisted that something was *wrong*. She was thrown hard against her crash harness, first in one direction, then another, then back again. She continued to grip her armrests, squeezing the fabric between her fingers.

Sam and White were both shouting. She couldn't make out the words over the alarm and the shaking of the ship. They seemed far away, and everything felt heavy—even the hair atop her head seemed to be weighing her down.

Spinning, she thought. *We're spinning out.*

It was the last coherent thought she had before she lost consciousness.

9

STRANDED

For a while there was nothing. No feeling. No thought. Not even nightmares.

Then, little by little, she became aware of pain. Dull at first, and distant, like a song you knew being played in another room at a low volume.

It was constant, like a low hum, but grew sharper and then duller again. Sharper, then duller again. There was also a sensation of cold. Rain. Water misting against her skin. And there was a sound—a hum, like someone speaking, but the words were just nonsense to her.

Goodwin opened her eyes. Sam was leaning over her. He was shaking her by the shoulder and asking questions. She didn't understand the questions, but really wanted to stop the shaking.

She groaned and batted his hand off her. She touched her forehead and her fingers came away sticky with dark fluid. She rubbed her fingertips together, trying to make sense of what she was seeing.

Blood. You're bleeding.

The words, the idea, somehow drew the world back into focus for her. She could understand what Sam was saying as he leaned over her, entirely too close for comfort.

"Oh thank God," he said. "You're awake."

Goodwin wasn't sure they ought to be thanking anybody just yet. She squirmed against the crash harness, and started to unbuckle herself.

"Don't try to move yet," Sam said. "I think you might have a concussion." He moved away, out of her line of vision. She heard him fumbling with something nearby.

"What happened?" she said.

"I'm not sure," Sam said. "But I think we were hit by lightning. It might've shorted our stabilizers. We spun out."

He returned, holding the bridge's first aid kit under one arm. He knelt in front of Goodwin and shined a penlight in her eyes.

"What are you doing?" she said.

"I'm looking at your pupils. Trying to see if you have a concussion."

She shook her head, then regretted it as fresh fireworks of pain burst in her skull. "That's a myth. Not a surefire way to test for a concussion."

He sighed, exasperated. "I'm no medic."

"Let's go to medbay. We can do a scan there."

"We don't have any power at the moment. All our instruments are dead."

"Must've been one hell of a crash," Goodwin said.

Sam grunted, a sound that might have been a weak attempt at a polite laugh.

"So no medbay," Goodwin said. "Get Compton. He's a perfectly capable medic."

Sam turned off the penlight, his mouth squeezed into a narrow line. He hung his head for a second, then pointed at a giant hole in the wall behind him. For the first time, she realized that part of the bridge was missing. Rain and wind were blowing in through an opening, along with weak, gray daylight.

"We suffered a hull breach during the crash," Sam said. "Compton was sucked right out. Like a bad magic trick. There one second, gone the next."

"No muss, no fuss," Goodwin said, and experienced another instance of immediate regret. Sam was nice enough to let the bad joke pass without comment. Instead, he cleaned the wound on her head, wiping away the blood and dabbing at the cut with antiseptic.

"This doesn't look too bad," he said. "You won't even need stitches."

"How's everyone else?" she said.

"It's sort of a miracle, really," Sam said. "Harris, White, and Cardona are all fine. You're the only one who took a hit."

"Me and Compton," she said.

"Right." He didn't seem to broken up about the loss of the android, but Goodwin felt it. He'd been a good companion—better than most humans. He was dependable, honest, and kind. Who cared if that's how he'd been programmed. It was who he was and always had been. And now he was just gone?

You don't know he's dead, she told herself. *He could've survived the fall. He might need some repairs, but he's not necessarily dead.*

Just most likely dead, another voice spoke up in her mind. *And you have no way to search for him. Better to just give him up for dead, kiddo.*

"Where's everyone else?" she said.

"Galley," Sam said. "Putting together supplies."

She let Sam finish bandaging her cut, then unstrapped from her harness and went to the galley. Her mind still felt foggy. Her movements were awkward. She probably *was* concussed. Great. Add it to the list.

She found Harris, White, and Cardona packing dry goods from the pantry into bags. White looked absolutely livid, but the other two seemed happy to see Goodwin up.

"Hey, Captain," Cardona said.

"Good to see you on your feet," Harris said.

"Wish I could say it felt good to be on them," Goodwin said.

"You took a big hit," Harris said. "Maybe sit for a minute? Take it easy?"

Goodwin did as he suggested, and sighed. "So," she said. "Have we made an assessment of the damage?"

"Stabilizers are completely fried," Harris said. "All of them will have to be replaced. Our electrical systems are all out, too. We'd need a jump to get them up again. But even if we got all of that fixed? There's a giant fucking hole in the ship where Compton used to sit."

"How'd we end up with a hole in the ship?" Cardona said. "I don't understand. Did something hit us? Aside from lightning, I mean."

"She's an old ship," Harris said. "Lightning, the storm, and gravity might've been enough, once we were spinning out."

Goodwin sighed again. "So we've crashed on DSJ-ten-twenty. Our ship is fucked. The only people who know we're here are the two marines in orbit, who've been paid to look the other way, and Roman Fade."

"Maybe Fade will send another rescue mission, when we don't report back?" Cardona said. "We have enough food here to hold out for at least a month, if we're careful."

"Even if that happens," Goodwin said, "assuming the ship makes it through atmosphere intact, this is a big planet. There's no guarantee they'd spot us, or vice-versa."

"Fuck," White said. They kicked the closest wall, and shouted. "Fuck! We're completely fucked."

"Cool it, White," Goodwin said.

White spun on her. "I said we shouldn't take this job! I said so! Did anyone listen to me? Did anyone care? And now we're stuck here, and we're probably going to *die* here, and it's all because no one would fucking listen to common sense." As they spoke, they edged in toward Goodwin, brandishing their index finger like a weapon, poking it in her face.

Goodwin didn't flinch. She stared the cargo handler down. Their eyes were wild. They were on the brink of losing control.

"You can calm yourself down, White, or I can sedate you," Goodwin said. "It's your call."

White's nostrils flared. The extended index finger drew back into a fist, and for a moment, Goodwin thought they were going to punch her. Then they dropped their hand to their side, drooped their head, and stalked away, to one of the dark corners of the galley.

"So what's the plan?" Sam said.

Goodwin considered, trying to think clearly through the brain fog. It was difficult. "Our best bet is to head for the colony. New Providence. It's presumably where Fade was headed, and it's our best chance of finding transport off this rock."

"Do we even know where we landed?" White said. "The colony could be on the other side of the planet. On a different fucking continent."

"We have some mobile equipment in storage," Harris

said. "We can rig it up to look for electronic signals—transponders, pings, SOS beacons, but also just electric current in the air. If there's any tech still running in the colony, we should be able to pick it up if it's within 200 klicks. We follow the signals, and hope we don't hit a body of water."

"What about the EVA situation?" Sam said. "There are only five suits. There are five of us but we wanted one for Bloch."

Goodwin shrugged. "If there's something in the air here, we're already exposed. Not much we can do about it now. You four are welcome to suit up if you want, but I'd rather not be encumbered. Our best chance is to make it to the colony as quickly as possible. Maybe they have a working medbay we can use to scan ourselves for contagion."

"Fuck," White said, but there was nothing explosive in the statement. It sounded reflective. Sad.

"Fuck," Goodwin agreed.

The crew packed as much food and medical supplies as they could comfortably carry, while Harris rigged up a motion tracker to search for electric signals. Goodwin took the time to dig her laptop out of storage. It was a warhorse of a computer—old, but the battery still held a charge despite long seasons of disuse. She grabbed the long disk that Fade had given her. It was still in the bridge console where she'd left it. It was cracked, and getting it out of the console proved tricky, but it still appeared to be in one piece once she had it out. She was curious whether the encrypted files would unlock now. She was eager to see what they said.

Once she'd packed her own gear, she joined Harris in the galley, where he was finishing up with the motion tracker. It was a handheld device with a small green display. He moved it back and forth through the air and it chirped at him.

"Any luck?" Goodwin said.

"Yes, as a matter of fact," Harris said. "I'm picking up a strong signal about fifty klicks south of us."

She squeezed his shoulder. "Good work."

"I know it," he said, smiling at the compliment.

10

DSJ-1020

It was about 11 degrees Celsius outside the ship. Cold, but not unbearably so. It was liable to get colder once the sun went down, so Goodwin ordered everyone to bundle up in their warmest clothing before they set out. They would probably sweat all day, but they'd be glad come nightfall. She wished that she had an ATV, something they could use as a pack mule for extra cargo.

Add it to the list, she told herself, and almost smiled.

Even the emergency electrical systems on the *Chariot* were screwed. Harris couldn't get the entry ramp to descend, so the crew were forced to exit the ship via the hull breach. They'd crashed into a rocky hillside, so they used a winch to lower themselves from the gap down to the closest level ground. One by one they descended. Goodwin went last. Once she was alone on the bridge, she put a hand to the damaged hull.

"I'll try to come back for you," she murmured. "I promise."

She made herself look up at the ship as she descended toward the ground. The *Chariot* looked so strange, wedged in at an odd angle among the hillside boulders. Her home. Her childhood home. Her livelihood. Dashed upon the rocks of an alien world. Completely dead. She had to find a way to fix it. To get the old girl running again. She owed it to her mother.

Only after she touched the ground did she look around. She stood in the bottom of a valley between two rocky peaks. The ground was grassy, interspersed with boulders. The storm seemed to have calmed somewhat, pelting the crew with a gentle, sprinkling rain.

"At least it's pretty here," Cardona said.

It was still daylight, although the sun was hidden behind heavy cloud cover, so it was hard to tell what time of day it was planetside. After consulting Harris's jury-rigged scanner, they started off in what they hoped was the direction of New Providence. They climbed up one of the steep valley hills, going slowly, their boots squelching in mud and occasionally slipping on wet rocks. None of them were experienced climbers, and Harris needed frequent stops to catch his breath. Too many cigars and too much junk food had caught up with the old man.

When they crested the hill, Goodwin and the crew found themselves looking down into another valley.

The next peak seemed less steep than the one they'd just climbed, but that was little comfort in the rain, and cold. Harris groaned.

"How far have we come?" she asked.

Harris checked his sensor. "About one klick. Still forty-something to go."

Goodwin looked skyward. She wanted to keep going, but the light was already failing.

"Let's get to the bottom of the hill, and we'll make camp for the night," she said.

At the bottom of the valley, they pitched their tents in a circle for the night. Maybe it wasn't such a bad thing, stopping this soon. Everyone must be fatigued, coming down from the adrenaline rush of the crash. A good night's rest would help. They could get in a better day's march tomorrow.

The rain had stopped by the time they finished pitching their tents. They set up a small, portable space heater in the middle of the camp, between the tents, and huddled around it, soaking up its feeble warmth. Goodwin could just make out everyone's faces in the dull orange light.

"Wish we could have a real fire," Sam said. "Like campers, back on Earth."

"No wood," Harris said.

"Even if we had wood, I don't know how to start a

fire," White said. "Do any of you?"

They looked around at one another. No one said anything. Everyone seemed sort of sheepish about it. Harris grunted a laugh. Cardona joined in. Then Sam. Then even Goodwin and White began to laugh as well.

The sound echoed in the valley around them. They laughed until Goodwin's sides ached and her head hurt even worse than before. She could barely breathe.

She couldn't explain it. It hadn't been a particularly funny moment. Under other circumstances, no one would have laughed. But for some reason, right now, it was the funniest thing in the world. She was laughing so hard she thought she might pass out.

Gradually the laughter tapered, and a heavy silence fell over the crew, as the reality of their situation reasserted itself.

"What should we do now?" Sam said. "Tell ghost stories?"

"Ugh, no thank you," Cardona said.

"We might as well turn in," Goodwin said. "Get some rest. Try to make better progress tomorrow."

"Should we set a watch?" White said.

Goodwin looked to Harris, who flipped on his tracker and set it to motion detector mode. He frowned down at the screen.

"I don't see anything moving anywhere near us," he said.

Goodwin frowned, too. That was odd. No movement

at all? No native lifeforms in the area? Not even birds? This was an Earthlike world. Surely *something* would've evolved here.

Unless the plague already got it, she thought.

"I'll sit up for a while," Goodwin said. "Keep an eye on things."

"I'll sit up with you," Sam said. "Since you might be concussed."

Goodwin would rather have had some privacy, but she couldn't argue with his logic. "Alright. Everyone else go to sleep. Sam and I will stay up."

Harris handed the motion tracker to Goodwin. The rest of the crew trundled off into their tents, leaving her and Sam sitting next to one another in the dim light of the space heater. Its glow was so weak, and the dark of the night around them so oppressive and strong. The winds were relatively gentle, but the unseen peaks around them amplified the sound, turned it into a steady roar. It would be difficult to see or hear anything approaching the camp, drawn to their feeble light.

She flipped on the motion tracker, and reassured herself that there was nothing moving within half a klick of their location, then switched it off again. She would have preferred to just leave it on, but it was probably better to save the battery.

"So," Sam said. He scooted closer to her, so that their hips were touching. "Want to tell ghost stories?"

"We should be quiet so the others can sleep,"

Goodwin said. "And anyway, I've got homework to do. You'll have to entertain yourself, if you can."

"Right," Sam said. He pulled his knapsack into his lap, and pulled a small rectangular device from it. Goodwin had seen it before: Sam's e-reader, a device developed purely for reading. They'd been in vogue on Earth briefly at the beginning of the 21st century. Goodwin had no idea how old Sam's was, but guessed it would qualify as an antique now. It probably cost him twice or three times what you'd pay for a low-end tablet, but Sam said he read better on the device's e-ink screen. He said it was closer to reading on paper, provided a purer experience.

He switched it on now, its screen throwing a blueish glow on his face as he settled into whatever he was reading—probably some fantasy novel, about barbarians and monsters in some prehistoric version of Earth.

Goodwin pulled her laptop from her knapsack. She powered it up, and inserted Fade's long disk. An error popped up on the screen: some of the files had apparently been corrupted. She swore as she cleared the error, and went to look at the files. As she feared, the corrupted files were exactly the ones she'd been worried about. The encrypted stuff that was supposed to unlock upon arrival. Only one of the files appeared to be intact. She opened it.

> **Bloch_Dossier_001**   ◄ ► X

My Dearest Roman,

If you're reading this, I'm already long gone.

I've been deceiving you for months now. It was necessary, to achieve my ends.

We've often talked about our mutual love of privacy and how hard we've fought to maintain it. We've also often joked about the books we could write. The scandals we could bring to light—you in the corporate sphere, me in the art world. We joked about selling our books to the big publishers on Earth, then stipulating that said books couldn't be published until after our deaths. How, from beyond the grave, we would get the last laugh.

I'm thinking about that now, as I write these words. I don't believe I'll ever actually write a book. This document, this manifesto, this whatever-you-want-to-call-it will be the closest I ever get. And I'm writing for an audience of one, because while I don't care what the world thinks of me, I do care about what you think, my love. I shouldn't. I really shouldn't. But I do. Because of that, I need you to understand why I'm doing the things I'm doing, even if no one else does.

You know more about me than anyone in the galaxy, but there's still a lot you don't know about my life. I want to fill in the gaps now. Firstly, because you deserve to know. Secondly, more importantly, I need you to understand why I've betrayed you, and stolen from you, after years of apparent happiness and intimacy.

So here, at last, is everything.

====

I was born on AF-617, a mining world in the Neroid sector. There aren't a lot of mining worlds in Neroid. It's mostly research stations and waste storage for the corps out there. Almost anything worth mining was stripped bare by the UPP years ago. But some surveyor or wildcatter found a pocket of helium that everyone else somehow missed, and Seegson set up a domed mining colony. They didn't bother installing atmosphere processors. They didn't bother naming the planet, or its colony. They didn't expect to be on-world long enough to need those things. Instead, they just threw up a dome over some prefabricated buildings and called it good.

Humanity shared this hunk of rock with a few endoliths—microscopic organisms that somehow managed to survive in its harsh atmosphere—but otherwise, we thought we had the planet to ourselves.

My father was a miner. My mother was a bartender at the local watering hole. It didn't need a name because it was the only bar on-world.

There's no great story to how my parents met. She was working, he was spending his pay. They went home together one night and liked it well enough that they made a habit of it. They never married, but by the time I was born, they lived together. I think they loved one another, in the way that ruthlessly pragmatic people can make room for one another in their hearts. I never saw them hug, or kiss, or heard them speak sweet nothings to one another, but I also never heard them fight or say a bad word about one another. I never saw them hit one another (as so many of my peers' parents did), or cheat on one another. Their affections and commitment seemed solid.

My earliest memories are of our apartment. It was a small space, with hard metal floors and walls. Mom did her best to make it cozy. She hung art prints on the walls, put rugs on the floors, bought candles and incense whenever the supply ships brought them.

During the first nine years of my life, I wasn't artistically inclined. There were no early warning signs of burgeoning genius. I drew and colored when there were supplies available, but no more than any other child. What I produced wasn't advanced, or particularly remarkable. You wouldn't have picked it out of a lineup of other children's art.

Me and the other colony kids went to school, where our teachers were Seegson Working Joe androids. We played hide-and-seek in the colony ventilation shafts, and occasionally stole tractors to go joyriding across the featureless surface of our home world. Sometimes, on windy nights, we gathered around a space heater in an empty classroom to tell stories about the creatures we imagined might be living out in the darkness.

It was a perfectly ordinary colony kid life—until the day Dad came home from his shift in the mines with a story that sounded like something we might've made up around the space heater.

The three of us—me, Mom, and Dad—were sitting around the fold-out dining table in our tiny apartment, eating a stew of protein bites in a thin broth. Dad had his customary Souta Dry open in front of him, and Mom and I had our cloudy glasses of water. Mom was excited because there was a ship due in—and not a company-owned ship, with its usual sad wares, but an independent contractor, called the *Chariot*, who might have all sorts of interesting things to sell. Mom was always desperate for new things to read, new movies to see, new tchotchkes to make our apartment homier. Moreover, the *Chariot* was captained by a woman named Alice Goodwin, who was apparently an old friend of Mom's.

Dad and I were being quiet, listening to Mom talk about all this. Dad never said much, so it wasn't unusual that he was quiet. What was unusual—and here I admit my memory may be lying to me, putting in foreshadowing where it didn't truly exist—was the pregnant energy coming from his side of the table.

When Mom got up to refill her water glass, Dad put down his spoon and shook his head. Mom somehow spotted the gesture from the kitchenette.

"What's wrong?" she said.

He took a sip of beer. Dad was never one to rush a task. "Damndest thing today at work. We drilled into a cavern."

"What's so unusual about that?" Mom said, re-seating herself at the table. "Don't you drill through empty pockets all the time?"

"Isn't that where you find most of the gas?" I said. We'd gone over gas mining at school as part of our lessons, but I was never a strong student. Even now, I'm not sure how gas mining works.

"Sure," Dad said. "But the sensor readout sent back some weird data. There was no helium in the cavern. What we got back on the sensors was air—actual, breathable air. Like Earth atmosphere air."

"Okay, that is strange," Mom said.

"We sent some probes down, to have a look," Dad said. "They found... things."

"What kind of things?" I said.

"It was sort of hard to tell from the video feed," Dad said. "But it looked like there was some kind of sculpture down there. A giant bald head. And around it, a bunch of, I don't know what you'd call them... vases, I guess? Black vases? Just tons of them, arranged in neat rows, extending out from the giant head."

I want to pause the narrative here, and point this moment out. The feeling I got, hearing my father tell the story, was the one I always *hoped* to feel when listening to my friends tell ghost stories on a windy night. Those stories always left me feeling a little disappointed, but I never understood why until this moment, at the dinner table with my father, listening to him describe a chamber which should *not have been there*, beneath the surface of AF-617. The tension between what should be, and what actually was, created a sudden frisson, goosepimples racing up and down my shoulders.

"What the hell is it?" Mom said.

"No idea," Dad said. "Nobody's ever seen anything like it."

"There's a lot of UPP worlds in this sector," Mom said. "Maybe something they left behind?"

"Maybe," Dad said. He said it lightly, but didn't seem convinced.

"Do you have a copy of the video?" I asked.

"No," Dad said.

"I want to see it."

I rarely showed interest in Dad's work, so maybe he was touched. He agreed to take me to the central mining office after dinner. Mom wasn't keen on the idea—afraid it would give me nightmares—but Dad overruled her. After we'd rinsed our dishes and put them in the washer, we donned our jackets and headed to the central mining office. There were a few administrators and managers hanging around for the night shift, but it was mostly quiet, and Dad found an empty desk where he could call up the recording for me.

We huddled before the little CRT screen to watch the video. It started with footage of a few miners gathered around a hole, testing the camera. One of the miners—a young man I recognized around station—waved and blew the camera a kiss before laughing and looking away.

The camera descended through darkness. For a long moment, there was nothing to see except craggy rock walls, lit by the camera's spotlight. The waiting only made it more exciting. I leaned in closer to the screen, so that my nose was only inches away. I didn't want to miss anything.

The camera finally emerged from the hole, into the cavern. The reception was glitchy, the screen plagued by little fits of snow, and the camera's light wasn't nearly enough to fill the chamber. I got impressions of images, little pieces of the picture, rather than the whole panorama.

From what I could tell, the chamber seemed massive. It stretched away in all directions, disappearing into the darkness. But close to the hole, near the only visible wall, there was a giant sculpture. Dad had described it accurately. A giant bald head, carved from dark stone. It reminded me of photos of the moai on Earth that I'd seen at school, but where those sculptures were crude and blocky, this was completely smooth, with fine detail.

The camera continued to descend toward the head, and as it did, I caught sight of the "vases" Dad had mentioned earlier. Rows and rows of them.

Then I spotted something Dad hadn't mentioned. It was only onscreen for an instant, but it caught my eye.

"Wait," I said. "Pause the tape?"

Dad did as I asked. Then I took over the controls, backing the recording up frame by frame. I moved back and forth, until, frustrated, I settled on the clearest image available. I pointed at the screen.

"What is that?" I said. "There, on the wall, behind the head."

The wall was black, like the vases and the stone head, but of a different texture—almost like spilled fluid, somehow flash-frozen before settling. It rippled and surged, as though in a strong wind. And at the center of this rippling, surging wall, a single figure seemed to emerge. It was difficult to see on the freeze frame, but slightly clearer in motion, once you knew where to look: roughly human in shape, but skeletal, as though it had no flesh, with long, narrow limbs, and an oblong, curved skull.

Dad leaned in beside me, squinting at the screen. "Huh," he said. "Nobody caught that."

A pleasurable shiver ran through my body. Even through the crappy resolution and bad lighting—or perhaps because of them?—I thought the figure on the wall was the most beautiful thing I'd ever seen. Here at last was a figure worthy of nightmares.

"Good looking out, kiddo," Dad said. He did a rare thing, then: he ruffled my hair. It was the last time he ever touched me.

====

I dreamt of the cavern that night, as Mom had worried I might. And I guess you would technically call the dreams nightmares. In them, I wandered the chamber of vases in the shadow of the ever-watching giant head. The figure on the wall moved. It beckoned to me, calling me toward some secret knowledge.

The next day was Saturday. Dad went to work— we needed the overtime—while Mom read a book on the couch and I shut myself away in my bedroom and started drawing. I'd always drawn, as children do, but for the first time in my ten years, I was taking it seriously. I had to get these images from my dreams down on paper.

When my mother finally came to check on me, I'd burned through almost an entire pad of drawing paper, had worn my black crayon down to a nub.

"You're never this quiet," she said. "What are you up to in here?"

Instead of answering, I watched her bend over and pick up a handful of pages I'd stacked on my bedside table. She rifled through them.

"Is this what you saw when you went with your Dad last night?" she asked.

Some of the pictures were things I'd actually seen—I'd done several studies of the giant head, for example—but others were riffs on reality. The figure from the wall, but set free from its Christ-like pose. Moving through the hallways of the colony. Lurking outside my classroom, barely visible in shadows.

She sighed. "I told him not to take you."

I wanted to tell her that yes, I'd had nightmares, but that they weren't the point. I didn't mind the nightmares. They—and the sights that had inspired them—had gifted me a glimpse into a larger world. It was like a curtain had been pulled aside—a curtain I'd previously been unaware of. Reality was bigger and stranger than I knew, and I was hungry for more.

But, at age 10, I lacked the words to express this. So instead, I asked if Mom would buy me more crayons at the colony store.

She glanced at the box on my desk, full of mostly-untouched crayons, then down at my nub of a black crayon.

"I should see if they'll just sell me one," she said. "Looks like that's all you need."

She went into the kitchenette and started on dinner. She liked to have it ready right when Dad got home. She was pretty good at timing it out, after all these years. It gave us time to eat together, before she had to head out for her night shift at the bar.

Only today, Dad wasn't home by the time she finished cooking. I set the table, and even put out a fresh, cold beer for him, but he had yet to clomp through the door.

"Maybe his shift ran long?" I said. But he usually called when that happened.

Mom went to our computer terminal, which sat on the bar between the kitchenette and living room. She dialed the number for the central mining office. It rang at least a dozen times, but no one picked up.

As I've previously mentioned, Mom was a pragmatic woman. She didn't show much emotion. So when she finally ended the call, the worried frown on her face disturbed me. It's funny—the alien artwork in the cavern didn't bother me, but my mother's face and my father's absence did. None of this was normal.

Mom stood, grabbed her purse from its hook by the door. She was already dressed for her shift, so there was no need to change clothes.

"Eat your dinner and then pack up the leftovers," she told me. "Your father and I will eat when we get back."

"I want to come with you," I said, but the front door was already sliding shut behind her. The door needed oil. It always creaked a little when it opened or closed, letting out a high-pitched little whine.

I did as I had been told. I chewed my way through my largely tasteless protein steak and re-humidified vegetables, then wrapped everything in foil and put it in the refrigerator. Afterward, I lounged around the apartment. Mom hadn't specifically told me not to leave, but there had been an energy around her exit that implied I ought to be here when she returned.

So I didn't go out. I didn't try to find my friends and join them in whatever mischief they were up to. I watched TV. The colony broadcast old shows and movies from Earth 24 hours a day, so there was always something on. Not necessarily anything good, but it filled the time.

I watched TV until I gave myself a splitting headache, then turned the set off and went to my room. I gathered up all my drawings, laid on my little bed, and looked through them. Each was familiar—when you've labored over a piece, you become more intimate with it than any scholar—but somehow alien. I knew the art had come from me, but I felt as if I were merely the conduit through which these images had flowed.

I know I'm not describing anything new. Plenty of artists have had this dissociative feeling about their own work. But it was a first for me, and I want to mark it here.

I stayed up far past my usual bedtime, studying and admiring my drawings while I waited for my parents to return. I worried for Dad, but that worry failed to quell my excitement about my drawings. I wish I still had them now. In my memory they're vivid, frightening things, presaging an entire career.

I must've fallen asleep at some point, because I was startled awake by the squeal of our front door opening sometime after 3 AM. I lay absolutely still, listening for the telltale sounds of my parents moving around. For the familiar hum of their voices. But I only heard one set of footsteps. Mom was home, but she seemed to have come alone. I listened to her hang her purse by the door, then go into our kitchenette. I heard the clank and crinkle of her removing the leftovers from the fridge, the scrape of food being put onto a plate. The beep of the microwave. And then a sound I didn't recognize. A sort of strangled gulp, followed by a low moan, and a single sob.

Crying. Mom was crying. It was the first time I ever heard it.

I got out of bed and went to the living room. I found my mother hunched over the kitchenette counter, one hand on her eyes, the other holding herself up on the countertop.

"What's wrong?" I said.

She startled—she hadn't heard me come in—and for a second, I saw her in a state of pure grief, her eyes red, cheeks tracked with tears, mouth a wavering, trembling line. Then she stood up, swallowed, and that vulnerability was gone. Her mouth was firm again, her eyes hard.

"There was an accident at your father's work," she said. "He's not dead. At least not that we know. Nobody can say for sure. Nobody knows where he is."

Was I worried about Dad? I think I was, somewhere deep in the mix of emotions. The main thing I remember being aware of was that curtain between myself and some greater truth. It was fluttering. Here was another glimpse.

"How can nobody know where he is?" I said. "What happened?"

At 10, I knew my mother well enough to know that she would tell me the truth. She wouldn't hide things from me to protect me. She wasn't that kind of mother.

"Nobody would give me a straight answer," she said. "But it sounds like the central office got orders from Seegson corporate today, telling them to send a crew down into that cavern and explore. Your father was part of the crew. Something happened, I'm still not sure what. And now your father is missing."

I went to her then, and put my arms around her. I didn't particularly want to—I wasn't that kind of son—but it felt like the right thing to do. She put an arm around my shoulders and squeezed me against her, one time.

"Will they send someone down to try and find him?" I said.

"I honestly have no idea."

"But they went down there on company orders," I said. "They'll want to rescue him, won't they? This is their fault."

She looked down at me. "There's a lot you don't know. Things you'll have to get used to out here in the colonies. Things your father and I haven't told you, because we wanted you to have a childhood—as much as you can have one, in a place like this." She turned and put both hands on my shoulders and looked me square in the eye. "Life is hard out here for normal people. Everything is run by big governments and even bigger corporations, and they consider people like you and me to be disposable. If they go after your father, it'll be because it benefits them somehow."

"Okay," I said, my mind already racing to the next possibility. "But he has friends at work. Other miners. They'll want to look for him, right?"

"I don't know," she said. "They seemed cagey about the whole thing."

"But maybe?" I said.

"Sure," she said, and gave me a weak attempt at a smile. "Maybe. We'll just have to wait and see what happens."

She walked me back to my room, and even tucked me into my bed, which she hadn't done since I was little.

"Try to sleep. You have school in the morning," she said. That was more jarring an announcement than her speech about the relative worthlessness of our lives. The idea that we would be expected to continue our normal routine. Then I realized what time Mom had gotten in. There was no way she would've spent nine hours at the central mining office. She'd gone to work at the bar. Maybe she'd been a little late to her shift, but she'd gone in. Despite what had happened to Dad, she was still working.

====

And so our worthless little lives went on. I went to school. Mom went to work. I would have liked to keep drawing, but I was out of paper, and my black crayon was more or less an unusable crumb of wax. So instead I goofed off with my friends. Played basketball in the rec center. Hide and seek in the air ducts. I got sympathetic looks from adults around the colony. A few words of comfort from my friends. Everyone acted like it was a done deal. As far as they were concerned, Dad was dead. Moreover, they acted like it had been a perfectly ordinary death. Miners died all the time. They acted like this was no different. Nobody referred to him as missing. Nobody talked about looking for him. As far as the colony was concerned, he was gone.

I think Mom grieved, in her quiet way. I didn't see a real change in her behavior during our daily routine, but sometimes I would wake in the middle of the night and hear her crying through the thin walls of our apartment.

Did I grieve? I don't think I did. I was mostly numb. I felt like I was existing outside of myself, watching my own life like a movie. I don't know that I was hopeful for Dad's return, but I was curious about that cavern, and the things inside it. What had happened during that ill-fated expedition?

Finally, the morning of the *Chariot*'s arrival, I skipped school and went to the central mining office. The front door was unlocked, so I walked right in, where I was met by the receptionist, Miss Leisure.

"Hello, sweetheart," she said, with a warm, sympathetic smile—the one I was seeing from all the adults in my life lately. "What can I do for you?"

"I want to talk to someone about my father," I said.

Her smile faltered. "I don't understand."

"I want to talk to someone who can tell me what happened to my father," I said.

"I see," she said. All trace of warmth and sympathy vanished from her face. "Just uh... Wait here a moment, okay?"

She got up from her desk and scurried back into the office. It was an open office, so there were no walls separating me from the people working. I heard lowered voices conferring for what felt like a long time. I spotted another miner hunched over a desk, doing paperwork at a computer, hunting and pecking at the keyboard with his huge fingers. I recognized him as Mr. Streitenfeld, one of Dad's drinking buddies. He glanced up from his computer terminal, made eye contact with me, and then looked away again.

Finally, Miss Leisure returned in the company of a man in a rumpled button-down shirt and crooked tie. This was Mr. Underwood, Dad's boss. He was the closest thing to a corporate suit on-station, and a far cry from the miners I knew. He was a small man, with messy dark hair going gray, dark bags beneath his eyes, and a permanent hangdog expression. He carried a coffee mug in one hand and a clipboard in the other, both of which he set on Miss Leisure's desk.

"Hey kid," he said. "Cory, right?"

"Corinth," I said. Nobody called me Cory.

"Sure, sure," Underwood said. He squeezed his nose and licked his lips, crossed his arms and leaned against Miss Leisure's desk, then seemed to think better of it, and stood up again.

"Shouldn't you be in school?" he said.

"I'll go when we're done here," I said. I was impressed by how confident I sounded. I didn't feel that confident.

"I understand you're worried about your old man," he said. "And I admire the gumption it took for you to come down here and ask about him. Very grown-up of you. But here's the thing: since it was an accident that happened on company time, none of us are allowed to talk about it. We're... still investigating. But once we have some more information—some direction from the higher-ups—we'll tell you everything we can. But until then, the best thing you can do is go to school, do your homework, and look after your mom. Let us do our jobs, okay?"

"Do you at least think he's still alive?" I said.

"As soon as we have something to report, I'll let your mom know," Underwood said.

I glanced past him, into the office. Everything I needed was right there. All I needed was a way into the computer system. I'd find reports. Video footage. Everything. Mr. Streitenfeld must've felt my gaze, because he looked up from his computer terminal at me again.

"Go to school, Corinth," Underwood said, drawing my attention back to him. "I don't want to see you around here again, okay?"

He put a hand on my shoulder, walked me to the door, and gave me a firm push into the corridor.

=====

I went to school, like he'd told me. I had to sign in tardy at the front office, but the secretary, who knew about my dad, gave me a pass. I walked in in the middle of science class. My teacher was talking about archaea (prokaryotes native to AF-617). I didn't even try to pay attention.

At lunch, I sat with my friends. Most of their talk was about the *Chariot*, and their hopes for what they might've brought to sell—toys, candies, new movies and TV shows to watch. I let all of it wash over me, focusing on my own thoughts until they were interrupted by my friend Leanna:

"Where were you this morning?"

I told her about my adventure to the central mining office, including the brush-off from Underwood.

"Something weird is going on," she said. "It's not just in mining. They reached out to my mom yesterday. Asked her to look at something they found down in that cavern."

Leanna's mother was the one scientist living in the colony. She was a geologist.

"What was it?" I said. "A rock sample?"

"Mom's not supposed to talk about it," Leanna said. "She seemed confused by the whole thing, though. Said that it was 'outside her area of expertise,' whatever that means."

That piqued my interest even further. Whatever the miners had given Leanna's mom, it didn't sound like a rock.

====

When I got home from school, I did my homework, diagramming the archaea native to the planet while Mom made dinner. We ate together, and then she went to her shift at the bar. I was expecting another long night alone, and was trying to figure out how to fill the space without Dad for company, when there came a knock at the front door.

I answered to find Streitenfeld in the corridor. He looked nervous.

"Hey Corinth," he said. "Can I come in?"

He wasn't a stranger, but I wasn't supposed to let people in the apartment while my parents were out. This gave me a moment's pause.

"C'mon kid," Streitenfeld said. "I don't wanna do this in the hall."

I stepped aside to let him in, and shut the door behind him.

He walked to the middle of the room, his hands tucked into his coat pockets, his mouth working as though chewing on something tough.

"Okay, look," he said. "I saw you come by the office this morning, and I heard Underwood give you the brush-off. But I figure you've got a right to know what happened to your dad. At least, as much as the rest of us know."

He removed a tape from one of his coat pockets. He started to offer it to me, then seemed to change his mind, and put it on the bar between the kitchenette and the living room. He left his fingers on top of it, though, as if he might pick it back up again.

"This is a copy of the tape from when we went down there," he said. "You'll have questions after you watch it. Don't ask me. Don't ask Underwood. Don't ask your mother. If anyone finds out I gave this to you, it's my ass. Do you think you can be a big boy and keep quiet, even if you see some things you wish you hadn't?"

I nodded. I'd have agreed to anything to get answers right then. I could feel the curtain fluttering.

Streitenfeld left his fingers atop the tape for another moment as he stared me down. Then, apparently satisfied, he left the tape on the counter, and swept across the tiny apartment, back to the front door.

"Don't contact me," he said. "And definitely don't come by the office again."

And then he was gone, and I was alone with the tape. I picked it up and looked it over. As a visual artifact, there was absolutely nothing remarkable about it. It was a simple magnetic tape. It didn't even have a label. And yet it held something vast and important.

I put the tape into the console on the bar counter. Here is another instance where I wish I had the original materials. I would love to include the tape here, so you can see what I saw, Roman. But alas, I have to make do with that old liar, memory.

The recording started abruptly—essentially as soon as the camera was turned on. Streitenfeld had given me the unedited footage.

It started with a shot of dark stone, and a pair of miner's boots, then swept up to take in five miners standing around a hole in the ground, over which they had set up a winch. A few of the miners, including Streitenfeld, waved to the camera. A couple of them smiled. My father did neither. He was fussing with the winch, and didn't seem happy with what he was seeing.

All of the miners on camera wore harnesses over their jumpsuits, but otherwise appeared to have no special gear. They didn't wear EVA suits, or protective masks and breathing apparatuses. I guessed that the cavern below was providing breathable air for them.

"Is that thing ready yet?" the camera operator asked my father.

Dad stopped frowning at the winch and instead frowned into the camera. "As ready as it's going to be. Stupid piece of junk."

The camera peered down the hole. It was wide enough that two men could have easily descended into it at the same time. It was impossible to see anything down there. The winch cable disappeared into pure black.

"Who goes first?" the camera operator asked.

Dad tilted his head and gave the camera a funny look.

"Fair point," the operator said. He hooked his friction control device to the cable, and Dad started lowering him into the cavern.

"Bombs away!" the operator shouted, his voice echoing off the walls around him.

The following minutes of the tape weren't super-revelatory. The operator descended into the cavern.

I saw the giant head again, surrounded by rows of vases. I got fleeting glimpses of the sculpture that seemed to be trying to emerge from the wall. It was all stuff I'd seen before, only now from a camera strapped to a miner's helmet, rather than a probe.

Three of the other miners, my father included, descended, leaving one up top to work on the winch. They approached the head, and now I finally got some detail I hadn't had before. It appeared to have been carved from stone, but had rough lines from the carving, as though it had been done with crude tools.

"What the hell do you think it's supposed to be?" the camera operator asked, pointing up at the half-sculpture in the wall. It was even more unsettling and magnificent up close. From my place at the bar, I reached out to touch the screen, as though I could reach through the glass and put my hand on the thing itself. The static buildup in my body caused a spark at my touch. A little jolt ran up my arm, further cementing the moment in my memory.

"No idea," one of the other miners answered. "But it's not the sort of thing I want to meet down in the dark."

Dad walked among the vases, looking to his left and right. They stood taller than I would've guessed from the earlier probe footage. They came up past Dad's knee. He paused halfway down the aisle, and knelt before one.

"Huh," he said.

"What?" the camera operator said.

"Come look," Dad said, and beckoned the guy over.

As the camera operator approached, I saw what Dad was trying to point out. A few of the vases near the back corner of the cavern had fallen over, and their contents appeared to have spilled. They lay in a mess of what looked like broken glass and black sludge.

Dad swiped one gloved hand through the sludge and then examined his fingertips.

"What is it?" the camera operator said.

"It's sticky," Dad said. He flexed his fingers together and apart. The black sludge seemed to stretch and retract in time with his movements. The camera zoomed in on his hand. Even when Dad was absolutely still, the fluid seemed to quiver in place, as if waiting for direction, ready to spring into action.

"But what is it?" the camera operator said. "Looks like oil. Is it oil? Like some kind of fuel?"

Dad wiped his fingers on his overall leg, smearing the goop across it in a black stain. "That is above our pay grade, my friend," he said. "How many of these things did Underwood say he wanted?"

"At least three," the camera operator said. He followed as Dad picked up an undamaged cannister, carried it to a gurney, and strapped it into place. He did this twice more, loading up the requested cannisters, and then he and another man affixed the gurney to the winch and gave the operator the signal to start pulling it up. As the gurney disappeared through the hole in the ceiling, Dad turned to the camera.

"Well I guess that's it for the field trip. Back to the grind."

"Oh joy," the camera operator said.

"On the bright side, we managed to kill about two hours on this little expedition," Dad said. "We're halfway to lunch already." Suddenly he frowned and looked at something off-camera.

"What?" the camera operator said.

"Do you hear that?" Dad said.

There was a long pause. The only sounds I could hear on the tape were the whining of the winch, and the camera operator's breathing.

"I don't hear anything," the operator said, finally.

Dad shook his head. "Guess it's nothing. I'm just getting the creeps down here. It's like a goddamn haunted house."

There followed footage of the other miners rising up the winch, until only Dad and the camera operator were left.

"You go ahead," Dad told the operator.

The operator hooked up to the winch. As he finished attaching himself to the cable, something moved in the darkness behind my father—something black moving against black, almost impossible to see. At first I thought it might be a glitch in the tape, a tracking issue. But then, as the camera operator began to rise, I saw it more clearly: a huge figure, moving with inhuman quickness.

The figure emerged into the light of the camera operator's flashlight, dimly visible behind my father. It's difficult to describe, because the footage was brief, and I don't have access to it today. It had a shape that was somehow familiar—like a bunch of oblongs strung together in a random order, somehow moving forward in a rolling pattern, almost like a ball, except clumsy, because it lacked perfect roundness. Its coloring was pitch-black, which made it difficult to see, even in the light.

"Bloch, look out!" the camera operator shouted as he began to rise. But it was already too late. The shape had washed over my father like a wave. He disappeared from view, subsumed in darkness.

I think he screamed. At least, I think he tried. The sound stopped almost as soon as it started, muffled as he disappeared.

"Jesus fucking Christ, what is that thing?" the camera operator said. "Get me out of here already! Help!"

He began to rise more quickly. The camera swept up through the roof of the cavern, and then everything was black.

The tape stopped there, right as I realized where I'd seen that shape before. It looked a lot like the diagram of an archaea that my teacher had shown us in science class that morning. But archaea were supposed to be microscopic. Not big enough to swallow a man.

====

I watched the tape over and over again. When I'd gleaned as much detail as I could, I ejected it from the console, took it to my room, and hid it deep in my closet, where Mom wouldn't find it. I didn't think seeing it would help her. I wasn't sure that it had even helped me. I'd watched it hoping for answers. Instead, I had more questions. The more the curtain revealed, the more confused I became.

I went to bed. I had no hesitations about turning out the lights, even after what I'd seen. It had been confounding, yes, and upsetting, but I still didn't feel frightened, exactly.

I lay awake in the dark for a long time, pondering. Something in that cavern had attacked my father. Some sort of creature. It had looked like a giant version of a microscopic organism. Maybe it was some life form that lived on the planet, that we just hadn't discovered yet?

Or maybe, I thought, *it came out of one of those broken vases*. Maybe that was what was in the black sludge? Horrible creatures beyond human imagination.

It was with this thought in mind that I drifted to sleep, and the dark dreams that lay beyond.

====

I woke some time later, to the sound of Mom re-entering the apartment. I glanced at my bedside clock. It was only 10 PM. She shouldn't be home for several more hours.

I got up and went into the kitchenette, where she was fixing herself something to eat.

She glanced up at me, then back at what she was doing. "You should be asleep."

"What's wrong?" I said.

"Everything's okay," she said. "We're just in lockdown. Management is worried about an outbreak. They want to make sure no one gets sick. But on the bright side? No school tomorrow. And I managed to swing by the *Chariot* before my shift. Check my purse, will you?"

I went to her purse, on its hook in the living room, and opened it. Inside I found a new sketch book, and a pack of colored pencils.

"So you won't be bored tomorrow," she said. "But do me a favor—try to use some colors other than black, okay? I can't buy a new pack every time you use up a single pencil."

"An outbreak of what?" I asked.

"They're not sure yet," she said. "That's part of why we're in lockdown."

I thanked her for the pencils and went back to my room. I set the new art supplies on my desk, and climbed back into bed.

I laid awake for a long time after that, listening to Mom eat her late dinner, watch TV, and then go to bed herself. I heard her crying, then snoring, before I managed to drift off.

I dreamt of shapes, things hard to make out, lingering in darkness, waiting for their moment to strike. I don't remember being frightened. I was fascinated.

====

The next day, I woke early and went straight to my desk to begin drawing. I drew the figure on the cavern wall. I drew the giant head. I tried to draw the shape that had taken Dad. I drew these things again and again, trying to get them right, to get down on paper what I saw in my mind's eye. To try and save pencil, I only drew in outlines. I didn't color anything in. It helped.

Around noon, my hunger was too great to ignore. I tore myself away from my desk and headed for the kitchen. On the way, I stopped by Mom's room and listened at the door. She was still snoring. She was always a heavy sleeper. She could sleep away entire days, if she had nowhere to be. I think it's part of what made her a good colonist. She didn't have strong desires, beyond the comforts of bed and unconsciousness.

In the kitchen, I fixed and ate a bowl of cold cereal. My mind reeled with the imagery I'd spent the morning recreating on paper. I thought about watching the tape again, to try and get a better look at the shape that had taken Dad, but what if Mom woke up and saw it? Better to leave it in my closet, at least until lockdown was lifted.

But maybe I didn't have to go the whole day without making progress into my investigation. Yesterday at school, Leanna had mentioned her mother receiving the vases from the cavern. Maybe she knew something.

After I finished my cereal and rinsed my bowl, I powered up the bar console and called Leanna.

She answered almost immediately, her brow creased with obvious worry. Her expression changed from worry to disappointment almost at once.

"Oh," she said. "Hi."

"Nice to see you too," I said.

"Sorry," she said. "I was just hoping you were Mom."

"What do you mean?" I said. "Isn't she in lockdown with you?"

Leanna shook her head. "She never came home from work yesterday. I've tried calling her office, but no one is picking up."

"I'm sorry," I said. "Do you need anything?"

"Nothing you can give me over a video call," she said. "We have plenty of food and toilet paper and stuff. I'll be fine. I'm just worried about Mom."

I thought about the tape in my closet. Should I tell Leanna about it? I wanted to tell *someone*, to share my questions, even if no one could give me answers. But I didn't think Leanna would be interested in helping me ponder these things now. Not when her own mother was missing.

"I'm sorry," I said again. And then, because I wanted to comfort her, I added, "I'm sure your mom's fine. She's just caught up at work. She'll be home soon, you'll see."

Leanna thanked me, and we hung up. I felt a little bad about what I'd said. I didn't know what was happening with her mother, Doctor Hixson, and what the good doctor might've discovered in those vases, but I sincerely doubted she was okay, or that she would be home soon. Something was happening on AF-617. I didn't know what, but I knew it was big.

====

I went back to my room after that, and drew until my hand ached. With each drawing, my subjects drew further into focus. I was surprised to see my abilities improve so quickly. It's amazing what obsession can do, when added to latent talent. However, while my depiction of the giant head and the bas-relief creature improved, my drawings of the creature that took Dad remained frustratingly vague. I just hadn't gotten a good enough look to copy it accurately.

I longed to get the tape from my closet. To put it in the console and freeze-frame the moment when the creature emerged into the light. I almost gave in to the temptation. I was in my closet, digging for the tape, when I heard Mom stirring in her bedroom.

It was already midafternoon, but I fixed her a pot of coffee and joined her in the living room as she gradually came awake. We lounged around in our pajamas and watched old sitcoms on the TV. Neither of us said anything. I won't say it was nice, exactly, but there was a numbing comfort to it.

After a couple of hours of this, the effect wore off for me. Mom seemed content to remain parked in front of the TV all day, but my anxiety and curiosity returned in full. I couldn't sit still any longer. I returned to my room, to keep drawing. I had started changing the imagery in my pictures. No longer copying what I'd seen. I created new scenes, using the elements I already had. I started adding miners to the pictures, interacting with the items in the cavern.

I was creating a picture of the miners, kneeling

before the bas-relief creature as if in prayer, when the console in the living room began to beep with an incoming call.

I ran to the living room, but Mom had beaten me to it. She hit the "answer" key as I entered the room, and I stopped as Leanna Hixson's face filled the screen. Her expression was no longer one of worry, but absolute terror. There was a pounding sound in the background, loud and insistent.

"Ms Bloch?" she said. "Please. I need help. I need someone to come. There's someone at the door."

"What do you mean, sweetheart?" Mom said. "We're in lockdown. Who's at the door?"

"I think it's..." she paused, and her mouth twisted as she wrestled with the next word. "... Mom," she finally finished, her voice thick with tears.

"You *think* your mother's at the door?" Mom said. She still seemed confused.

"There's something wrong with her," Leanna said. "She looks wrong somehow. Ms. Bloch, I'm afraid."

"No one should be moving on-station," Mom said. "If you're afraid, you should call Security."

"No one's picking up," Leanna said. "Please, Ms. Bloch." The pounding sound grew louder on her end.

"Sweetheart, I don't know what to do," Mom said. "Don't answer the door, don't—"

She was cut off by a great crashing sound on Leanna's end, and a groan of bending metal.

Leanna screamed and ducked out of view. The call remained connected, the camera pointed toward an empty frame as the screaming continued, a sort of incoherent begging in counterpoint to a heavy grunting sound.

"Please," Leanna kept saying. "Please, Mommy. Please."

I had been slowly approaching the console during the length of the call, and I came to stand beside Mom as the screaming increased, and then ceased. The heavy grunting eased to a labored breathing sound. Mom had a hand pressed to her mouth. Her eyes were wide, and glassy.

A figure lumbered into the camera's view. They were only visible from the shoulders down, and seemed human in shape. They wore medical scrubs, which had been stained black and red in several places. We could hear nothing aside from the heavy breathing. Then the figure leaned forward and looked into the camera, and I saw what had scared Leanna so badly.

The figure's head was only vaguely recognizable as Doctor Hixson. It had changed shape, distended and bloated so that its features had become monstrous. It stared into the camera now with eyes full of dull malice.

"Kacey?" Mom said. It was barely more than a whisper.

The thing on the other side of the screen grimaced at hearing its name. It growled, and Mom took a step away from the console. I took a step closer. I wanted a better look.

Doctor Hixson—or what was left of her—roared, and struck out at the camera. She hit it again, and again. On the third strike, the call disconnected, and our console returned to its home screen, green text on a black background.

"What the fuck?" Mom said. It was barely more than a whisper. A tear ran down her cheek. "What the fuck is happening?"

"It's the cavern," I said, turning back to Mom.

I told her what Leanna had told me, about the vases from the cavern that had been delivered to Doctor Hixson's lab. I was tempted again to tell her about the tape in my closet, but saw no reason to upset her further. She already knew Dad was gone. What would be the point of shading in more detail?

Mom turned around and went back to the TV in the living room. She turned it to the "main" channel, where management made colony-wide announcements. A calm, disembodied voice spoke over an image of the Seegson logo:

"... Repeat, we are experiencing a medical emergency, and recommend that all non-essential personnel shelter in place until you receive other directions."

The message looped again, providing no additional detail, no indication of what the emergency was, or when it might be over.

"Screw this," Mom said. She turned and took me by the shoulders. "Go to your room and pack a bag," she said. "Only things you need. Clothes. A jacket. Go."

"But the message said—"

"I know what it said," she interrupted. "But that thing—Doctor Hixson—saw us on camera. For all we know, she's headed here next. I'm not going to wait here to be slaughtered."

I ran to my room, dumped all my school supplies from my backpack, and threw a bunch of clothing into it. After a moment's consideration, I also grabbed all my recent drawings and colored pencils off my desk, and the tape out of my closet. I didn't want to lose any of it.

In the living room I found Mom back at the console, a bag over one shoulder as she made another call. When it connected, it showed the image of a woman with long dark hair tied back in a ponytail. She had a pronounced nose, strong jawline, and serious dark eyes. I didn't recognize her from on-station.

The woman frowned in confusion. "Molly?" she said.

"Alice," Mom said. "I need a favor."

"What's up?" the woman (Alice) asked.

"Prep the *Chariot* for launch. Things are going bad here and we need to get out."

"Is this about the lockdown?" Alice asked.

"Yes," Mom said. "I don't have time to explain. Do you have room for two more?"

"Sure, but quarantine protocol—"

"We're not infected," Mom said. "But something is after us and we need to get off-world. *Please*, Alice. It's me asking."

Alice looked down, apparently debating with herself, then sighed. "Fine. You've got half an hour, and then we're leaving, with or without you."

The call disconnected and Mom turned to me.

"We head for the docking bays," she said. "Straight there, okay? We get to the *Chariot*, and Alice will take us off-world."

I wasn't so sure about that. I knew Alice was an old friend of Mom's, but if the *Chariot* was still on-world, it would be grounded and locked down, too.

I didn't say any of this. I reasoned that, if Mom could talk us aboard, the ship would be as safe a place as any to wait out this disaster.

I did point out the one flaw I saw in her plan, however: "They'll probably have the trams shut down," I said. "As part of the lockdown."

"Then we'll make the trip on foot," she said. "It'll take a little longer, but it won't be bad. You up for a hike?"

We left the apartment. Mom locked the door behind us. I've often wondered about that decision. Was it force of habit? Or did she really think we'd be coming back?

We started off at a brisk walk down the corridor. We passed the tram station and made our way to the tunnels that connected the different hubs of the colony. They were long concrete and steel passages, mostly used for safely transporting goods from the mines to the docks—things that they didn't trust to the rail system. The lighting was minimal, and we moved through shadows, our footsteps echoing off the walls. The echo made it sound as though we were being followed. I kept looking over my shoulder to make sure that wasn't the case. I never saw anyone, but the shadows in that tunnel were oppressive. It was hard to tell what might be lurking, either behind or ahead. The sounds of my own breath seemed to come from all around me, mixed with the tunnel's own shifting and groaning. All of this combined to make me feel exposed and naked.

We didn't run, but walked quickly. My legs began to burn from the effort. The tunnel seemed endless.

"How much further?" I asked Mom.

"We're almost there," she assured me. We rounded a wide bend in the tunnel, and her words proved true. The doors to the hangar bay rounded into view—still at least a few minutes' walk away, but blessedly open. Through these doors—large enough to drive a truck through—I could see part of the underside of an unfamiliar ship. A man in a leather jacket hurried about beneath the hull, disconnecting umbilicals and sealing hatches. I assumed this was the *Chariot*.

God, Roman, it was so close. At the pace we were walking, we would have been at the ship in another few moments. But as this open door came into view, so did something else: a figure crouched in the middle of the corridor, squarely between us and the hangar door.

The figure was positioned so low to the ground that, if you were only looking up, you might have missed it. It was folded up in a way no human body was meant to be arranged—head forward, near the floor; legs somehow stretched under, around, and then atop the torso, so that the feet were planted on either side of the head; arms beneath the knees, stretched out to either side.

It wore a miner's jumpsuit, which was now black with cavern goop, and red, with blood. It wasn't Doctor Hixson, but something that seemed to share her condition. It was lying in wait, curled up like some terrible spider, ready to pounce on anyone fleeing for the hangar.

The figure's head tilted up to regard us. Her face

was so much worse in person. The flesh had a melted, burnt look, like cheese that's been cooked too long and turned leathery. The forehead bulged, giving the skull a shape not unlike a shelled peanut. But the eyes were worst of all. They looked up at us from their position near the floor, and contained no recognition. No warmth. Only a blank, seething rage.

Here again, memory fails me. I know the figure stood. It somehow untangled that mess of limbs in one smooth motion and rose to a fully upright position, but I can't remember how those things happened. One moment, it was on the ground, and the next, it was face-to-face with my mother, preternaturally still. Something in its bearing reminded me of the half-sculpture from the cavern wall. It wasn't as regal or beautiful, but it carried itself as though it were the most important thing in creation.

Mom met the monster's gaze, and stood her ground. She only looked away to glance at me.

"Run," she told me. Then she turned back toward the figure, and gave it a shove.

The figure roared. It rocked backward with the shove, but then retaliated with a balled fist to the side of Mom's head. I stood frozen, unable to look away as my mother flew backward, her head turning away from the punch, blood exploding from the point of contact. I heard the crack of bone, and as

Mom hit the ground, I could see that her jaw was no longer completely connected to her skull. It hung loose and ajar on one side.

Mom's eyes were glazed over. I don't think she was dead, but she was no longer completely conscious and aware. I think that was a mercy.

I took more time than I should have to look at her like this. The moment is frozen in my mind's eye. And unlike so many of the things I saw on AF-617, this image isn't one I wish to see any clearer, or more often. I'd banish it if I could.

The figure pounced on Mom. It landed on her chest, pinning Mom's arms with its knees. It raised both fists into the air and brought them down with a terrible crunching sound, onto Mom's face.

That crunch finally yanked me back to my senses. I became aware of other sounds. Someone was shouting, and voices were echoing in the corridor. I turned and looked at the docking bay. With the figure fixated on Mom, my way was clear now. The man with the clipboard was shouting and waving me toward him. I couldn't understand what he was saying, but his intent seemed clear enough. He was offering me the safety of the ship, but wasn't going to come get me himself.

I turned away from my mother, and ran as fast and hard as I could. My footsteps echoed around me. My breath was loud in my ears. Sweat beaded on my forehead, in my armpits and along my spine. My sneakers squeaked against the concrete floor. My arms and legs pumped. My lungs burned. My cheeks were wet, and I realized that I was crying. After days of fascination and dark wonder, I was finally upset. I was finally frightened.

As I left the corridor and entered the hangar, the man outside the *Chariot* grew more frantic in his gesticulations. I didn't understand, and, confused, glanced back. The figure had apparently lost interest in my mother. It loped along after me now, running in an awkward but powerful gait. Our gazes locked, and it screeched.

I turned back to the *Chariot*, and my heart sank. The ramp was still down, but the man with the clipboard was gone. He'd probably fled for the safety of the ship. Would they still let me aboard? The ramp was still down. I had no choice but to find out.

I pushed my body harder than I ever had before, but couldn't resist another glance back. The figure was closing the distance between us. It was only a matter of seconds.

The ship was so close now. I was almost there.

Something grabbed hold of me and yanked. My shoulders lurched backward with the strain. The figure had hold of my backpack. I wriggled free and the creature collapsed onto it, buying me maybe an extra second.

It howled with rage, and I stretched my arms forward, like a kid playing tag, reaching for home base. As though, if I could just touch the ship, I would be saved.

Fingers—cold and bony through my thin shirt—closed around my shoulder. This was it. The monster had me.

The figure threw me to the concrete floor. I hit it hard, my head bouncing off the surface. I saw stars. Through them, I was dimly aware of the figure above me, staring down with those hateful eyes. I raised my hands and squeezed my eyes shut in a feeble gesture of defense, knowing it was useless, but unable to stop myself—

A deafening thunderclap split the air, and the weight disappeared from my chest. I could breathe again.

I opened my eyes, and found myself staring at the hangar ceiling. I lifted my head, confused, and looked around. The figure lay on its back a few meters away, writhing. I sat up and looked behind me. A woman stood at the bottom of the *Chariot*'s entrance ramp. She had long, dark hair tied back in a ponytail, a pronounced nose, and a strong jawline. She held a shotgun, which was pointed toward the doctor.

"Get up, kid!" Alice Goodwin shouted at me. "Get inside!" I scrambled to my feet, tripping over them and nearly losing my balance anew as I stumbled past Captain Goodwin and onto the ramp.

As soon as I crossed the threshold, still looking back over one shoulder, I bumped into someone and startled. I nearly fell over again trying to back away, but the person I'd bumped into—the man I'd seen in the leather jacket—grabbed me by the shoulders and steadied me.

"Come with me," he said.

I let him lead me through a few corridors of the ship and onto the bridge, where men and women were strapped into their stations, running through preflight checklists.

One of them—another man—looked up from his station. "I thought we were taking on two passengers," he said.

The man who'd been guiding me gave his interlocuter a hard look and said, "Henderson."

Henderson, understanding the look and the man's tone well enough, looked back at his console.

My guide strapped me into a seat near the rear of the bridge. "Stay here," he said.

Once he was gone, Henderson looked up again. "You're not sick, are you? Are you going to get the rest of us sick? Like that woman out there?"

I heard him, but the words might as well have been in another language, for all my ability to respond. I sat in silence, dazed, watching the crew prepare. Outside the ship, I heard more muffled shotgun blasts, and voices shouting. Eventually, both sounds stopped, replaced by the sound of the entrance ramp closing.

Alice and the clipboard man came running onto the bridge. Alice was still carrying her shotgun. The clipboard man had a pistol. Both were spattered with blood.

"Henderson, get us out of here," Alice said.

"What the hell happened to you?" Henderson said. "I thought there was only one of those things out there?"

"The noise attracted others," the clipboard man said.

There came a pounding sound from outside the ship, hard and irregular. It seemed to come from all sides at once.

I unfastened my harness and got out of my seat. I walked up to the bridge's viewport. The docking bay was awash with figures like Doctor Hixson—former humans, misshapen now, gazes blank with hate, with malice. They were mobbing the ship.

"Should we call air traffic control?" Henderson said.

"What do you think?" Alice shouted. Then she noticed me, got up, and dragged me back to my chair. "Gotta be safe, kiddo," she said, strapping me in before rounding on Henderson. "Henderson, *get us the fuck out of here*!"

The ship shook as the engines rumbled to life. The comm system began to chime with an incoming hail. Captain Goodwin opened the channel. It was air traffic control, demanding we power down at once. The whole colony was in quarantine until management said otherwise.

"What do I do, Captain?" Henderson said.

"They don't have any weapons systems," Goodwin said. "They can't stop us."

At this point, things get fuzzy for me. I sort of "went away". I'd just lost my mother. For all I knew, my father was one of the creatures trying to get into the ship and kill us right now. I wanted to let the adults handle the details of our escape, and so was only vaguely aware of the shake of the ship around me and the shouts of the *Chariot*'s crew.

Eventually, the ship's rumble settled into a soothing hum. Someone touched me gently on the shoulder and drew me back to the present. I looked up into Alice Goodwin's face again. It wasn't a kind face. There was nothing maternal about her. But she did seem concerned.

"Hey," she said. "Are you hurt? Are you alright?"

I looked myself over. "I think I'm okay," I said. And then, sounding far more like a kid than I would have liked, I asked, "Is it over now?"

Her expression broke into a sympathetic grimace.

"Let's get you to medbay. Get you checked out,

make sure you're not sick like those people back there. But yeah, kiddo. I think it's over."

I looked past her, at the stars outside the viewport, and breathed a sigh of relief.

But she was wrong. Nothing was over. At least, not for me. For me, it was all just beginning.

11

THE FIRST DAY

Goodwin startled at a shuffling noise to her left. She looked away from her laptop, blinking bleary eyes, as Cardona emerged from her tent. The younger woman settled in front of the space heater, rubbing her arms for warmth.

"Have you been up all night?" Cardona asked her.

Goodwin glanced at her watch, before realizing it was a useless gesture here. Instead, she looked to the sky. It remained overcast, but was starting to brighten into a lighter shade of gray.

"I guess so," she admitted. "But you know. Possible concussion and all. Kind of had to stay up just to be safe."

"Yeah, but shouldn't someone have been up with you to watch out?"

"I had Sam," Goodwin said. She gestured at the

pilot, who lay curled up in his sleeping bag, between Goodwin and the space heater, snoring softly. She was pretty sure he hadn't meant to fall asleep down there. He'd just been trying to stay warm, and had drifted off. She hadn't had the heart to wake him. He looked so peaceful. And besides, she'd gotten caught up in the Bloch dossier, and had appreciated a chance to read in peace.

Goodwin glanced back at the laptop screen, where the dossier was still open. The contents—what she'd read so far anyway—were a lot to take in. Was it possible that this was all true? It would make sense, she thought, to find out that all of this was fiction. She'd seen Bloch's work. She knew he had a hell of an imagination.

But he'd mentioned her mother. Alice Goodwin. And Henderson, her mother's old pilot. Goodwin remembered Henderson from when she was a girl. He'd crewed for her mother for a long time. Goodwin wished, again, that her mother was alive. She'd love to ask the old woman about AF-617. About Corinth Bloch.

But, putting aside thoughts of Alice Goodwin—what if Bloch was telling the truth about everything? What if this was really how his parents had died? What if this really was what had happened to the colony where he'd been born? Goodwin had gotten around, in her years hauling cargo. She'd heard her share of rumors, about strange lifeforms on distant worlds. But she'd never heard of anything like what was described here. Ancient temples full of breathable air, featuring art both human and inhuman. Vases full of something that could—what? Somehow change the essence of a lifeform? Warp it into something terrible?

Was that what had happened here, on DSJ-1020? Had the colonists discovered another one of those temples?

Goodwin wanted nothing more than to keep reading the dossier. There was still so much of it to get through. But now the rest of the crew was stirring. Sam's eyes opened. He lifted his head and looked around, and his expression fell.

"Oh shit," he said. "I fell asleep."

"It's okay," Goodwin said. "I survived."

He sat up, rubbing his eyes like a little kid, as White emerged from their tent.

"I was having the best dream," they said. "Then I woke up and remembered that we'd crash-landed on a hostile plague world." They collapsed, cross-legged, in front of their tent, hands extended toward the space heater.

"Someone tell me we thought to bring coffee," Harris said, emerging from his own tent.

"Coming right up," Sam said. "Cold, and instant, but caffeinated."

"Yay," White groaned.

Goodwin put the laptop away and let herself be sucked into the crew's conversation for a while. They were grumpy, but rallying as well as could be expected. Sam made everyone cups of cold instant coffee, and they used a battery-powered hot plate to warm them up. At least they were afforded that small luxury. She wished she could give them more. They deserved more.

After coffee and a light breakfast of ration packs, they packed up camp, checked Harris's motion tracker, found the electronic beacon, and set off in that direction, up and out of the valley. They went slowly, carefully, as they'd done the day before, moving up the steep hillside, bending over to use their hands to pull themselves when necessary. The ground remained slippery from yesterday's rains, but while the sky threatened new showers, it didn't make good on the threat during their climb.

As they crested the hill, dirty, cold, and out of breath, the crew found themselves on level ground, at the outer edge of a wood that seemed to stretch for miles before them.

"Oh good," White said. "We pass the gauntlet of the never-ending hillside, and now we get to try the impenetrable forest."

Goodwin pulled her laptop from her bag, and opened a topographical map of the planet. She was better with star charts than land maps, and anyway, they had no good way of knowing where on the planet they'd crashed, aside from the fact that they were close to the colony (assuming Harris was picking it up on his tracker, which was more hope than fact). She rotated the map a few times, then sighed. There were woods both north and south of the colony. Both patches looked large on the map. Going around would be a hassle.

"I don't think we've got any choice," she said. "We don't have the time or the supplies to go around. We go through." She looked at Harris. "Assuming that through is the correct direction?"

Harris flipped on the tracker and stared down at the screen for a second. He pointed straight ahead, into the woods. He opened his mouth, then shut it quickly and frowned.

"What is it?" Goodwin said. "What's wrong?"

He frowned at the tracker for another moment before returning his attention to Goodwin. "Nothing," he said, then pointed straight ahead. "Signal's coming from that direction. Fastest way is through those woods."

Goodwin shifted her backpack, and led the crew past the tree line. As they pushed into the forest, the world grew dark around them. After several minutes of diminishing light, Goodwin glanced up, and was unsurprised to find she could no longer see the sky. The trees grew thick and close here, and their branches blocked the view.

She switched on a flashlight, and the rest of the crew did the same. They tromped forward into the new darkness, winding single-file between the trees, carefully stepping over roots and fallen branches. Despite the abundance of flora, they encountered no signs of fauna. No droppings, no nests, no bodies.

After an hour's march, Goodwin had Harris check the tracker again. She wanted to confirm they were still heading in the right direction, that the forest hadn't somehow shunted them aside, turned them in the wrong direction.

Harris booted up the tracker, and again he frowned at it for what seemed a long time.

"You know, when you make that face, you're not exactly inspiring confidence," White grumbled.

Goodwin was annoyed with her cargo handler, but they weren't wrong. Harris's expressions were worrying her, too.

"What's up?" she said.

"It's nothing," Harris said. Goodwin stared him down until he sighed and added, "At least, I think it's nothing." He gestured at the tracker. "Every time I boot it up, it picks up movement nearby. But only for a second, and then it disappears."

"That's not ominous at all," White said.

Harris shook his head. "This thing's older than you are, kid. It's got to be a glitch. Why else would it keep disappearing?"

"Why, indeed?" White deadpanned.

"Calm down," Goodwin said. "Harris is right, it's probably a glitch. Another thing to replace when we get paid. Don't get spooked. In the meantime—Harris, are we heading in the right direction or not?"

"The signal's a little jumbled in here," Harris said, turning his eyes back to the tracker and moving it from side to side. "Must be the trees. But yeah. Yeah, I think so."

"Then let's keep moving," she said.

The crew continued on their path for several uneventful hours. As the valley had slowed them down yesterday, the forest slowed them down today. The trees remained close, and hard to pass between. The forest floor never opened up before them, never gave them room to breathe.

They checked the tracker once an hour to make sure they were still on the correct path. Twice they had to redirect themselves, after taking a wrong turn. This did nothing for anyone's mood.

Despite the day's trudge, Sam and Cardona kept up a steady stream of cheerful chatter, for which Goodwin was grateful. It was entirely too quiet in these woods. It was too easy to imagine one of Bloch's 'transfigured' people lurking just out of sight in the darkness, ready to pounce.

They stopped once, in a tiny clearing, to rest and eat a midday meal of ration bars. After another six hours of walking, even Sam and Cardona had stopped talking. Everyone was exhausted—Goodwin doubly so. She hadn't slept last night and her body was practically screaming for rest. They settled down in a tiny clearing, set up the space heater, ate a quick dinner, and went to bed. Cardona agreed, reluctantly, to take first watch.

Goodwin settled into her sleeping bag beside Sam, laptop open. She wanted to try to read at least a little more of the dossier before she drifted off.

She failed in this ambition. Sleep took her quickly, barely giving her time to shut the laptop before she went under.

Her nightmares gained further clarity that night. Shapes emerged from the textured darkness, making crunching sounds as they broke free. They were almost impossible to make out in the pitch of the dream world, but what Goodwin could see was beautiful: extending long and elegant through the black in line, they seemed almost more designed than grown. A machinist's stylized dream, caught in a darkly gorgeous ballet. Goodwin, who was so often merely an observer of her dreams, felt herself here in the dark. She longed to reach out, to touch these half-glimpsed miracles. She found herself wondering if she had a body here in the dream.

Then the screams dragged her awake.

She opened her eyes with a sharp intake of breath. It was completely dark in the tent. She could feel Sam wake beside her.

"What the fuck," he said, but she barely heard him. She was already moving. She'd fallen asleep with her flashlight at hand, and she switched it on now as she fumbled with the tent zipper and stumbled out into the small clearing. She banged her shin against the space heater and swore as pain shot up her leg and the night air hit her like a fist to the chest. It had been chilly in the tent, but it was fucking *cold* out here.

She whipped her head back and forth, trying to figure out what was going on, only catching glimpses in the sweep of her flashlight beam: a bit of tent here; trees there; darkness everywhere. Darkness just like her dreams.

Focus. She needed to focus. The screaming—it was a woman's voice. That could only mean Cardona. And it was already fading.

White poked their head out of their tent, looking as discombobulated as Goodwin felt.

"What the hell's going on?" they said.

Harris emerged from his own tent, wearing his long john underwear and his boots, and picked up the motion tracker off the ground. It wasn't even turned on, and he flipped the power switch now.

"Tell me you can see her on that thing," Goodwin said. The screams continued to fade. It was getting hard to tell what direction they came from.

Harris looked at the tracker. "She's moving like a goddamn bullet."

"Give it to me," Sam said. He'd snuck up on Goodwin, and stood at her elbow now. "I'll go after her."

"Now hang on a second," Harris said, pulling the device out of Sam's reach.

Sam looked confused, and more than a little angry. "Harris. Something grabbed Cardona. If we don't hurry we're gonna lose her!"

"And what's your solution?" Harris said. "To take our one tool for finding a way out of these woods, and go barreling off into the dark after Cardona and whatever is making her scream? That seems like a good idea to you?" As he spoke, the motion tracker continued to chirp, sounding the location of Cardona and her abductor.

Sam made a frustrated sound. "Okay, then. We all go together. Right now."

He looked at Goodwin, clearly hoping for her support. She sighed and shook her head.

"Harris is right," she said. "Whatever grabbed Cardona is—first of all—big enough to carry off a grown woman. Second, it moves fast as a motherfucker, even through these dense woods. It took us a day to walk a few klicks, and now you want to go off, undressed, and try to match its speed?"

"So what?" Sam said. "We're just giving up on her? Sorry, Cardona, bad luck?"

"We're not giving up," Goodwin said. "But we're not going to do something stupid just because we're panicked and worried about a crewmate." She knew this last word was the wrong one as soon as it was out of her mouth, and she regretted it at once.

"Crewmate?" Sam said. "I thought we were supposed to be family."

"We are," she said. "I just misspoke."

He glared at her. She stared back, unflinching. The chirps from the motion tracker grew further and further apart, as the signal moved further away from their location. At last, the chirps stopped. When that happened, Sam finally looked away, turning his glare on the ground.

Goodwin didn't feel good about winning the staring contest. She cared about Sam, and Cardona for that matter. She admired her pilot's desire to help the young cargo handler. But she couldn't back down on this. Going after Cardona like this would be suicidal.

She approached Cardona's tent, which stood directly across from her own. The front flap was sealed. She walked around it, squeezing past a tree to do so. The rest of the tent was intact, too. Whatever had taken Cardona had done so while she was outside. On watch. Goodwin turned to look at Harris, White, and Sam. All three had been in their tents when Cardona was taken. The motion tracker had been on the ground. Had she heard something, and reached for it, only to be snatched by a wild animal?

"Jesus fucking Christ," she muttered. How stupid

could they have been? They needed to get smarter and fast, if they were going to survive this mission. "Alright," she said. "From now on we take the watch in pairs, and we leave the motion tracker on at all times, so we can see if something's approaching."

"You sure?" Harris said. "This thing's old. I don't know how long the battery'll hold out."

"I'm sure," Goodwin said. "White, Kurzel—" she used Sam's last name here, because it was time to be a goddamn captain, "—you two get some more rest. Harris and I will take the next watch."

Sam looked like he wanted to argue, but the use of his last name in front of the others had chastened him. He ducked his head and went back to the tent. White went, too, but not before taking a parting shot:

"This is so beyond fucked up," they said.

Goodwin and Harris sat on the hard forest floor with the space heater quietly humming between them. They said nothing to one another, staying quiet to allow the others to at least try to sleep. The hiss from the motion tracker was the only indication it was on. It didn't chirp again that night.

Harris stared out into the darkness. He held a mug of coffee, but never seemed to actually drink from it.

To pass the time, Goodwin opened her laptop, and began the next file of the dossier.

Bloch_Dossier_002

I'm afraid the next phase of my life wasn't nearly so exciting, dear Roman. I'm tempted to leave the story at my "secret origin." The dark, foreboding exploration of an ancient temple. The disappearance of my father. My encounter with the transfigured Doctor Hixson. My mother's final sacrifice. My frankly thrilling escape from AF-617 aboard the *Chariot*, with Captain Alice Goodwin and her hardy crew. Surely it would be enough to explain why I am the way I am?

But there are other pieces of the story I want you to have. You can decide what's necessary and what's pure indulgence, once it's finished.

So where to pick up the thread? I suppose a quick summary of what happened next is as good a place as any.

Immediately after we departed AF-617, Captain Goodwin ordered me to the medbay on the *Chariot*, where I underwent a full body scan. Everything came back clean. I was carrying nothing—or at least, nothing the ship's instruments could pick up.

After the medic released me, I returned to the bridge, to find Captain Goodwin editing the ship's transponder signal. She wanted to hide that we'd just departed AF-617. If word got out about what had happened on the colony, other places might not let us land or dock. Furthermore, changing the transponder signal would help us hide from Seegson corporate ships or Colonial Marines looking to prevent news and/or contagion from spreading.

Once the change was complete, the crew set a course for a nearby trade hub, and we all went into cryo.

My dreams there were disappointingly vague. While on AF-617, I'd felt close to a great discovery. That feeling had extended into my sleeping hours. In cryo, my dreams were dark, but fuzzy. The revelations which had been pulling into focus were now sliding out again.

I should have been grateful. After my near-death experience, I was safe and moving away from the horror. Instead, I felt as if I were being deprived of answers to the great mystery.

We arrived at our destination—a place whose name I've forgotten, if I ever knew it—and stayed there for a couple of weeks. Captain Goodwin and the crew were kind to me. They gave me little jobs to do around the ship—mostly cleaning, or running out into the station to pick up supplies for the crew, but occasionally I was given some mechanical task, to change things up. I appreciated it. The work kept my mind in neutral, prevented me from dwelling on recent events.

Was I sad about the loss of my parents? Absolutely. I loved them. They had been good to me. They hadn't deserved what had happened to them. And yet, my grief was muted by an overwhelming sense of dismay. I'd lost the tape of Dad's disappearance, as well as all my drawings. My dreams continued to fade and grow diffuse. I still knew what I'd seen, but its immediacy was fading in my mind's eye. I got ahold of pencils and paper and tried to recreate the drawings I'd done back home, but everything looked wrong. Like a copy of a copy. Too far removed from the real thing.

While this was happening, Captain Goodwin tried to figure out what to do with me. I appreciate that she took the time. She could've dumped me on the station, turned me over to some colonial office as an orphan. It would have saved her time and money when she could've been lining up her next contract. Instead, she asked me about my family. As far as I knew, I only had one person, aside from my parents: my mother had mentioned a sister. An aunt.

Eventually, Captain Goodwin found the woman, on a planet in the New Eden sector. Captain Goodwin reached out, and, after an exchange of messages, my aunt Lucy agreed to take me in. So we made another jump, which meant another jaunt in cryo, and my dreams grew no clearer. Something was slipping away from me—perhaps forever. It was my first real taste of heartbreak—a feeling I'd recognize later, as my early love affairs inevitably went awry. Strange that my first experience with the sensation had nothing to do with matters of love, or romance, but with art, and inspiration.

The *Chariot* arrived at a world called Welkin. Captain Goodwin had me gather up my few belongings in an old backpack the crew had donated—some clothes the captain had bought me, a few toiletries, my art supplies, and my feeble attempts to recreate the temple on AF-617.

Once she'd received confirmation that my aunt had arrived, the captain walked me to the ship's loading ramp. While we waited for it to lower, she put a hand on my shoulder, and looked down at me.

"Listen, kid," she said. "You've been through some shit. Shit nobody should have to go through. I think your life's about to get a lot easier. Easier than you could possibly expect. But no matter what happens—you've got to keep your mouth shut about what happened on AF-617. You never know who might be paying attention out there, looking for news or refugees. The corporations don't like loose ends. You don't want anyone trying to tie you off. So here's the official story: your parents died in mining accidents on AF-617, and you came to stay with us because I'm an old friend of your mom's. If anyone asks, you've been with us for months, not weeks, because it took us a while to locate your aunt. When you tell your story, you don't bring up any ancient caverns, or creatures that used to be human. You don't know anything about a quarantine on AF-617. You keep all of that to yourself, and if anyone brings those things up, you shrug and say it's news to you. If you start talking about what really happened, you'd be putting me, my crew, yourself, and your aunt in danger. Do you understand?"

I said that I did.

"Good man," she said, and let go of my shoulder.

The ramp had finished lowering by then, and we walked down it together, onto the docking bay floor. I was surprised by how different it looked from the trading hub where we'd spent the last few weeks. That place had been dark and dirty, the technology old, the people tired. The dock on Welkin was brightly lit and clean. Everything looked brand-new. The ship workers still looked dirty and tired, but the dock employees wore clean, crisp, matching uniforms, and seemed lighter of step here. It was my first hint at the divide between those with money, and those without. I'd understood before that there were rich people and poor people, but I hadn't understood just what that *looked* like.

I stopped at the bottom of the ramp where I found

myself before a woman in soft, flowing clothes and open-toed shoes. Despite having never seen a picture of her before, I recognized my aunt Lucy at once. She looked like a prettier version of my mother—softer of feature, fuller of figure. Here was my second glimpse into the world of money. Aunt Lucy had led a soft life. Hard labor hadn't robbed her of her beauty; indeed, cosmetics (and surgery, I presume) had helped enhance and preserve it.

Lucy stood next to a large man with a hard face. He wore an immaculate black suit and tie. I wondered if this was Lucy's husband, my uncle Reuben.

She came forward, as though she meant to hug me, but something made her stop about a meter short. The man in the suit followed about a step behind, his face impassive.

Aunt Lucy gave me an uneasy smile. "You must be Corinth," she said.

I nodded, and she extended a dainty, manicured hand with long red nails.

"I'm your aunt Lucy," she said. "It's so nice to meet you."

I took her hand, shook it, and smiled.

Lucy shook Captain Goodwin's hand as well, and thanked her for bringing me safely to Welkin.

"Of course," Captain Goodwin said. "Your sister was a good friend of mine. I couldn't have lived with myself if I hadn't gotten Corinth home."

Goodwin threw me a small salute. "Be good, kid," she said. Then she walked up the ramp, back onto the *Chariot*, and there she, her ship, and its crew pass out of my tale, although all three remain close to my mind and heart to this day. I often wonder what became of Captain Goodwin and her ship. Perhaps, if I survive my current ordeal, I will try to find out.

But all of that is beside the point of my current narrative. Once Captain Goodwin had taken her leave, Aunt Lucy introduced me to the man standing behind her. He was not, in fact, her husband, but rather, her chauffeur. His name was Stanley.

Introductions made, Lucy said, "Let's get out of here. I can't stand being in such a dirty place. Do you know what I mean?"

I nodded to be polite, but was perplexed. I followed her and Stanley back to her car, a sleek, shining red vehicle which looked fancier than anything I'd ever been close to in my life. I'd showered and was wearing clean clothes, but still felt too dirty to be close to it. And yet, Stanley held open a door for me on the rear driver's side, and then for my aunt on the passenger side. We slid into the backseat. He shut the door for us, then climbed into the driver's seat.

He drove us away from the docks and the industrial center and out into a flat, warm, grassy countryside, dotted only sparsely with large houses behind large gates. I was overwhelmed by the sight. I'd never seen actual houses before, outside of old Earth media. Everyone I'd ever known had lived in apartments.

Aunt Lucy's house was as big and splendid as any of the homes we passed during the long drive. It was a massive, two-story structure, with a wide, pillared front porch and a giant circular gravel driveway with a working fountain in the middle.

Lucy gave me a tour, showing me the major rooms of the house, and introducing me to the servants we met in the hallways and kitchens. After this, she took me up a winding staircase to the second floor, where she introduced me to my uncle Reuben.

He was in his office, bent over a computer. He was a far cry from Stanley. Where Stanley was large and impassive, like a block of granite, Reuben was small and nebbish, with graying hair, heavy bags under his eyes, pronounced lines around his mouth, and a perpetual scowl. He barely looked up when Lucy announced our presence. I merited a glance—a brief one.

"Oh yes," he said. "Lucy said you'd be coming. Make yourself at home." And having made his pronouncement, he waved a hand through the air to dismiss us.

Lucy led me out of the room. "He's always so

busy," she said. "He works so hard. You'll get to know him. He's a good man."

I said I was sure he was.

Then, as the last stop on the tour, she brought me to my own bedroom.

"It used to be a guest bedroom," she told me. "I thought about decorating for you, but I thought you might like to pick things out yourself, instead. That could be fun, right?" She seemed as nervous around me as I felt around her, as she opened the door upon a room larger than my family's entire apartment on AF-617. A four-poster bed stood against the far wall, bordered on either side by floor-to-ceiling windows with heavy maroon drapes. A desk stood on the wall to my left, and a wardrobe on the one to my right. There was enough space between the room's three pieces of furniture that several couples could have comfortably waltzed. Through an open doorway to the left of the wardrobe, I saw the bathroom. I had my own bathroom.

"Will this do?" Lucy said, giving me a hopeful look.

I nodded, my mouth dry, any words caught in my throat.

"I'll leave you to get settled," she said. "Let me know if you need anything."

I could spend thousands of words on my early days in that house. I could tell you about the strangeness of settling into that massive house, with more space than I could possibly use. The alien feel of snuggling into my new bed for the first time. Being swallowed by its vastness. How quickly I grew used to being waited upon at mealtimes, at having my room cleaned by maids. The shopping trips into the cities of Welkin, where my aunt bought me new bedding, new curtains, new clothes, and every type of art supply I desired.

Lucy and I never grew close. She was always kind, and I was always well behaved and grateful, but there always remained a distance between us. An awkwardness we could never seem to overcome. We often ate together (joined about half the time by workaholic Uncle Reuben), and shopped together, but otherwise spent most of our time apart.

It didn't worry me. I think Lucy was that way with everyone. Even she and Uncle Reuben seemed to prefer their privacy from one another. They slept in individual bedrooms, and if Reuben ever visited Lucy in the night (or vice-versa), I didn't know about it.

I continued to draw, and also made my first clumsy attempts at painting and sculpture. I chased after the figures from my memories of AF-617, and grew increasingly frustrated as my efforts fell short of capturing their dark wonder. When Lucy realized the intensity of my interest in art, she enrolled me in classes. My technique began to improve, but the final results looked less and less right, somehow.

After a few months, Lucy decided I'd spent enough time in quiet contemplation and mourning, and sent me away to an elite private school across the continent from their palatial home.

Pena Academy was, itself, another change of pace. Even though it was only a few years old, it had a lot of money behind it, and most of its students were the sons and daughters of corporate bigwigs. It was built to look like an old Earth private school, a smattering of brick buildings spread across miles of grassy lawn, and dorm rooms that were small enough that they put me in mind of AF-617.

However, the dorms were the only part of Pena that was like my old home. The classrooms were comfortable, with large desks and soft lighting. The teachers were strict, and the lessons difficult. No longer could I just space out during class, and make up for it by acing my homework and tests. I had to pay attention, and keep up. I rose to meet the challenge. I made good grades. My teachers liked me. They wrote nice things in my progress reports, which Aunt Lucy loved.

I took art classes, but was careful not to make my "real" art here, in the presence of so many others. I focused on honing my technique, but kept my subject matter safe. I painted vases of flowers, bowls of fruit, portraits of handsome classmates.

In short, I kept my head down and did my work—until my senior year, when I got in trouble for a paper I wrote.

====

The assignment was simple: write an essay about someone who changed the world—or should have.

It was a "gimme" assignment. I could've written about Peter Weyland, or Hideo Yutani, the founders of the modern age, as at least half of my classmates had. But I went another way. I can't say what possessed me. After years of following Captain Goodwin's advice and staying relatively innocuous in my home and academic lives, something wild in me, which had lain dormant for years, suddenly struck out. I was seized by the need to write something true. So I painstakingly researched a paper, then wrote it in a white heat. When I turned it in, I was genuinely convinced I'd done the best work of my life.

For a few days after I turned the paper in, life went on as normal. Then something shifted. Where before, teachers would smile and say hello in the halls, they now gave me odd looks. They stopped calling on me in class, even if I raised my hand. And after about a week, I was called into the headmistress's office.

Doctor Fell was an energetic young woman with dark hair and wide brown eyes. She was given to smiling when I saw her in the halls, or during school assemblies, but she wore a deep frown now as she sat behind her desk with her hands folded.

"Please sit, Corinth," she said.

I settled into a small chair in front of her desk. I kept my hands in my lap, a little anxious but mostly curious. What could possibly warrant this level of seriousness? I hadn't done anything wrong, as far as I knew. Did she perhaps want me to inform on another student? Was I being selected for some honor? I had no idea.

"Do you know why I've called you in here?" Doctor Fell said.

"No, ma'am," I said.

She nodded slowly, and then picked up something off her desk. It was a small stack of pages, stapled together. I could read the title on the front page from where I sat:

OTBD: Duncan Fields and the Warning Against Colonization

It was my history paper. For the first time since turning it in, I felt a twinge of discomfort.

"This is your paper, isn't it, Corinth?" she said.

"Yes, ma'am," I said.

"Now do you understand why you've been called in here?" she asked.

"Not really," I admitted. "Is there something wrong with my paper?"

I was quite proud of the paper. I'd worked hard on it. I'd dug up as much information as I could about the prophet Duncan Fields and the Earthsavers cult. I don't know if you remember them, Roman, so if not, please forgive me a brief history lesson:

In the late 2000s, a man named Duncan Fields began experiencing persistent nightmares about life among the stars. He saw horrible monsters in these dreams. He came to believe that these nightmares were visions, a promise of things to come if humanity left the cradle of Earth and insisted upon colonizing other worlds. That these monsters would spell the end for humanity.

Fields was able to attract a small army of converts to his cause. These converts called themselves Earthsavers, and lived by a simple credo: OTBD, or, "Out there be demons."

In 2103, the Earthsavers made several attempts to sabotage or otherwise prevent the Weyland-Yutani colony ship, the *Covenant*, from leaving Earth to settle the distant world of Origae-6. The cult ultimately failed in its attempts, and most of its members were rounded up by law enforcement. Colonization exploded under Weyland-Yutani's watch. Humanity spread across the stars.

Now, in Doctor Fell's office, she shifted in her

seat, and her mouth worked for a moment.

"Corinth," she said. She kept saying my name, and it was beginning to irritate me. "Your assignment was to write about someone who changed the world—or should have. You turned in a paper lionizing a terrorist organization."

I hadn't really considered the Earthsavers by that term before. I'd thought of them as fanatics, and cultists, but never terrorists. It gave me pause now.

"No," I said after thinking it over. "I don't think I agree."

Doctor Fell bent over my paper. She flipped through the pages until she found what she was looking for:

"'It would be a mistake to say that humanity's expansion beyond the Sol system has come without a great cost,'" she read. "'I began to wonder—has this expansion been worth it? And in my researches into the early days of colonization, I found that humanity had been given at least one warning—a warning which went entirely unheeded, and has been largely forgotten by history.'"

"I wrote the paper," I said. "I don't need you tell me what it says."

Her head whipped up and she gave me a withering glare. It took all my courage to keep my head up and meet her gaze.

"I'd never heard of the Earthsavers until your

history teacher alerted me to your paper," Doctor Fell said. "And frankly, once I did a bit of research on my own, I was alarmed. This group killed people," she said. "And you're writing about them in a way that doesn't condemn their actions."

"I'm trying to examine the subject with some nuance, doctor," I said. "Did you read the entire paper?"

"I did," she said.

"Then you should know I'm not praising the Earthsavers," I said. "I think it's terrible that they took human lives. Unforgiveable. But I'm also trying to understand what could compel them to do what they did. I'm trying to look at the evidence with objective eyes."

"What evidence?" Doctor Fell said. "Corinth—"

"Doctor Fell, why did you call me in here?" I said.

"Young man?" she said, as though confused.

"Why am I here?" I repeated. "Is it just so you can yell at me? Or did you want some sort of explanation for my actions? If the former, fine, I'll sit here and take it, but I won't apologize for my paper. Duncan Fields, by all accounts, led a normal life for a long time. He showed no signs of mental illness or antisocial tendencies. He was an adjuster for an insurance company. White collar. Paunchy. Someone you wouldn't look twice at if you passed him on the street. And yet one day, this ordinary man began to have dreams. Persistent dreams, brilliant in detail. He tried to dismiss these dreams, through therapy, through drugs both legal and illicit, through natural remedies. And yet his nightmares persisted. He came to believe that they were more than the production of a troubled subconscious, but rather, visions. A promise of things to come, should humanity leave the cradle of our solar system. Terrible monsters that would wipe out humanity, if we made contact."

"You're not making a compelling case so far," Doctor Fell said. "People can be as old as their sixties before manifesting symptoms of psychosis."

"But we're not just talking about one man, here," I said. "This chubby little insurance adjuster managed, by the strength of his visions, to enlist a small army of followers."

"Crazy people can be compelling," Doctor Fell said. "Look at Adolf Hitler or Osama bin Laden on old Earth. Objectively bad men who managed to convince others to help carry out their insane schemes."

I sighed, frustrated. "Yes, I considered that. But here's the key difference—those men were hungry for power. They became leaders within their respective organizations. From all accounts, Duncan Fields was far removed from the leadership of the Earthsavers. He sat on the sidelines while they planned and committed the violence. We're not talking about a power-hungry despot here. We're talking about a man tortured by visions of a future—a future that actually *came to pass*."

"Came to pass?" Doctor Fell said, incredulous. "You and I are currently sitting here, on a colony world far from Earth. We're both clothed, comfortable, and safe. We're not in fear for our lives."

"Doctor Fell, we're not the only colony," I said. "And with all due respect to you and your position at this school—you haven't seen the things I have. I don't think you appreciate just how wrong things can go."

"I know that colonial life is often difficult and dangerous," Doctor Fell said. "Bad things happen. It's the cost of the life we've chosen. Technology fails. Ships go missing. Occasionally we encounter a dangerous species, like the Swarm. But Duncan Fields believed in indescribable monsters. In all the years of humanity's expansion into the Middle Heavens, there's been no recorded mention of creatures like the ones Fields feared."

I saw Captain Goodwin's face in my mind's eye. I remembered her telling me to keep quiet about my origins, my past. Her warnings about what happened to people who spoke up. I was a hormonal teenager. I was angry. But I knew the captain was right. I'd miscalculated, and I should let this go. Instead, I said:

"There's a dark secret at the heart of this galaxy. Whether it comes to light in our lifetimes? I have no idea. But it's out there. Peering at us from the shadows. Waiting for its moment."

Throughout this conversation, Doctor Fell's expression had vacillated between frustrated and enraged. Now it changed to a mixture of sympathy and fear. It took her a moment to find her bearings. She licked her lips a few times, then folded her hands on her desk.

"Corinth," she said. "It's clear you feel strongly about this. Let me talk to your instructor, and your mother—"

"My aunt," I corrected her. "I live with my aunt. My mother is dead. One of those casualties of colonial life that you brushed aside. Technology fails, right?"

"Right," Doctor Fell said, her gaze dropping back to my paper. "Of course. Let me talk to Doctor Simpson, and your aunt, and we'll meet again to discuss next steps here."

====

I left the headmistress's office feeling discombobulated. I'd gotten worked up. I'd lost control. I'd said too much. Hell, I'd given away too much just by writing that paper. That had been stupid of me. Even if I was right, what had I been hoping to prove? How had I expected my instructors to react?

I didn't understand myself then, but I think maybe I do now, with some hindsight. I had had a religious experience on AF-617. It had profoundly shaped and changed me as a human being. I'd gotten a glimpse behind the curtain, and was looking for answers. I'd actually come right out and said so to Doctor Fell, when pressed. There was a dark secret I would never be able to stop pondering, or trying to uncover.

My story had taken another turn. I was that much further down the road to darkness.

12

THE LITTLE STRANGER

Goodwin and Harris's watch passed in relative peace. The motion tracker didn't pick up any new movement. No strange noises came from the woods. She finished reading the second file of the Bloch dossier undisturbed before it was time to wake Sam for his shift.

When Goodwin let herself into their tent, lighting her way with a flashlight, she found Sam wide awake. He lay on his back, hands behind his head, glaring at the fabric ceiling.

"Have you slept at all?" Goodwin said.

"No," Sam admitted. "Don't think I'm getting any sleep tonight."

He sat up and began to pull on his boots. She squeezed his shoulder, but he shook her off. She sat back, startled. He usually leaned into her slightest touch like an eager puppy.

"Listen," she said. "I know you think I'm being cold about Cardona."

"You're the captain," he said, keeping his back to her. "You don't have to explain yourself to me."

He let himself out of the tent, zipping it closed behind him to join White on the watch.

Goodwin collapsed back onto her sleeping bag, stung. She told herself to get over it. Sam was an emotional person. He didn't have Goodwin's talent for locking down feelings. The events of the last couple of days had gotten to him. Of course they had. Shit, they were getting to her, too. She couldn't expect him to brush all that aside just because she squeezed his shoulder.

Still, she'd been hoping he needed to be touched as badly as she'd wanted to touch him. She could've used his warmth in this cold place, even if it was just for a moment.

It's what you deserve, a small voice inside her said. *You're the cold, hard captain. This is what it gets you.* The voice sounded like her mother.

"Shut up, you old hypocrite," she mumbled under her breath. She knew Alice Goodwin had been softer than she'd appeared. After all, the old woman had rescued Corinth Bloch from AF-617. She'd saved his life and helped him find his family. That wasn't exactly the behavior of a cold, hard captain, now was it?

Maybe she ought to take a page from the old woman's

handbook. Say 'fuck it' to the mission, and try to find Cardona. Shit, maybe they could find Compton, too.

To what end, though? Even if they could find their missing friends, she and her crew would still be stuck on DSJ-1020 without a ship. No, the best hope—for everyone—was to make their way to the colony, find supplies and a working ship, then search for the others. Any other path would be suicide.

And if taking the smarter path meant Sam gave Goodwin the cold shoulder? Goodwin would just have to live with that. She was, as he had helpfully pointed out, the captain.

The thought brought her no comfort, here on the cold, hard forest floor, with only a bit of fabric between her and the elements. She closed her eyes and sighed.

It's more than being smart though, isn't it? Mom's voice asked. *You don't want to cry off your current quest for purely practical reasons. Deep down, you want to meet him. You want to meet Bloch.*

She sighed again and turned onto her side. It did nothing for her physical or mental comfort. The voice was correct. Goodwin wanted to meet Corinth Bloch. The things he wrote in the dossier spoke to her. Although she hadn't seen anything like what he'd encountered on AF-617, something about his descriptions—and the art he'd made, inspired by his experiences—felt *true* to her, in a way that most things, she now realized, did not. She didn't quite understand what that meant, but there was no other way to put it. The surface world, the one she'd participated in for the last thirty-odd years of her life, felt like a show. A veneer, cast over something else. Something darkly beautiful, only visible at the edges of things, in the corners. Something she'd only glimpsed in her dreams. She'd never met anyone else who could put this feeling into words—this fog through which she'd lived her life. She *had* to meet Corinth Bloch. Had he found answers here? Had he unlocked the dark secret at the heart of the galaxy? And if he had, what would that mean?

Despite her agitation, Goodwin fell asleep almost at once. Her dreams were the sharpest and clearest they'd ever been. In them, she wandered dark, humid corridors that looked grown or carved, rather than built. They seemed to be made of some organic material, wet and sticky to the touch, although the floor beneath her feet seemed to be man-made metal—identical to the flooring in countless space stations and colonies.

Figures moved through these dark corridors—massive and hunched over and hard to discern in the darkness—as though at some great task, but the task itself remained mysterious to Goodwin. There was beauty and synchronicity to the figures' movements, as though they were dancers performing a well-rehearsed routine. Goodwin moved among them, sidestepping their graceful movements, careful not to interrupt the dance. They didn't seem to notice her—or if they did notice her, they didn't seem to care. They were too focused on the task at hand, and so she moved unmolested through their corridors, pausing occasionally to wipe sweat from her brow. She knew she was drawing closer to… something. Some presence at the center of all of this. The final answer. Goodwin longed to see it, and felt, in some way, that it also longed to look upon her.

She searched and searched through the hallways of her dream, always sure she'd find what she was looking for around the next corner. She was still searching when Sam came to wake her, and yanked her rudely from her quest.

"Sun's coming up," he said, while she blinked at him, trying to reorient herself in the waking world. "Figured we ought to get moving."

She nodded, to acknowledge that she'd heard and understood him, and that she agreed. He looked for a moment like he might say more, but instead he left then, and Goodwin was alone in the tent again. She pulled on her boots, and rolled up both sleeping bags before she came out.

The morning air hit her like a splash of cold water, chasing away the last wisps of sleep. Sam, White, and Harris were already packing up the campsite, taking down tents. They'd left Cardona's standing, however.

"Make sure to bring that one with us," she said, pointing to it.

"Why?" White said. "It's just extra weight."

"Cardona's part of this crew," Goodwin said. "We're not giving up on her."

White rolled their eyes, but Sam smiled a little. Just a little, and the expression vanished quickly, but Goodwin caught it. It was why she'd given the order. White was right—this was almost certainly a futile gesture, but it was one that mattered to Sam. If it kept his morale up—and more importantly, kept Goodwin in his good graces—then it was worthwhile.

Harris checked the motion tracker. They were only about ten klicks from the signal now, and could reach it in the next day or so, depending on how the woods treated them today.

"Imagine," Harris said. "If we get to the colony, we might be able to take a hot shower. Sleep in real beds."

"Assuming it's safe to go in there," White said.

"It's been a couple of days and I feel fine," Harris said. "Are you feeling sick?"

"No," White said. "But that doesn't mean anything. Some viruses, you don't know you're sick for days, or even weeks."

"You're a barrel of cheer, kid," Harris said.

"I'm just saying," White said. "Don't get too comfy with the idea that everything is fine once we get to New Providence. Whatever went wrong here? It probably started there."

"Quiet, both of you," Goodwin said. "We'll see what there is to see when we get there. No sense worrying about it until then."

They marched in silence after that. A soft rain began. The tree cover protected them from the worst of it. The droplets made a soft pattering sound against the leaves. It was a soothing sound. The sort of thing Goodwin could have thrown up on the picture window at the hotel where she'd stayed with Sam. What had that place been called? It was only a few days in the past, but it already felt like a lifetime.

The Bowers. They'd stayed at a hotel called the Bowers. God, the bed in that room had been so soft. She'd been so cozy, nestled in the blankets next to Sam.

And yet, Goodwin wouldn't trade her current situation for that one. Even after all the misfortune that had befallen the *Chariot*. She had a feeling that, for the first time in her life, she was *exactly* where she was supposed to be.

Travel through the woods remained difficult and slow. It was dark, and the overcast skies did little to help even when the tree cover occasionally broke. There were frequent points when the crew had to move single file between the trees.

The day went almost entirely without incident, until

mid afternoon, when the crew were moving single-file through a patch of dense forest, and the motion tracker chirped.

Goodwin, who was currently leading the party, stopped and turned to look back at Harris. He was at the end of the line, behind Sam and White. He was frowning down at the screen of the tracker. It continued to chirp.

"I've got something incoming," he said. "Not just a glitch, it's a steady signal. Moving relatively slow." He pointed off to his left. "Coming from that direction."

The frequency of the chirp increased. Whatever it was, it was getting closer.

"What do we do?" White said.

Goodwin pulled her mother's revolver from its holster in her jacket. She turned off the safety and wrapped both hands around the grip, then pointed the weapon up toward the trees. The beeping was now a steady clip. Goodwin strained to try and hear any additional noise. Was it coming on the ground? Was it up in the trees, moving that way? She strained, but heard nothing over the persistent chirp.

"We're not really just going to stand here, are we?" White said. The whole group was sort of wedged between two lines of trees. They'd had to turn sideways to traverse the tight space.

"There's not really much we *can* do right now," Harris said.

"Fuck this," White said. "Fuck this to death."

"White, shut up," Goodwin said. "I'm trying to listen."

White did shut up, although Goodwin felt them staring daggers at her. The chirping from the motion tracker was so constant now that it was almost a steady tone. Goodwin adjusted her grip on the revolver, and at last, heard something beyond the chirping sound—a quiet crunch. Footsteps on the forest floor.

Goodwin braced herself, and put her finger on the revolver's trigger. She kept her head turned as far to the left as she could, trying to see. This might be it. Where she died. Stuck between two trees, unable to get a proper shot off at whatever was stalking them. She braced herself.

The source of the signal emerged from the dark, and Goodwin at first only processed it as a bundle of movement, low to the ground. She cocked the revolver and swung it toward the thing.

"No!" Sam shouted. "Don't!" he slapped the gun from her hands and sent it off into the dark.

Goodwin nearly punched him. He'd killed them, prevented her one chance at defending the crew, and she would express her displeasure before she died, by God. Then her mind at last made sense of the thing she'd almost shot, and she let out a short, sharp laugh.

It wasn't some unspeakable horror, like those described in Corinth Bloch's memoir. It was a dog. A golden retriever, if she wasn't mistaken. It had a thick yellow coat and plaintive dark eyes. It looked a little skinny, but otherwise healthy. No visible injuries.

The dog moved between the trees with ease. It approached Goodwin and then sat at her feet, wagging its tail and looking up at her expectantly.

She knelt—a difficult proposition, between the trees where she was currently wedged—and put out a hand for the dog to sniff. The dog licked her palm, then rubbed its face against her fingers, almost like a cat. She scratched the dog's chin and ears, and its tail thumped the ground harder.

"I nearly shot you, you dummy," Goodwin said.

"But you didn't," Sam said. "And now you have a new friend."

"Another mouth to feed, more like," White said, but they sounded relieved.

Goodwin wasn't sure how she felt. Her heart was still pounding in her chest, from the tension and anxiety of the moment before. She knew that, at a basic, animal level, her body was experiencing relief, at knowing it was safe again. She also knew she ought to be glad to see this dog. It was the first living thing they'd encountered since setting down on DSJ-1020, and although the dog seemed a little underfed, it was otherwise happy.

But another part of Goodwin—the part that was devouring the Bloch dossier with such hunger—was disappointed. She'd been hoping to see something she'd never seen before. Something extraordinary.

The dog rolled over onto its back, exposing its belly. Goodwin quickly deduced that the animal was male.

"Hey, little man," Sam said. "What are you doing out here?" He pulled half a ration bar from his jacket pocket and offered it to the dog. The dog rolled back up, approached the pilot, and eagerly plucked the food out of his hand. It vanished in one bite.

"Little fucker probably didn't even taste it," Harris said.

"What's to taste?" Sam said. "Those things are disgusting."

The dog looked at Sam expectantly, hoping for more.

"That's all for now," he said. "You'll have to wait until we stop to get anything else."

They spent a little time hunting for Goodwin's revolver, and eventually found it nearby on the forest floor. Once she'd secured in its holster, the crew set off in the direction of the electric beacon again. The dog kept pace with them, trotting along, seemingly happy for the company (and eager for any more food they might share). The forest remained dense and dark and difficult.

The rest of the day might've gone without incident, if the forest layout were slightly different. If they'd squeezed between different trees. But they went the way they went, and in the early evening, Goodwin led the group into a small clearing—and stopped dead at what she saw. She stopped so abruptly that Sam bumped into her from behind.

"What's wrong?" he said.

She held up a hand to silence him. The truth was, she wasn't entirely sure what she was seeing, and needed a moment to process it.

The first thing she noticed was that the clearing was roughly circular in shape, which gave the whole milieu a sort of dark fairytale energy. The second thing she noticed were the people. The first human beings she'd seen since crashing on DSJ-1020. They were fastened to the trunks of the trees by some shiny, glassy substance. Each person had a hole in the middle of their chest. Each was clearly dead, their eyes glassy, mouths distended in grimaces of pain or screams of terror.

Goodwin put a hand to her own sternum, and thought of Bloch's sculpture, *Transfiguration*. The figure depicted there had had a distended chest.

On the forest floor, in front of each one of these bodies, were large, oval-shaped objects, sort of like eggs. They looked tough, like maybe they were made of leather, but also slick, as though covered in some sort of viscous substance different from the rain that had been falling all morning.

The top of each egg appeared to have opened, four

corners folding back to expose the interiors. Goodwin crept forward now, for a better look at the inside of the closest one. As she did, something wrapped around her boot and dug into the top of her foot.

She shouted and tripped backward, landing hard on the forest floor, catching herself on her hands and sending lances of pain up both arms.

The spiky sensation on her foot stopped as soon as she fell. She drew her legs back until her knees were pressed to her chest, and looked at what had grabbed her. It was some sort of crablike creature, yellowish in color, with four fingerlike legs on each side, and a long, whip-like tail. It didn't seem to have any eyes, and while most of its body seemed hard, its underbelly was soft and meaty.

Something touched Goodwin on the shoulder and she shouted again, lurching forward. She looked back and saw it was only Sam.

"Relax," he said. "I think that thing is dead. You just triggered a reflex." He picked up a stick off the ground and poked the crab thing's soft underbelly. Its legs closed around the stick in a grasping gesture.

"See?" Sam said.

Goodwin looked around. There were several more crab things scattered across the clearing, all apparently dead. Everything in the clearing was dead, except for Goodwin and her crew.

White and Harris approached one of the bodies fastened to the trees.

"What the hell happened here?" Harris said.

"I think I'm gonna be sick," White said—and, true to their word, they turned aside and emptied their stomach onto the ground.

"I guess we've found our plague," Goodwin said. "Why no one's allowed to approach or leave the planet."

Sam continued to poke at the crab-thing on the ground. "You think these are the things that took Cardona?" He sounded doubtful. He dropped the stick and went to check on White, who stood with their hands on their knees, still loudly retching.

"So we have the eggs, right?" Harris said. "And then, the crab-monsters. And then these poor souls." He gestured at the human bodies positioned around them. "With gaping chest wounds. How does this add up?"

"I don't know," Goodwin said, as she climbed back to her feet. "Maybe there's some piece to this we haven't seen yet?"

She glanced back into the woods, and noticed for the first time that the dog hadn't come forward. He remained in the relative safety of the trees, head lowered, whining.

"It's okay," Goodwin said to him. "I don't think anything here can hurt you."

The dog's hackles went up. It bowed forward, as though it might pounce, and exposed its teeth in a snarl. A low growl rose from its throat.

"Okay, okay," Goodwin said. "Stay there, then."

She turned back to the eggs. For some reason, they

put her in mind of the vases that Bloch had described on AF-617. The neatness of the arrangement. The feeling she had, that they had contained something... potent. Dangerous. None of it made perfect sense, but she could feel the connection. In her mind, it was undeniable. Somehow, all of this must tie together. Maybe Bloch could make it make sense.

She wished they had a camera. She wanted to take pictures of all of this. She was no artist. She wouldn't be able to reproduce what she was seeing with pencils, paints, or clay. Instead, she would have to do her best to remember. To keep all of this in her mind's eye.

"This is so fucked up," White said. They'd apparently recovered from their bout of nausea, and had joined the dog at the outskirts of the clearing.

"No argument here," Harris said.

"Can we leave?" White said. "I want to get away from this place. This is a bad place."

Harris and Sam both turned to look at Goodwin, the question plain on their faces. She could've happily stayed here for hours—this was the closest she'd been to Bloch's great mystery. She was hesitant to leave these semi-answers behind. But they had a destination. A goal. And she couldn't justify staying here just because it felt *right* to do so.

"Sure," Goodwin said. "Let's get out of here."

* * *

Since the dog refused to enter the clearing, Goodwin and the crew had to double back and go around it, to get their furry companion to come along. Once they had the dog's cooperation, however, Goodwin noticed a shift in the animal's allegiance. Whereas before, it had walked beside her, it was now hewing closer to White, perhaps sensing a kindred spirit.

The dog stayed close to White for the rest of the day, and when they finally stopped for the night, he lay at White's feet, only getting up when offered scraps of food from the rest of the crew. He would come to you if you held out food, but immediately returned to his new best friend after. White, for their part, seemed happy to have a new friend. They were considerably cheerier now than they'd been at the start of the mission. They even gave the dog a name, dubbing him 'Quilbo.'

"Quilbo?" Sam said. "Is that a family name or something?"

"No," White said. "Just the name of a character I played in a game when I was a kid. Quilbo was a heroic ranger. Good at moving through the woods, just like our new friend here." They ran a hand along the dog's flank, scratching near his tail. Quilbo's tail thumped the ground a few times, but then Goodwin offered him a bit of her dinner, and he got up to accept the proffered food.

She wondered again how Quilbo had gotten out here. Had he come all the way from the colony, looking for help? Or had he been with other people, out in these woods? People who'd been snatched by the same thing that had taken Cardona? The dog seemed to recognize the eggs and bodies in the clearing were bad business.

If only you could tell us, she thought, watching him return to White's feet.

Goodwin and Sam took the first watch, letting Harris and White sleep. White took Quilbo into his tent with him, leaving Goodwin and her lover alone, sitting on opposite sides of the space heater.

"You don't have to sit so far away," Goodwin said, and patted the ground next to herself.

"I know," Sam said, but didn't move.

"That was my way of asking you to sit next to me," she said.

"I'm good over here, thanks," he said.

She nodded, licked her lips, and ran her hands over her thighs and knees as she tried to decide how to respond. She could feel him waiting for her next move. He wanted her to say more, to draw him close again with soothing words and apologies. She wouldn't do it. She refused to play that game. She'd invited him over. If he wanted to be cold and alone, that was his business.

She pulled her laptop from her bag, opened the Bloch dossier, and began to read.

```
Bloch_Dossier_003                    ◄ ►  X
```

After my confrontation with Doctor Fell, I was ordered into counseling at school. In my sessions with the counselor, I realized that nothing I said would convince the adults in my life that I was correct about the Earthsavers cult. So, because it was expedient, I apologized for the paper. I wrote a new one, about Peter Weyland, and the advent of the modern android. I purposely avoided mentioning Weyland's mysterious disappearance and presumed death. I also didn't mention the problems that resulted from the early David androids. I shied away from anything controversial or difficult, because I understood the adults in my life wanted easy answers. They wanted pre-digested truths that could be passed on ad infinitum. They didn't want to think hard, or ask uncomfortable questions.

So I kept my head down. I finished secondary school. I got serious about my art. Aunt Lucy enrolled me in classes on my breaks from school. My dreams remained fuzzy and diffuse, and my memory an unreliable narrator, but I grew better at capturing the essences of things, even as more work grew less representational and more stylized.

I stopped working with pencils and began to use paint, and that was a turning point for me. Suddenly my work had a vibrancy and liveliness it had formerly lacked. I knew, without my teachers having to tell me, that I was growing.

After I graduated high school (without distinction), Aunt Lucy wanted me to apply to universities. I held her off, and asked for two years to pursue my art. She discussed it with Uncle Reuben, and they agreed to fund a trip for me, with the understanding that I would start college at age twenty.

I had no intention of honoring this bargain, but agreed to it because—as you might guess—it was expedient. I was also convinced, with the arrogance of the very young, that I would become rich and famous before those two years were up. I had no solid path to this goal, no concrete plans. Only an overpowering optimism, a faith in my talent, and a vague sense that destiny was on my side.

I spent the first six months of my journey bouncing around the New Eden sector. I stayed close to home, where things were comfortable. I rented luxurious apartments. I ate sumptuous meals, and went on shopping sprees with Uncle Reuben's money. I went to art shows. I got to know other artists, and dealers. I made friends. I rented expensive studios, far beyond my needs, envisioning myself filling them with stacks of paintings and armies of sculptures.

But in truth, I worked little. Maybe an hour or two a day, at best. I completed some paintings. A few sculptures. I continued to try and recreate the nightmarish visions I'd lived through as a kid. Technically, my work was impeccable. I knew this. So I began to submit to galleries. Only the biggest, most famous places. The places where the masters were showing. After all, I was a Great Artist. Why bother starting at the bottom?

The galleries didn't laugh me out of the building, which was a kindness, but they also made it clear that they weren't interested.

At the last stop on my rejection tour—at my "safety" gallery, "Rebirth" on Alexandria (a gallery that catered to rich patrons with conservative tastes), the owner took me into her office and sat me down across from her desk. I had an acute dense of déjà vu, like I was right back across from Doctor Fell in high school.

The woman's name was Mabel. I considered her a friend. I'd been to plenty of shows at Rebirth, had even been to parties at her home. She had gray streaks in her dark hair, and I remember, at age 18, thinking she must be impossibly old. In truth, I think she was in her mid 30s, and had made the aesthetic choice not to dye her hair. As usual, I am embarrassed by my younger self.

"Corinth," Mabel said. "Please take this advice in the spirit with which I'm offering it." She leaned over the computer on her desk, turned the monitor so we could both look at it, and called up the portfolio I'd submitted. She slowly clicked through a gallery of my recent work. A painting of a large, bald, stone head; a painting of a row of black vases. A painting of a man in mining gear, examining a vase, while in the background, a creature that looked like a collection of giant single-celled organisms prepared to pounce.

"You have immense technical skill," she said. "I don't think anyone would deny it. For your age, you're one of the most competent craftsmen I've ever met."

"Thank you," I said.

"But there are two problems here," she said. "First—" and here she pointed at the painting on her monitor, "—why are you trying to peddle this sort of subject matter to my gallery? We sell paintings of sailboats and horses to rich people. They're not interested in pulpy horror. I mean, did you really walk in here today thinking I was going to give you a show?"

My face grew warm. That was exactly what I had expected.

"Second of all—even if you were in the right place to sell this kind of art?" She leaned forward on the desk to force me to look her in the eye. "This stuff? It's all... empty. Missing something vital."

I looked at my lap, ashamed. The very thing I'd feared, now given voice by this woman.

Mabel stood up and walked around the desk to put a hand on my shoulder.

"Look, kid," she said. "There's something about you and your work, but I can tell it hasn't bloomed yet. You're about one breakthrough away from becoming something. You're still young, which is good, because it means you still have plenty of time to get that breakthrough. But you're also rich, and that's the part that worries me."

"What do you mean?" I said. Even at eighteen, I was aware of the myth of the starving artist. Artists tended to be happier and more productive if they had a belly full of food and enough money to live on. Most success stories in the arts were stories about people with money.

"I mean, you've been comfortable all your life. You haven't seen anything."

I opened my mouth to tell her that wasn't true, but for some reason held back. I wanted to hear her out.

"You haven't seen what the galaxy is really like," she went on. "You want to talk about darkness? Get out there and see some of it for yourself."

She walked me all the way out of the gallery and

out onto the street, where she wished me luck and told me to think about what she'd said.

I went straight from the gallery to my favorite dive bar, where I did some serious drinking, alone, on an empty stomach. The first drink helped numb the pain of rejection. The second drink opened me to Mabel's advice. The third drink convinced me that she was entirely right. Yes, I had seen some terrible things—but that had been eight years ago. I'd been delivered from my trauma to a world of softness, luxury, and comfort. Whatever hard edges I'd gained on AF-617 had been sanded down. Now I had to make a choice. The way I saw it, I had three options:

One, I could give up this ridiculous quest to become a great artist. I could go back to Welkin early, apply to schools. Go get a degree in something useful, and maybe go work for Uncle Reuben, doing whatever the hell he did (even after all the years of living with him, I still wasn't sure).

Two, I could continue pursuing my path as an artist, but change my subject matter. Learn to paint the sailboats and horses that rich people liked to buy.

Or three—I could go out into the galaxy and try to get my edge back. Hunt down the truths I'd only glimpsed so far.

I closed my tab, and tipped well. After all, why not? I was paying with someone else's money. Then, trying to look sober, I hailed a cab and took it to the docks. It would have been more demonstrative of my new mindset to have walked, but I had no idea where I was going. Wandering a strange part of the city, possibly being mugged or murdered, would have done me no good.

At the docks, I got directions to a local office that found employment for workers looking to ship out. I walked in, trying to look sober, filled out some forms, and submitted to a background check. I was worried that my lack of experience and expertise would prove a hindrance, but I was offered three different positions right away. I took the one that started the soonest—as a cargo handler on a ship called the *Jackalope*. They were departing in two hours. I signed my contract there in the office.

I made one stop on my way to my new posting— for coffee. I didn't contact my landlord at my apartment or my studio. I didn't let Aunt Lucy or Uncle Reuben know where I was going or what I was doing. I was afraid I'd lose my nerve. I had to act now, while I had my courage.

When I arrived at the *Jackalope*'s loading ramp, the first person I met was my new boss, Captain Nathan. He stood at the foot of the ramp, smoking a cigarette and looking at a tablet. He had longish gray hair, a salt-and-pepper beard, and his mouth was fixed in a half-smile around his cigarette as he looked me up and down.

"Bloch, right?" he said.

"Yes, sir," I said. And because I wasn't sure of the protocol, I saluted him. He made a sound somewhere between a laugh and a cough. A plume of startled-looking smoke puffed from his mouth.

"You are green, aren't you?" he said. Then his smile disappeared. "Look, are you sure you want to do this? Once you're onboard, there's no turning back."

"I signed the contract," I said.

"You did," he said. "But you're not the first rich drunk kid to stumble up my ramp, either. You boys sometimes turn out to be more trouble than you're worth. You show up, trying to prove something, and after a few days you get tired of hard work, and end up costing me time and money. I mean look at you. You're not even dressed for this work."

I looked at myself. I was wearing designer slacks, and a fashionable shirt. My hair was styled with expensive product. My shoes were soft leather. I realized how ridiculous I must look to this serious working man.

I waved at myself. "I know this isn't a great look. But give me a chance. If it doesn't work out, I'll buy out my own contract, so you don't lose any money."

His eyebrows went up. "You can afford to do that?"

"This isn't about money for me," I said.

"Why would you do this if you don't need the money?" he said. "I sure as shit wouldn't."

"It's hard to explain," I said.

He sighed, then jerked his head toward the ramp. "Go on, then. But you have to change clothes. Check locker 4 in the galley, I think we have some spare jumpsuits and boots you can wear until you get your own."

"Thank you, Captain," I said. "You won't regret this."

=====

Fifteen minutes later, I was wearing a jumpsuit that was at least one size too large for my narrow frame, and helping strap down crates of cargo in the ship's hold. I acquitted myself well enough for a beginner, and the rest of the crew seemed to feel I'd passed the audition.

An hour later, we were in space and undressing for cryo. I was used to private cryo pods when traveling. The group pod situation aboard the *Jackalope* was rather alarming. There were eight of us—three women, and five men, myself included—and there we were, practically naked in front of one another. No one else in the room seemed to think it was a big deal, so I tried to act like I didn't care, either.

Soon after, I was deep in cryo, and dreaming my boring, diffuse dreams.

=====

For the next year, this was how my life went. Moving from system to system. Asleep for weeks at a time. Waking up to help move cargo onto and off the ship. Drinking with my crew mates in the local dives.

I didn't paint or sculpt during this year. All my worldly possessions fit into a backpack that I kept in my locker. I didn't throw away my ID or credit cards or try to hide who I was. I kept everything that I had brought aboard with me. But I made a point of not using Uncle Reuben's money anymore. I lived off my own pay.

Speaking of Uncle Reuben, I did eventually let my family know where I was. It was an awkward call. Neither my aunt nor uncle had noticed anything amiss, despite the fact that I had stopped spending money.

Uncle Reuben expressed vague pride. He said he admired my attempt at independence, and that "doing some hard work" would give me "an appreciation for what real life was like." Aunt Lucy expressed concerns about the danger of the work, and the class of people with which it would force me to associate (forgetting, of course, that my parents were exactly those type of people). I promised to be careful.

My friends—the fellow artists I'd met during my six months pretending to be a genius—were a little more surprised and alarmed. I'd been omnipresent in the art world, and had disappeared abruptly. Most were happy to hear I was alive. My landlord was happy to hear I would pay off any back-owed rent and the cost of storing my belongings. But at least one friend questioned my choice, and was even more confused when I admitted that I had no art supplies with me and wasn't currently creating. He was a fellow painter, one who'd had a bit of success already. He hadn't had a show of his own yet, but had sold pieces here and there.

"You want to be an artist, don't you?" he said.

"More than anything," I said.

"Then shouldn't you be making art instead of hauling cargo?"

"Not yet," I told him.

"When?" he said.

"When I find my voice."

I continued life as a cargo handler. Sleeping away the days between ports. Fastening and unfastening crates of food and drink and other goods, to be moved in and out of the cargo hold. I learned how to play cards. How to drink cheap beer and like it. I had a few sexual encounters (don't be jealous, dear Roman—it's just another part of the story)—some with fellow crew members, others with strangers I met in bars. I tried both men and women, and found quickly that I preferred men.

Most of my crewmates led relatively insular

lives. They ate and drank and played cards together, and didn't venture far from the *Jackalope* when we were in port. This was their job, and most of them were just marking time between trips back home to their families. I was the weirdo who spent time exploring the stations, cities, and colonies where we stopped. I never lost sight of my mission. I was here to see what life was like. To get my edge back.

I paid attention everywhere I went. I tried to record the details of the streets I walked down. The neon signs with burnt-out letters. The beat-down expressions on people's faces as they traveled to and from their punishing daily toils. The dirt under their fingernails. The worn-out knees of their jumpsuits. The run-down heels of their boots. I tried to take it all in, commit it to memory while drawing none of it.

I grew reacquainted with discomfort, with need, in a visceral way. It was bracing, to be surrounded by the poor, after having been rich. When I was a child, I hadn't really understood the difference between rich and poor, beyond the most obvious (rich people got to do and have whatever they wanted, while the poor had to work to get by). I saw now the massive divide between those who had, and those who did not. I saw hundreds (thousands) or people struggling from paycheck to paycheck. Hell, I had to watch my own money carefully, and I was one of the "lucky" ones without dependents or debts to worry about. I finally understood the real qualitative difference between rich and poor. To be rich meant security. It meant you were allowed to feel optimistic about the future, because good things were probably going to happen to you. It meant sunshine, good food, fine clothing. It meant doctors when you were sick, and lawyers when events didn't go your way.

To be poor meant a grind. From day to day, week to week, month to month, year to year, birth to death. Massive corporations governed your existence, made fortunes off your labor, and paid you a pittance in return. It meant that you prayed not to get sick, because a medical emergency could bankrupt you. It meant that you kept your head down and tried not to get noticed—because if the rich or powerful noticed you, and decided to make your life hell? You had no recourse.

I tried to take all of this new perspective and incorporate it into my worldview. It seemed like an important piece of the greater picture I'd been chasing all my life. The great secret at the heart of creation. I wasn't quite sure how it all fit together yet, so I continued to refrain from making art. I knew I wasn't ready yet. But I was getting closer.

Then came the day I met the street preacher.

We were in port on Torrin Prime with rations. I'd

finished unloading the cargo, and was out exploring the city when I saw him.

He wasn't the first street evangelist I'd ever encountered. Spend any time traveling, and you run into every type of person, again and again. The preachers I'd met in the past were usually selling variations of the traditions of old Earth—Christianity, Buddhism, Judaism, Islam, and the like. They were often loud, but it was easy enough to ignore their shouting about Jesus and Allah, even if they had a megaphone.

I almost passed this preacher, too—I had no interest in engaging with a religious nut in my time off—but he shouted a single word that stopped me in my tracks:

Dragon.

I turned to look at the preacher. He was small, dirty, and completely bald. There was a wildness in his eyes I recognized as religious fervor. I'd seen enough of it out here that it was familiar to me. The only thing unfamiliar here was the content of his speech.

"Yes, the dragon cometh, friend!" he shouted. "*They* don't want you to know. *They* want you to keep being good little boys and girls, going to work, spending your money, making their fortunes. But we know the truth, and we will not be silenced!" As he spoke, he waved a small book back and forth through the air in his right hand.

I felt the curtain between myself and the great mystery flutter.

I approached the little man. I towered over him by probably 20 cm, but the light in his eyes made him seem larger.

"Tell me," I said.

He smiled up at me, revealing several missing teeth.

"A fellow truth-seeker," he said. "I know the look. Hello, friend. What's your name?"

"Adam," I lied. Despite my curiosity, I didn't want to give this possibly crazy stranger any information about me.

"Well, Adam," he said, "my name's Zachariah, and you came up to me for a reason. Something I said spoke to you, yes?"

"You shouted the word 'dragon,'" I said. "Not a word you hear very often, outside of storybooks."

He laughed. It was a goofy sound, deeply uncharismatic.

"Too true," he said. Then he frowned. "Adam. An interesting name. One could argue that he and Eve were the original truth-seekers, yes?"

"I suppose so," I said.

"And they were punished for seeking greater truths. Cast out of the garden, doomed to suffer and toil upon the surface of the Earth. A cautionary tale for all of us. Truth-seeking is a difficult path. The higher powers—be they Gods or megacorps—don't want us looking beyond our places, do they?"

"No, they don't," I said. Despite my initial misgivings, my deep suspicion of anyone trying to sell their religion on the street, my curiosity about this man and his message increased. The curtain continued to flutter.

"So before I say anything more, Adam," Zachariah said, "let me ask you—what are you willing to risk, to find the truth at the heart of this galaxy?"

"Everything," I said.

"Are you indeed?" Zachariah said. He gave me a shrewd look. "Well, I guess we'll see about that."

"Enough with the circumlocutions," I said. "What are you selling?"

"The unvarnished truth," he said, and he offered me the book in his right hand. It was small. Barely more than a pamphlet. I read the cover: *Space Beast* by Robert Morse.

"This is the book no one wants you to see," Zachariah said. "The true firsthand account of the sole survivor of Fiorina-161. Robert Morse. The man who saw the dragon and lived to tell about it. I could be arrested right here and now just for holding this. It's banned across the galaxy. Weyland-Yutani's done their best to keep it buried. But I'm risking life and limb to give you the opportunity to see it now."

I reached for the book, and he held it out of my reach.

"I deserve some recompense for this book of truth, don't I?" he said.

"Most religious organizations give their texts away for free," I said.

"I'm not part of an organization," Zachariah said. "I'm out here doing this on my own, and I have to eat, don't I?"

"How much?" I said.

He named his price.

"Fuck you," I said, and named another, much lower price.

We haggled, met in the middle. He was still gouging me, but not as much.

He insisted that we make the exchange in a nearby alley, so we wouldn't be seen. I followed, somewhat warily, fully aware that if he were going to mug me, I'd be at his mercy. I had no weapons, and he had the energy of a madman. I had no doubt he could beat me to death if he wanted to.

Still, he had my interest. I was on the hook. I wanted the book. I wanted to know about the so-called 'dragon.' So I followed him.

Luckily, he wasn't interested in hurting me. He took my money, and gave me the tiny book. At his suggestion, I shoved it into my backpack.

We walked back to the somewhat better lighting

of the street. Zachariah started to walk away, but stopped when I called his name.

"You said you're not part of an organization," I said.

"So what are you doing, selling this thing out here?"

He shrugged. "People deserve to know the truth about what's out here in the stars. And what the megacorps are doing to hide it from us."

He walked away. I never saw him again, although I often wonder about him. What became of him? Did he really believe what he was selling, or was he just trying really hard to sell it? Is he still alive? Still risking arrest by proliferating *Space Beast*? Or is he more like me than I suspect? Did he eventually go in search of the truth behind the book, get a glimpse behind the curtain, and find a darker fate? I would love to be omniscient. To know.

I returned to the *Jackalope* and hid in one of the galley bunks, pulling the privacy curtain closed to hide my illicit activity.

Space Beast was short—so short that it was held together by staples. But I think that, even had it been long, I'd have read it in one sitting. I was transfixed from the very first lines:

I'm writing this book because it's what happened. I'm a bad person and I'll spend the rest of my life banged up, but one thing I do have that most of you stupid lags don't is that I survived the end of the world. A monster came and ate all my mates. It sounds like a fairy story, but it's exactly what happened, and since it doesn't matter a tin shit whether or not you believe it, you might as well. I'm a lag but no liar.

The book was ostensibly written by a man named Robert Morse. Morse was a convict who'd been part of a skeleton crew assigned to take care of a closed-down Weyland-Yutani lead-smelting factory on a planet called Fiorina-161 (more commonly called 'Fury-161'). He and his fellow convicts were religious men (although the details of their religion, as depicted in the book, were vague and hard to pin down).

Another frustratingly vague point in Morse's book: after introducing the other main characters in his story (including a doctor named Clemons, and the cult's ostensible leader, Dillon), Morse alluded to the arrival of a woman named Lieutenant Ripley.

Morse didn't linger long on Ripley's arrival on Fury-161. He quickly moved on to the tale of "what [Ripley had] brought with her." Convicts began to die in violent ways—first a man cleaning a ventilation tunnel, then two of the three men who were sent to investigate the death. Everyone assumed the third man—the survivor, Golic—had killed the other two. They took him to the infirmary and strapped him to a bed, while he babbled about "a dragon" having killed the others.

There was that word again: *Dragon*.

But right after that, Morse wrote, "He wasn't wrong though, was he? Dragon, Xenomorph."

Xenomorph. That was a new word, one I hadn't heard before. There in my bunk, I mouthed it silently to myself, trying it out on my lips.

After that, the dragon (or Xenomorph) subsequently killed the madman, the prison's doctor, and the warden.

Ripley and the convicts regrouped after that. Since they had no real weapons or tracking technology on Fury-161, they decided to trap the beast in an unused toxic waste storage tank. Here, Morse gave a few more details about this dragon. Apparently, it was afraid of fire. Apparently, it walked on all fours, which made it different from "the beasts she'd seen," which implied Ripley had encountered these creatures before. Apparently, the beast went about on all fours because a dog had been its incubator. That was also news—that these creatures incubated inside of others.

The creature could "run on the walls and ceiling as easily as on the floor," and "it moved and leaped like nothing should be allowed to." Still, Morse refrained from ever properly describing the beast, which was frustrating. He likened it to a spider, but never said if it was hairy, or smooth, short or tall.

In any case, the convicts' subsequent attempts

to trap the beast came to naught, and resulted in the deaths of ten additional inmates. After that, the survivors were inclined to hole up and wait for rescue—Weyland-Yutani was sending a crew to retrieve Ripley. But Ripley let loose a little more of her past. When she'd first encountered these creatures, she'd been working for Weyland-Yutani. The company was so fixated on preserving the creature, they considered her and her entire crew expendable. If Weyland-Yutani considered Ripley and her friends expendable, how would they value a motley group of convicts?

Hence Ripley and the survivors devised a plan to trap the monster toward the lead works, where they would try to kill the beast. A lot of men died including their leader, Dillon, but they *were* able to lure the creature into the mold and kill it.

Weyland-Yutani operatives subsequently arrived with the intent of taking Ripley into custody. Morse claimed to be the only survivor but had some interesting details about Ripley's death. She jumped off the gantry into the molten lead rather than be captured, but as she fell, something exploded out of her chest—a tiny version of the creature that had been terrorizing the inmates for the past few days.

Morse was taken into custody, moved to a different prison. As he put it himself in his closing paragraph, "I get by, but I don't sleep so good. [...] It doesn't matter what we do or don't, the end comes for all of us."

And there the book ended. As I said, it was short.

After I finished, I lay in the bunk aboard the *Jackalope* and pondered what I'd just read.

There was some surface-level similarity between Morse's book and AF-617 (insular community, disrupted by the arrival of monsters), but otherwise, they were fairly distinct. Although Morse was vague when it came to specifics of the appearance of the 'dragon,' it didn't *sound* like the things I'd seen. I'd been chased onto the *Chariot* by monsters that had once been human. Morse described a creature that moved about on all fours (although to be fair, Morse's account seemed to imply that Ripley had seen 'upright' versions of the beasts in the past). The amorphous black thing that had snatched Dad seemed to be 'upright,' if such a term could apply. Also, this business of the space beasts incubating inside a host—I hadn't heard of anything like that, either.

And yet, despite its discrepancies from my own experience, I believed every word. This book chronicled something that had really happened to someone. An incomprehensible terror had arrived from the stars, to humble humanity. It had to be connected to the vases, the giant head, the bas-relief in that cavern on AF-617. I didn't know how, exactly, but I suspected (and still suspect) that if I can answer that question, I will come to understand the dark secret at the heart of all things.

Something shifted in me then—two plates in my heart that had previously been misaligned suddenly clicked into place, making a contiguous, continuous surface. I knew that I'd spent enough time on the *Jackalope*. I'd seen what I needed to see. It was time to get back to work.

13

COMPLICATIONS

Goodwin wanted to keep reading, but her concentration was broken by the sound of whimpering from White's tent.

She and Harris both looked at the tent, then at one another. White had taken the dog in to sleep with them just a couple of hours ago.

Goodwin thought about the people they'd seen today in the forest—the ones with holes in their chests. With a twinge in her gut, she stood up, set her laptop on the ground, and drew her pistol from its holster.

She took one step toward the tent, and then a horrible yelp sounded from inside. It was a cry of pure, pathetic pain, and it wrenched something in Goodwin's heart.

"White?" she called. "White, can you hear me?"

"Get out of that tent right now," Harris said.

"Captain," White said, their voice barely audible

through the tent. "There's something wrong with Quilbo."

There came another yelp, but this one was choked off.

"We know," Goodwin said. "Just… just come out here, okay?" She leveled the pistol at the tent and thumbed the safety off. Then, afraid she might shoot White, she pointed the gun skyward. She swallowed and her throat clicked.

From the tent came another semi-choked yelp, followed by a pounding, and cracking, tearing sound like a rack of ribs being torn apart.

"Oh Jesus fuck," White said. Their voice remained barely above a whisper. "Oh Jesus, oh Jesus, oh God."

They continued this mindless, half-formed prayer. Harris leaned forward as though he meant to unzip the tent and retrieve White if necessary. Goodwin grabbed him by the shoulder and gave him a sharp shake of the head. Harris didn't look happy about it, but stayed back as the tearing sounds from inside the tent grew louder, and louder—and then stopped. There followed a moment of absolute silence. Goodwin could hear her own heart pounding.

Then came a horrible, high-pitched shriek. It didn't sound like the dog. It had an inorganic, metallic quality—almost like the cry of a machine.

Scrambling sounds came from the tent. White continued to invoke the Christian god and savior as they fumbled with the zipper. They got it a quarter of the way down before the metallic shriek sounded again. White screamed. This sound was all too human.

The zipper stopped its descent. The tent rattled and shook as though a great struggle were taking place inside. White continued to scream as more tearing sounds came from within, punctuated by the metallic shrieks.

Then White's screams subsided into weak cries. Then grunts. And then they made no sounds at all.

Goodwin wasn't sure what to do. The animal part of her—which couldn't think further than surviving the next few seconds—wanted to lean forward, grab hold of the tent zipper, and yank it back up, to trap whatever was still inside. The thinking part of her knew better. Whatever was in there had killed the dog and White. A polyester tent wasn't going to hold the thing if it wanted out.

So she stayed one step away from tent. She leveled the pistol at the entrance, finger over the trigger, waiting for the slightest indication of movement. Her own breath was thunderous in her ears.

The tent zipper jangled as something brushed against it. Goodwin squeezed the revolver trigger three times in quick succession, as something punched through the fabric, almost too fast to see—a tiny, pink-gray streak that burst from its self-made opening, moved between Goodwin, Harris, and the trees, and disappeared into the dark, shrieking. It took all of Goodwin's good sense not to swing the gun around and fire after the thing. She might hit Harris, or Sam, who'd emerged from his tent. And she only had so many bullets.

Sam. He'd kept quiet until now. He finally spoke:

"What the hell is going on? Captain, do you mind not pointing that gun at me?"

Goodwin realized she still had the revolver pointed level before her. She pointed it at the ground instead.

"Sorry," she said.

"Something... got White and the dog," Harris said, answering Sam's question.

Sam passed Goodwin and knelt at White's tent. He paused to touch the hole it had punched through the tent entrance, with a thoughtful frown.

"I don't think you wanna see, son," Harris said.

Sam ignored him and pulled the zipper all the way down. He parted the tent flaps and stuck his head inside. He stayed that way for what felt like at least a minute, then emerged. He remained on his knees, his head bent forward. He pinched the bridge of his nose and closed his eyes.

"Something came out of the dog and killed White," he said.

"Yeah," Goodwin said. And then, because the word sounded far away to her, she repeated herself, to make sure she'd spoken. "Yeah."

"Fuck," Sam said. "Just... fuck. We saw the people

with the holes in their chests. Why did we let White take that dog into their tent?"

"We didn't know," Harris said. "We're all tired. This is all new."

"Yeah, well, we should've thought about that," Sam said. He stood up and wheeled around to look at Goodwin and Harris. "We've lost half our fucking crew on this mission. We're all that's left. How many more of us have to die before we get smart about this?"

"I'm doing my best," Goodwin said.

"Your best?" Sam said. "Your best? Captain, you've been a space cadet since we landed. You haven't been at your best in months."

"Calm down, kid," Harris said.

"Fuck you, Harris," Sam said. "We're stuck here, and if we don't get smart, right now, we're all going to die on this fucking rock."

"You're right," Goodwin said.

Sam's eyebrows went up. He clearly hadn't been expecting that.

"You're absolutely right," Goodwin said. "We've got to get smarter. We saw the bodies yesterday in the forest. We saw how the dog reacted to them. It was like it had seen this kind of thing before. And we didn't connect the dots, and now one of our friends is dead. We've got to do better."

Sam nodded along as she spoke, as though agreeing with her. He seemed to calm down a little more with each passing sentence. By the time she finished, he no longer seemed full of rage.

"So what do we do now?" Harris said. "Try to get some more sleep? It's another few hours until dawn."

"I think I'm done sleeping for the night," Sam said. "But I understand if you two need some rest."

Harris looked at his tent and scowled. "Not gonna lie. I'm tired as hell. But I don't think I could actually sleep after all that." He gestured at the omnipresent motion tracker in his hand. "We're only about three klicks from the signal. If we start now, we could make it there by dawn, maybe. Find some actual cots to sleep on at the colony. With walls and doors around us, to keep out things like..." He gestured toward White's tent. "... things like that," he finished.

The plan made sense to Goodwin. She didn't think she'd be able to sleep, either, and she was eager to get to New Providence. She wasn't sure how much safer she'd be in the colony—after all, the whole planet was quarantined—but she wanted to see if Bloch was there. If he'd survived the trip.

"Let's get moving," she said.

They packed up their campsite, leaving White's tent behind, and set off toward the signal—toward what the others hoped might be safety, and Goodwin hoped might be answers.

I honestly don't care if I live or die, she thought. *As long as I get some answers first.*

That's pretty fucked up, kiddo, her mother's voice rang in her head. *You sure this is the path you want to go down?*

The going was slow and difficult, and took them most of the rest of the night. They stopped once, about one klick out from the signal, to take a quick rest. When they did, Sam sat next to Harris, clearly putting distance between himself and Goodwin. Goodwin noticed it, but was surprised to find she didn't care much. It didn't hurt like she expected it to—like it would have even a few days ago.

She took a moment to ponder this change in herself. Sure, she was tired, and stressed out. These were extraordinary circumstances, so it stood to reason that the crew's behavior might be strange as well. But shouldn't the stress be bringing Goodwin and Sam closer together, rather than driving them apart? Didn't people huddle up when the dark closed in around them? Shouldn't they be fucking like bunnies every chance they got? Lord knew they'd done so when circumstances were easygoing.

You've been acting like a cold, hard captain since you crashed, her mother said. *Every time that boy looks to you to act like a human being, you drive him a little further away. And that's not all, is it? You know better.*

She did know better. It was the Bloch dossier. It was having an effect on her. Finalizing a process that had begun long ago. Goodwin had always felt *apart* from the people and worlds around her. The waking world had always seemed less real and immediate than the textures, feelings, and half-formed images that comprised her nightmares. And so she'd always held everyone and everything at arm's length, refusing to engage too fully.

Bloch's memoir was the first thing she'd encountered that seemed as real as the nightmares. He seemed to have the same basic, dim view of the universe, and to be actively seeking the dark secrets she'd always suspected, but never been able to articulate. Bloch was the first true kindred spirit she'd ever encountered. And now that she'd found him (his memoir, his work, if not the man himself), she felt even more distant from the rest of the galaxy. Sam and Harris were... well, it would be cold to call them a waste of her time. She didn't wish them any specific harm. She wanted them to survive this experience, if possible. But she was less interested in their survival than she was in making it to the colony, and finding Bloch. She needed to know what he knew. To discover the dark secret at the heart of everything. And if Sam and Harris got in the way of that? Well, she'd find a way around them.

Sam continued to glance at Goodwin from his spot next to Harris, as if hoping she'd get up and come sit next to him. She ignored his looks, and instead opened her laptop, to continue reading Bloch's dossier.

```
Bloch_Dossier_004                    ◄ ►  X
```

And so what came next, dear Roman? I bought my way out of my contract on the *Jackalope*, and returned to Welkin. Using my old accounts with Uncle Reuben's money, I rented a studio, and I got back to work. For months, I painted, and sculpted. I didn't tell any of my old friends that I was back. I didn't want the distraction. When I ate, I ate simple meals—dry goods, things that didn't need to be cooked or refrigerated. When I slept, I slept on a cot in one corner of the studio, using my backpack for a pillow and my old *Jackalope* crew jacket as a blanket.

When I wasn't eating or sleeping, I was working. I painted and sculpted. I didn't bother with still lifes or portraits of interesting-looking people. As before, I tried to give voice to the dark things that had obsessed me since childhood. I could tell something was different this time. Before my stint aboard the *Jackalope*—before reading *Space Beast*—everything I'd created had been a pale copy of my faded memories. Now, after seeing a bit of the galaxy, and reading Morse's book? The visions flowed through me.

I still painted the things I'd seen as a boy—the giant head, the temple full of vases, the giant microbial creature that had stolen my father—but I also found new subjects: the downtrodden colonials, with dirty clothes and faces ruddy from years of too much drinking. People whose entire lives could be boiled down to their functions in the greater machine of galactic capitalism. I painted them at play, in the bars, at work, in the factories and reactors, and in the in-between spaces, walking the dirty metal and concrete streets as they headed to or from another exhausting shift, for which they'd been paid entirely too little.

As I shifted in my subject matter, I also shifted my style. I abandoned any attempts at realism, at reproducing things exactly as I'd seen them. Instead I shifted to reproducing how those things *felt*. My attempts yielded an entirely new style—a sort of lurid, cartoonish grotesquerie, full of vivid colors and exaggerated features—mouths too wide, eyes too large, teeth too crooked. And yet, I tried to paint these cartoonish figures with dignity, the way renaissance painters might've treated the portraits of saints.

I emerged from the cocoon of my studio after six months of work, and started visiting galleries again. I reconnected with old friends—fellow artists and patrons and gallery owners. After my absence, I was worried I wouldn't be allowed back into the circles I'd previously occupied, but that worry turned out to be for naught. I was given a warm welcome. Friends bought me drinks. People invited me to parties. Everyone was eager to hear about my adventures slumming among the working poor. They also wanted to know what I'd been working on, if anything. This last question was always asked with a mixture of hope and trepidation. it seemed everyone had been waiting to see if I would develop into an artist of worth. some were in my corner, and others were hoping I'd fizzle out, become just another rich boy hanging around with the real talents. So when I explained that yes, I was working on something new, I got a variety of reactions. Verbally, they were similar: usually, the person I was talking to expressed happiness. It was their eyes that told the real story—genuine good cheer, or hooded jealousy. Here I was, another potential competitor.

When I started querying galleries to show my work, I was surprised to get invitations from most of the places that had snubbed me before. I had expected to be snubbed again. Looking back, I think I understand: it was in my bearing. It was probably in my eyes. The gallery owners saw the change. They wanted to see if it had carried over into my work.

When I took my work to these galleries, I didn't bring any of the "dark truth" work. Instead, I brought the series I called "Life among the stars," my portraits of colonial life. And to my delight (if not exactly surprise), I was offered a show at the very first gallery I visited. It was a mid-level space on Welkin called Visions. They specialized in real art (not the safe stuff that new money tends to buy, but high art that challenges and confounds).

I invited all my friends. I also invited Aunt Lucy and Uncle Reuben. They'd both been banging the 'university' drum since my return to Welkin, but they hadn't cut me off yet. I wanted them to see what their money had bought.

The show, simply entitled 'Life Among the Stars,' was my debut. Thanks to some buzz from an early review—an art critic friend named Natalie Carr—the gallery was packed on opening night, with friends and strangers. Aunt Lucy and Uncle Reuben arrived early, and I took them on a tour of my work. I said little, mostly answering questions if they asked, but otherwise letting the paintings speak for themselves.

They said little throughout the tour. After I'd finished showing them around, I took them to the bar, and got them both a glass of wine. They both sipped in silence, looking pensive. I kept silent, too. I refused to ask them what they thought. If they wanted to share an opinion, that was their choice.

Aunt Lucy spoke first. "They're... interesting." She gestured toward the gallery with her wine glass. "Like nothing I've ever seen before. It's like..." She pursed her lips and furrowed her brow as she tried to think of the right comparison. When she made this face she looked so much like my mother that my heart broke.

"These paintings," Lucy continued. "They're ugly. But also deeply beautiful? I can't think of any other way to say it. I'm not sure they're anything I'd want to hang in my own home, but I understand why they might be important to other people."

"Thank you, Aunt Lucy," I said, suppressing a smile at the backhanded compliment.

Uncle Reuben, who'd been silent until now, gave a frown of his own.

"I don't know shit about art," he said. "But walking through the gallery tonight, and looking at these paintings... I can't deny your talent, Corinth. This is big. This is important." He paused as he gathered his thoughts, and cleared his throat. "The time you've spent since you left school? It was well spent."

What more to say of my big debut? There isn't much. I sold everything by the end of the following week. There were more reviews from other publications. Mostly raves. I was hailed as "a major new voice for the voiceless." Individual paintings were singled out as "masterpieces." I was, overnight, not rich, exactly, but more than a working artist.

I finally returned my aunt and uncle's credit cards to them, and moved into an apartment of my own on Welkin. I could afford it now.

And for a few years after that, this was how my life went: I spent time alone, in my studio, painting and sculpting, bringing the things I'd seen to light. Then I would have a show, sell my art, and make a bunch of money. I would meet more and more rich people. People far, far up the financial ladder. As my fame grew, I met people who made my aunt and uncle look like paupers. The real movers and shakers of the galaxy. They offered me outrageous sums for my work, and I happily accepted.

News outlets wrote stories about me. They said I was "putting a spotlight on the common people." They called my work "socially responsible." But I can tell you, Roman, since it's just the two of us here: I don't know that there was anything responsible about my work. I was selling paintings to the people who created (or benefitted from) the horrible working conditions across the galaxy. I was taking their money, and what was I doing with it? Was I opening orphanages? Or schools? Was I funding libraries, or creating food banks? No. I was hoarding a fortune of my own.

I continued to live in the same apartment, and work in the same studio. I lived simply, and barely made a dent in my bank account. The only real money I spent was on travel. While I worked, I kept an ear to the ground, waiting to hear about disasters. Colonies that suddenly went quiet, or were emptied of civilians, with little explanation. The corporations do their best to cover these things up, so it was rare for news to actually reach me. But when it did, I would hire a ship, and try to go to those places. I wanted to see what had happened.

Often the results were disappointing. There were plenty of times when a colony really seemed to have been wiped out by some virus. And those were the worlds where I was allowed to land. Often, when my hired ship arrived at our destination, there would be a Colonial Marine frigate to turn us away.

These expeditions weren't fruitless. I started to notice some patterns. First, the reports about what was happening in these places were never widespread. To find out about them, you had to be faster than the major news organizations (which are owned by the major corporations). There would be reports when things went wrong, but they usually vanished within hours (if not minutes). I spent a good chunk of my new fortune paying for a professional-grade news-alert service to send me each new story as it was posted to the wire. I had the stories sent to an email address individually. No digests. I waded through endless talks of politics, war, and commerce, looking for key words: "quarantine"; "ancient"; "infection"; "creatures."

The second thing I noticed was that whenever one of these colonies went silent—be it in the United

Americas, the Three World Empire, or even the Independent Core System Colonies—it was almost always Weyland-Yutani sweeping in to do the cleanup. Occasionally a different company would show up—usually Seegson, but once in a while, Lasalle Bionational—but Weyland-Yutani almost always got to the scene first, before even the military. Just like in Morse's book.

It stood to reason that the corporations were the ones working hard to keep these events from becoming widespread knowledge, and paying the Colonial Marines to keep looky-loos (like myself) from getting close to any of these events. The corps were after something.

After a couple of years of fruitless voyages, being turned away from plague worlds by heavily armed ships, I finally understood what I would have to do. I would have to make a contact at Weyland-Yutani. Someone high up the corporate ladder. Someone who would know things, and be willing to share them (or who was lazy and trusting enough not to notice if I stole a few secrets here or there).

I wasn't without resources in this regard. I was, by now, a very well-known artist. I was invited to parties with politicians and business people. I'd just never targeted any of them specifically.

I made my play now. All the artwork I'd been creating but keeping to myself? All the paintings of cyclopean temples, and long-limbed terrors? Of dragon-like beasts that moved around on all fours? I now deployed it all in a new show. You remember what I called the show, Roman, of course: 'OTBD.'

I didn't explain my cryptic title to the gallery where the show took place, nor to any journalists who interviewed me. They all asked, and were all frustrated. I was surprised, when I read the interviews after the fact, that no one had stumbled on the answer. Wasn't it out there, for anyone searching the networks?

So I did a search of my own at that point. I looked up the letters "OTBD" and found nothing. Then I searched for "Earthsavers," which brought up no results regarding the cult back on Earth. Finally, in a fit of pique, I searched for "Duncan Fields." That search yielded results on plenty of people with that common name across the galaxy, but nothing about the prophet. So I was forced to conclude that someone had wiped Fields and the Earthsavers from the public record. They'd been forcefully forgotten.

I was nervous ahead of OTBD's debut. This was the first time I was showing my true work to the public. It was different from anything I'd done before. If my previous work had an "elevation of the common working people" theme, this show had a much darker one. Here I was stabbing at the curtain between myself and the truth, and titling my show with a bit of deliberately erased history. I was famous, but not powerful. I'd been deliberately provocative in creating and naming the show. I wanted Weyland-Yutani's attention. I wanted their executives to come to the show.

I was scared. What if I'd gone too far? What if this drew their ire? They had the resources to make me disappear, like Duncan Fields. This could be the end of my career—maybe even my life.

These thoughts kept me up late on the nights before the opening. I passed the time reading early reviews. They were—to put it kindly—mixed. A few proclaimed this "a bold, fresh vision for Bloch." A few others seemed confused as "a retreat into dark fantasy, after years of brave social commentary." Advance praise didn't exactly set the galaxy afire.

And yet, the opening had the usual strong turnout. Regardless of the mixed reviews, people wanted to see the new Corinth Bloch show. My name still had the draw. As I walked through the crowds, I eavesdropped on my patrons, trying to get honest opinions when they thought I wasn't listening. I heard phrases like "darkly compelling," and "wondrous." That was all well and good. But none of it meant anything unless I'd roped in someone from a megacorp.

I began to despair, that despite my having put everything on the line, I had not, in fact, drawn the megacorps' eyes. That this, in the end, would be nothing more than another show for me—an interesting footnote to anyone writing my biography, but forgotten in the larger body of work by all art historians.

And then, dear Roman, you walked in.

How to describe you, so that you can see what I saw? How to tell you about that first night? You lived it, too, but you always say you have a terrible memory. So maybe some of this will refresh it for you, or at least give you a new perspective on old events. I'll do my best to entertain.

First, I should say that you were not what I was expecting. I was expecting a younger man. A corporate executive on the rise. A man with a handsome, unwrinkled visage, a generic smile full of perfect teeth. Someone still trying to make his name. A himbo I could talk circles around.

But there you were, Roman. The unexpected patron. Average height and build. Wearing a suit that was probably worth as much as Uncle Reuben's house. Your hair was short and silver. You were clean-shaven, with a strong chin, sharp nose, and sparkling green eyes. You weren't smiling when you walked in, but you had one of those faces that seemed to communicate good humor regardless of expression—as though there were a smile just out of sight, ready to emerge at the slightest provocation—and when our gazes met for the first time? That smile came out at once, and all my prepared spiels and little monologues left me, and I stood staring at you.

You'll call me a liar, Roman, but you were the most beautiful thing I'd ever seen in my life up to that point (yes, you've been supplanted in the meantime—but that's why I'm writing this memoir—so you'll understand. There are things I have to do. Things I think maybe I was born to do. Those things mean leaving you. But I do hope I'll see you again, once I've fulfilled my terrible purpose. Hopefully you can begin to understand?).

Our eyes met. We were only standing a few feet apart. I'm not sure what would have happened next, if good old Mabel (the gallery owner to whom I owed my career) hadn't intervened.

She stepped between us then, extending a flute of champagne to you, Roman. Her black hair was severely short that year, and she wore giant earrings that looked like chandeliers. I worried about the stress on her earlobes. She was a short woman—in heels, she only came up to our chests—but she knew how to fill a space.

"Roman, my dear!" she said. "I can't believe you made it!" She turned to me. "Corinth, this is Roman Fade—one of my oldest and best customers. He almost never makes it to the openings!" She leaned in closer to me and held up a hand to give me a conspiratorial aside: "He hates the public. I usually sell to him after hours, at private showings."

"Well," you said, smiling down at her, and then at me. "I read a review about the show, and it caught my eye. I was worried everything would sell out if I waited for our usual arrangement."

"Roman," Mabel said, gesturing at me. "This is Corinth Bloch, the man of the hour."

We shook hands. Your grip was dry and firm as we murmured the usual pleasantries. Could you feel my desire even then? Did you reciprocate it yet? These are things I wish I'd asked you when I had the chance. Please think on your answers, my love, and be ready to tell me when I return. I promise not to be upset if you didn't feel what I felt (as long as you're not mad at me for all the things I've done recently).

"Thank you so much for coming out, Mr. Fade," I said.

"Call me Roman," you said.

"Alright, then. Thank you for coming, Roman." I realized that I was still holding your hand, that I'd had it in my grip for far longer than normal or socially acceptable. I let go and cleared my throat.

"What kind of art do you like?" I said. "What's your usual taste?"

You looked to Mabel, who threw up her hands. "I can never tell," she said. "I just show him everything."

"I know it when I see it," you said, and laughed politely.

"Well, I hope you'll see something here that you like," I said.

"Why don't you show me around?" you said. "You can talk me through it. Sell me on it."

My normal response would have been haughty. I would have told anyone else that good work sold itself. I wouldn't have said the words "fuck you," but they'd have been heavily implied.

Instead, to you, I only nodded. "It would be my pleasure."

We walked back to the gallery entrance, and I gave you the tour. I told you the name of each piece, and a little about how each was created—the paints I'd used, the canvas, the technical challenges. It wasn't until the third painting that you interrupted me.

We were standing in front of a piece called "Anticipation." In the foreground, a dragon-like beast was curled up, legs tensed, as though ready to pounce. In the background was a long corridor, opening on a single door at the end. Through the door, bright reds and oranges were visible. They might've been the fires of hell.

The creature itself had brown scales, and was somewhat difficult to make out against the dense black background, even in the brightly-lit gallery.

"This is all very fascinating," you said. "I think I've learned more about the technical side of painting in the last few minutes than I've learned in the last fifty years. But I was hoping you'd tell me what these pieces mean to you."

"What do you mean?" I said.

"All this dark, fantastical imagery. It doesn't exactly jibe with your earlier work, does it?"

"So you know my earlier work?"

"I may have done a little research before coming to the show," you admitted.

"I'm flattered," I said.

"You're avoiding the question," you said. "Charmingly, but still."

I dropped any pretense at charm. "I don't believe in spoon-feeding meaning to my audience. The work speaks for itself."

"How noble," you said, with only a slight hint of mockery. "Maybe tell me this, then: which one should I buy?"

"How much are you looking to spend?" I asked.

You cocked an eyebrow, but didn't answer. So I walked you to the biggest, most expensive piece in the show. It was on a canvas as wide as four men, and so tall it stretched from the ceiling to the floor (it'd been tricky getting it into the gallery at all). It depicted a spaceship lifting off in a massive hangar bay. Its engines were pointed toward the ground, holding it aloft. At the bottom of the frame stood several figures in silhouette, watching the ship depart. The figures were basically human in shape, but oddly proportioned. Their heads were large, and bulged in strange places. Their limbs were a little too long. Their gazes, fixed upon the departing ship, were meant to unsettle. They unsettled me, and I was the one who'd painted the damn thing. I'd kept a large drape over it in my studio, so I wouldn't have to look at it.

I looked over at you, watched you take in the painting. I saw your mouth quirk a couple of times. Perhaps something amused you. Perhaps you had questions that you were quelling. Finally, you stepped to the left of the painting, to read the card beside it, which had only the title of the piece. You read it aloud:

"'Destiny,'" you said, and looked back at me. "This is the one you're selling me?"

I shrugged. "It's the best one."

You nodded. "It's a deal."

After that, you stopped needling me to explain each painting to you. And to my credit, I stopped hammering you with craft talk. We walked from painting to painting in companionable silence. Here was another green flag I noticed that first evening: how easy it felt to be quiet around you.

Of course we were interrupted. Other people

wanted to meet me, congratulate me, impart their observations about my work. You were gracious. You always stepped away when someone wanted my attention. But you never went far, and you always returned at the end of the interaction—sometimes with an hors d'oeuvre, sometimes with a fresh glass of champagne. I drank more than I usually do at one of my own shows. By the end of the night I was fairly drunk, and when you asked me if I wanted to join you for another drink, I said yes.

It was a good night for me, professionally. By the time the gallery closed, we'd already sold several pieces. Not as many as we usually sold on an opening night, but these were a drastic departure for me. Gone were the grotesques. Here instead was the great mystery. And here I was, hugging Mabel goodnight after she locked the gallery doors.

"He likes you," she said, as I leaned down to wrap my arms around her. She didn't have to explain who she meant.

"I think I like him too," I said, standing up again.

She smiled. "Good. I was... worried about this show. It looks a lot like the stuff I rejected when you first rolled up. But you have the name now. The fame. The cachet. You get to decide what you want to paint, and where to sell it. And based on the reviews—and the receipts—it looks like you're going to be just fine. But still, I worry about you.

The entire time I've known you, you've been..." She pursed her lips while she considered the next word. "... driven," she said finally. "You've thought of nothing but getting to this moment. And don't mistake me—that sort of determination is what separates the successful artist from the talented amateur. Talent is cheap. Discipline is rare."

She hugged me again, and then we went our separate ways—her, to her expensive loft, and me, to the car that would take me to the bar where I would continue drinking with you.

Welkin is a warm planet, for the most part, but it was one of the cooler seasons. I remember, as I left the car outside the bar, that the weather was a little too cold for just a shirt. I had no jacket and shivered in the delicious cold air. The skin on my arms goose pimpled.

I walked into the bar. It wasn't one I'd ever been to before. It was called Taanstaafl (confusingly short for "There ain't any such thing as a free lunch," I would learn later). The walls were artificial wood paneling. A few pool tables lurked in the corners, and the walls were covered in Grateful Dead memorabilia. It wasn't the sort of place I usually went with my own friends, and definitely not the sort of place where I would've expected to find you, Roman. I took you for a high-end kind of man. And yet you'd asked me to meet you in a dive.

You were sitting at the bar, sipping a tall glass of beer when I walked in. You raised it to me in a toast as I crossed the room and sidled up next to you.

"This is... an interesting rendezvous location," I said.

"I like this place," you said. "It reminds me where I came from."

"You came from this?" I said, gesturing around us.

"I had working-class parents, yes. I'm one of those dreaded 'self-made men,' I'm afraid. What about you? Where do you come from?"

"My mother was a bartender and my father was a miner," I said. "After they died, my aunt Lucy and uncle Reuben took me in. They have money."

"It must've been quite a shock," you said. "Rising in the economic hierarchy."

I shrugged. "You get used to being rich."

You laughed. "Isn't that the truth? You get used to it fast. That's why I like to drink here. No one bothers me, for one thing. But more important, it gives me a reminder of what life is like for most people in this galaxy."

"How noble of you," I said. "If you care about the poor so much, why not give away all your money? You could ease some of the suffering."

"Even if I gave away every cent I had," you said, "the condition of the poor wouldn't change much. And then I'd be poor, too, and that's no way to live.

No, I give away plenty of money every year, for all the difference it makes."

"A pragmatist with a heart," I said.

Your mouth quirked as you tipped the last of your beer down your throat. "And what about you?" you said, as you set the glass down and gestured at the bartender for another.

"Me?"

"Sure. From what I've read, you've made a tidy nest egg selling paintings of the poor. The downtrodden. How much of it have you given to charity?"

"I'm doing okay," I said. "But I'm not 'give vast swaths of money away' rich. I'm more, 'if I didn't sell another painting for two years, I could still afford to eat,' rich. If my reputation took a nosedive tomorrow, I'd have to find a real job. I'd be back among the working poor."

"The tenuous life of an artist," you said. "Are you looking for a wealthy patron?"

"Are you offering?" I said.

Our conversation was interrupted before you could answer, as the bartender came to take my order. She was young, and cute. She didn't look like my mother, but I thought of my mother anyway. How she must've looked to my father, when they first met. Before life ground them both down.

I made a conscious effort to turn away from her, and back to you. "What is it you actually do?" I said.

"How did you get so rich, if you came from nothing?"

You looked at the bar, and moved your head from side to side, as though considering how to phrase what you wanted to say next.

"I'm... a capitalist," you said. "In the truest sense. I look for ways to make money, and then I go make that money. But most of my income comes from contracts with Weyland-Yutani."

There they were. The magic words I'd been waiting for. I tried to keep a straight face, to hide my delight.

"And what is it you do for Weyland-Yutani?" I said.

"A lot of different things," you said. "Manufacturing. Power and utilities. Correctional facilities. Mining. Defense research."

Two more magic words. Morse's book had mentioned that Weyland-Yutani wanted the 'dragon' for their weapons program. Could you have something to do with that?

I decided right then that I would do my damnedest to find out.

We drank a couple more rounds. Then you asked me if I wanted to come home with you. I said I did. You took me to your house, a mansion that made Aunt Lucy and Uncle Reuben's look like a rustic shack. We kissed our way from the foyer up the stairs and into your bedroom. We made love, twice. I was impressed with your stamina. I'd expected less, since you were an older man, but I guess when you're rich, old age is no barrier. Pharmaceuticals will get your engine revving no matter what.

The sex was good. That wasn't a surprise. What was surprising was what happened after. My drunken, ill-formed plan had been to ask you questions, or try to find your office and pillage it for secrets. But afterward, you spooned against my back, one arm draped across my chest, your breath soft against my neck—short at first, then long and measured, as you fell asleep holding me.

Biology is a funny thing. When you click with someone, what is it? Pheromones? Some alchemy of personality and physical attraction? I don't know. But I know that it felt right, there in your arms. I found myself unable to move, even after I thought you were deeply asleep. I couldn't make myself get up to go snooping. I was paralyzed by contentedness.

I told myself I would just lie like this for a little while. Maybe catch a catnap, then get up and try to find some answers.

Instead, I drifted off. There in your bed, in your arms, in your big fairytale castle of a house, I slept the night away. And for the first time in years, I didn't dream.

We must've drifted apart in the night, as we went on our separate sleep journeys, our bodies pushing us to different poles of the bed, because I woke the next morning on my back, with you draping an arm and leg across my body, and kissing me softly on the cheek. Your stubble whispered against mine as I fully returned to consciousness.

"Good morning," I said.

"Breakfast?" you said.

Here again I broke with my tradition. Normally I wouldn't have stayed the night, and on the rare occasions when I did allow myself to fall asleep at someone else's place, I always made a quick exit the next morning. Instead of fleeing, however, I sat on your veranda with you and ate eggs and toast and drank orange juice. That strange peacefulness of the night before—the spell you cast over me, dear Roman—remained unbroken. It was the happiest I'd ever felt.

We spent the weekend together, lounging around your mansion. When we got hungry, we ate. When we were overcome with desire, we made love. The weekend passed in a blissful haze. And on Sunday night, as we lay together in your home theater, watching an old movie, I found myself dreading the week to come. You would inevitably return to work, and I would have to leave, and figure out what to do with myself when not in your presence. I know it sounds dramatic, but it was a state of mind I usually fell into after a new show opened. I was always at loose ends. Not ready to get back to work, but with all the reviews and publicity behind me for a while, I didn't know what to do with myself, and as a result, I tended to get depressed and drink too much for a few weeks, until the melancholy passed and I started to feel the itch to paint again.

There was also a confusion mixed up with the melancholy. I'd meant to seduce you and get your secrets. And here, instead, I was watching a movie with you and holding your hand, and worrying when I might see you again. What was happening to me? To my grand plans and ambitions?

You seemed to notice something amiss and turned to me.

"What's wrong?" you said.

I meant to say something cool. Something dismissive. To show that I wasn't falling in love. Instead, the truth came tumbling from my lips:

"What is this?" I said.

One side of your mouth quirked up in an almost-smile. "Beg your pardon?"

"I mean, what are we doing here?"

"We're having a nice weekend," you said. "Although I'm feeling a bit blue since it'll be over soon."

"Tell me about it," I said, and gave you a rueful smile. "But what I meant is—is this just a weekend? What happens tomorrow?"

"What do you want to happen tomorrow?" you said.

"I don't want this to be over," I said.

"Me neither," you said. "But before I can commit to spending more time with you, there's a conversation we need to have. We should've had it at the bar on Friday night, before I let you into my home, but, well..." Your mouth quirked again. "You have an effect on me."

"You have one on me, too," I said. "But what's this talk?"

You pursed your lips, and for a moment, your grip on my hand loosened. You looked me dead in the eye.

"Out there be demons," you said.

In reaction, my own grip on you loosened. I felt a sudden urge to stand and back away, for some reason. I controlled myself, though, and remained seated.

"I beg your pardon?" I said.

"OTBD," you said. "The name of your show. That's what it means, right?"

I considered lying. But after a weekend of decadent living, several glasses of wine deep, my mind wasn't nimble enough for it. So I nodded instead.

"My friends at Weyland-Yutani have paid a lot of money to have those words stricken from the public record," you said.

"Why?" I said.

"You know why," you said. "Or at least, you have a pretty good idea. Don't you? It's why you used the letters 'OTBD' as the name of your show. You wanted some attention."

You studied me for a moment, clearly giving me space to respond. To deny your allegations or confirm them. I said nothing.

"Do you want to tell me what you saw?" you said. "What you experienced? What you know?"

Now I did let go of your hand, as an icy feeling spread through my stomach. I understood how arrogant I had been to come here. To think that I had the advantage over you. The rich man with connections to the most powerful corporation in the galaxy. Had you been toying with me all weekend? Softening me up? Enjoying me, before having me killed? Who else was in this giant house with us? It was massive. There could be hired killers in the next room and I wouldn't know.

"What are you going to do to me?" I said.

"That depends on you," you said. You folded your hands in your lap and regarded me with a strange mix of shrewdness and kindness. "You wanted Weyland-Yutani's attention. Now you have it. The question is, what do you want with that attention?"

"Answers," I said. "I just want the truth."

You grimaced. "That's going to be a problem.

There's a reason they wiped OTBD from the public record."

"Because it's true," I said. "There is something out there. Something dark."

"Something we don't understand. Yet," you said. "Something that, if word got out too soon, would be hard for them to make the public understand."

"Something the company wants for themselves," I said.

"That too," you conceded. "They want it for themselves so they can make decisions on how best to use it. Is there something wrong with that? Seems like good business to me."

"Except people are getting hurt, and they're covering it up."

"Why cause a panic?" you said. "Who does that help?"

"It helps people if they know what can happen," I said. They can make informed decisions about starting a new life in the colonies, or taking risky shipping jobs."

"And all of that hurts Weyland-Yutani's bottom line," you said. "You see why they can't have that, right?"

I understood well enough. Life was cheap to these bastards. Which begged the real question, which I asked again now:

"What are you going to do with me?"

"Like I said before, that depends on you," you said. "Weyland-Yutani have done their homework. They put the timeline together. They know you lived on AF-617. That you escaped right around the time that world experienced an event. It happened in Seegson territory, so they're not sure the exact nature of that event, but they know you've seen something. And now you're threatening to say something about what you've seen. The company wants you quiet."

"Why send you to do their dirty work?" I said. "You work with them, not for them."

"I volunteered for this, Corinth," you said. There was such gentleness in the way you said my name. It made my heart hurt. "I looked you up. I saw your work. I saw pictures of you. I was intrigued, so I volunteered to look into the matter for them. And you're lucky it was me, and not someone directly employed by the company."

"Why's that?"

Your face softened. "Why do you think, you silly man?" You reached for my hand again, and against my better judgement, I let you take it. "This weekend? It's all been real for me. I haven't faked a single moment. Have you?"

"No," I admitted.

You sighed with apparent relief. "Okay, then. I have some leeway in how I handle this. Weyland-Yutani wants you quiet. They have a few different methods for ensuring this. One is publicly discrediting you. Ruining your career. They have the resources, Corinth. They could do it. They could also ruin your aunt and uncle. Turn them into paupers, so you'd have no recourse but to join the working poor. Do hard labor until you were ground to dust, completely forgotten, your artistic legacy destroyed. And that's the option where you get to live, Corinth. You understand what I'm saying?"

"They could kill me," I said. "You could kill me."

"I wouldn't do it myself," you said. "But if I decided that was the correct move in this case, yes. I would make a call. You'd be dead that day." You squeezed my hand. "But there is another option. See, you haven't gone too far yet. In all the press you've done, you haven't actually explained 'OTBD' to anyone. None of your paintings reveal anything classified. You've danced around it. I can go back to Weyland-Yutani tomorrow and tell them you've agreed to stay quiet."

"And they'll just believe you?" I said.

"They will, if you stay with me," you said.

"What?" I said. "Like a prisoner?"

"Darling boy," you said. "Of course not. Like a companion." You leaned forward. "Be with me. Be mine. Weyland-Yutani needs me. They wouldn't dare displease me. If you're my partner, and you stay quiet, it will have to be good enough for them.

Oh, don't look at me like that," you said, in response to what must've been my horrified face. "You can continue to paint and sculpt. You can have gallery shows. You can make a name for yourself. And you'll have me. My support. My money. My love. All you have to do, to keep all of this, is come to live with me, and never do something like OTBD again. You'll also have to understand that there are things about my work I'll never be able to talk about. You won't be able to ask your questions. You'll never know the truth."

I made an intuitive leap, then. You never said so, but I understood that you were tied, somehow, to the 'demons,' in 'Out there be demons.' I didn't know how, exactly, but I understood it to be true. And that this was why you were so valuable to Weyland-Yutani. Why you could get away with saving my life and career, if you wanted to.

"What do you think?" you said. "Does that sound so bad?"

I looked at our hands, our fingers still intertwined, and I looked at you. What did I feel in that moment? It wasn't closeness, Roman. Or happiness. No, what I felt then, was the divide between the rich and the poor. The difference between how our lives were valued. You were rich. I was not. Other rich men wanted me 'dealt with.' But you looked at me, and you felt something. So you'd decided, rather than murdering me, to buy me.

The spell of the weekend was definitely broken. I saw my worth. I was a commodity. Chattel. Maybe you felt something for me. Maybe that would even develop into love. But it would never be a partnership built on respect. I'd be your pet.

But then again, what choice did I have? I could be yours, or I could have my life ruined, or ended. So what did I do? I squeezed your hand and smiled.

"No," I said. "That doesn't sound so bad at all."

I moved out of my studio, and into your mansion, Roman. I lived with you, as your companion, if not your partner. We ate well. We travelled. We spent your money. I continued painting my portraits of colonial life. The reviews of my work accused me of "growing stale" and repeating myself, but the paintings continued to sell. I was famous. A known quantity. Even if I wasn't the darling of the art world anymore, my work still commanded a certain price. I kept my own bank account, and the money piled up. I didn't spend any of it, preferring instead to spend from your seemingly bottomless coffers. I still saw my friends in the art world—I went to shows, and drank at bars, sometimes with you, sometimes by myself.

You and I had sex regularly. It was fine, but never achieved the heights of that first weekend, when I thought we might be genuinely falling in love. Before I became your property.

For my own sake, I pretended to be happy. To be content. That the spell of our early days together hadn't broken.

Years crept by, in a semi-comfortable haze. More and more lines began to etch themselves on your handsome face. I began to find gray hairs in my own dark mop.

We were together for over a decade. In that time, did I ever develop love for you?

It's an interesting question. Can you truly love someone if you're afraid of them? I suppose it's possible. The human heart is complex and contradictory. Children long for the approval of bad parents. People stay with abusive partners.

But did I love you? Do I love you? Maybe it's better to say I grew accustomed to you. Your moods, your expressions, your habits, your body. Even as I write these words, I find myself missing the feeling of you, next to me in our bed. Your snores—quiet and cute on the good nights, untenable on the bad ones. The sandpaper feel of your cheek as I kiss you goodnight. We had something, Roman. Something real. After all, here I am, writing this memoir for you, as if you deserve any sort of explanation.

When I made the decision to accept your proposal, I thought I was deliberately killing a part of myself—the part that longed to see Morse's dragon and get to the truth at the heart of all things. I saw this murder as necessary to my own survival. I had to let the truth go or die in its pursuit.

But, though I may have stopped the quest, may have stopped painting my visions, the visions continued to haunt me. I had my nightmares, full of dark, wet figures moving in onyx tunnels. I felt a presence. It seemed to call to me, across the stars.

I kept these dreams to myself. I didn't paint or draw what I'd seen, even in the privacy of my studio. I didn't write them down. I was afraid of what might happen to me, if I did. I didn't know how closely you were watching me. Whether you had spies checking in on my work, to make sure I was behaving. So I locked them away in my mind, that last truly free part of myself.

I won't say I planned, or schemed, because I didn't. I had no concrete idea how to get out of this gilded cage you'd built for me. But I did wait. And I did watch you. I paid attention to everything you said and did in our twelve years together.

Here's the thing about getting comfortable around another person. You let your guard down. You get sloppy. And you, dear Roman, were no different. In the early days, you never talked about work in front of me—or if you did, you did so in very general terms. You always went into your office to take calls, and shut and locked the door behind you. You did this for maybe three or four years.

Then, I suppose, you got used to the idea that you'd conquered me. That my apparent happiness and comfort were synonymous with compliance. You talked about work with me a little more. You would admit if you'd had a hard day, or if a client was making trouble for you. You began to take calls while I was in the room—not all the time, but occasionally. I silently noted these things. I wasn't sure if you were testing me, to see what I'd do, or if you were genuinely relaxing. So I tested you right back, and did nothing but notice, and wait.

Around year five of our relationship, you stopped locking your office door when you left the house. Again, I noticed and did nothing. What if there were cameras hidden in there? Or you had some sort of monitoring software on your computer, which would log any access attempts I made? There were too many variables. Too many ways I could fuck myself and end up dead.

I guess this is where my scheming started. When I met with friends at bars, on the nights when you stayed home or worked late, I began to ask questions. To see if they knew anyone in the tech industry, who could help me with things. I said that you might be cheating on me. That I wanted a program that could spy on your computer. Record your activity. See if you were trading messages or calls with a secret lover.

My friends were happy to introduce me to hackers. The first one I met sold me a package of stalkerware that would record everything that happened on your computer, and send reports to my own. The hacker promised it was stealthy, would fly beneath the radar for most antivirus software, and even if discovered, almost impossible to remove without wiping the computer itself. Best of all? It was supposed to be easy to install. Like child's play.

I bought the stalkerware. But still I bided my time. I waited for my moment.

That moment came in the middle of our twelfth year together. You ate some exotic cuisine on a business trip, and came home with an acute stomach bug. You spent the morning and afternoon locked in one of our second-floor bathrooms, making terrible sounds, and generating smells I'll not describe here.

After making a perfunctory check on you, and asking if you needed anything, I walked down the hall to your office. The door was open, so I took a deep breath and entered, knowing that if you did have cameras, I was now screwed. But I'd made my choice.

Installing the stalkerware on your computer was a simple thing. It took me less than five minutes. When I finished, I walked down the hall again, past the bathroom where you continued to groan and moan, and into my own little studio. I sat down at my computer, and opened the stalkerware client on my desktop. It was a perfect reflection of your screen, and it was recording everything.

You got over the bug, although it took a few days before that bathroom became suitable for human use again. I waited, anxious, to see if you would confront me about entering your office. If you would show me footage of myself, sitting at your computer. You did neither. You acted as though everything was normal. I'd gotten away with my subterfuge.

I remained careful. When you were home, I limited my computer use to games and work emails. I waited until you were out before opening the stalkerware client and checking out what you were up to.

For several months, you kept to boring business. Sales reports. Shipping manifests. Project proposals. But then, one day, sandwiched between messages requesting in-person meetings (so many people so desperate for your time), there was a message entitled "Project Providence."

One thing about this stalkerware—it didn't allow me to take control of the stalked computer. I had to wait for you to open the message before I could read the contents. Luckily I didn't have to wait. You opened it almost as soon as you received it.

The message was from someone named Alvarado, on the Weyland-Yutani security concepts team. It was brief:

> *Mr. Fade,*
>
> *My subordinates tell me that all monitoring equipment is now in place on DSJ-1020, and that we're go for Project Providence. It's a peaceful world with no military presence and only rudimentary communications equipment, which should make it easy to quarantine. Conditions are ideal for creating and then documenting an outbreak of the XX121 creature.*
>
> *My superiors have authorized me to request five Ovomorph samples from you, to be deployed during the next supply run to the colony. Please respond ASAP to let me know if this will be possible.*

You responded that you would make it your top priority, once you'd received payment from the company.

I took note. I recorded the world's name: DSJ-1020. I looked it up. A small colony world. Wet, cold, and stormy, but habitable by humans. There were approximately 200 people living there, trying to set up agriculture. The world was meant to produce crops. Food for people to eat.

I marked the coordinates, because I knew all too well what happened to the star charts when Weyland-Yutani was through with a world.

After that, I sat and pondered the terms in the Alvarado message. *XX121. Ovomorph.* I'd never heard or read of either thing in any of my research or wanderings. I cursed my stalkerware, which let me spy on your computer, but not search it. I was sure you had files explaining all of this. Records of times you'd delivered Ovomorphs to colonies before. But all of that was beyond my grasp.

Still, I was on to something here. This wasn't some plain delivery. The message mentioned quarantine and outbreaks. This was the part of your work you meant to keep secret, dear Roman. And now I had leads. More words to look for. Breadcrumbs to follow.

I followed the DSJ-1020 developments on your computer. I watched you send messages to your employees. People working on a space station in an isolated part of the frontier. Ordering them to prepare 'five eggs' for pickup by Weyland-Yutani personnel. You sent encrypted files explaining the 'XX121 life cycle' to Alvarado and company.

After Alvarado and his team took delivery of these eggs (Ovomorphs?), things went quiet for a while. It was frustrating, but made sense. Alvarado had only contacted you for a delivery. Your part in this story was done. Weyland-Yutani owed you no further updates.

Desperate for more information, I did another

search for DSJ-1020. As I'd predicted, the world had disappeared from the official records. Whatever Weyland-Yutani had planted, it was coming to fruition.

I understood my own next moves, then. If I meant to know more about the XX121, I would have to travel to DSJ-1020 myself. I would have to find a way past the quarantine. And I would have to go soon, in case Weyland-Yutani decided to clean up after themselves.

It took a little time to put all the necessary pieces together. I would need a ship, but I couldn't ask anyone else to go into danger with me, so it would need to be something I could pilot myself. Luckily, I'd learned how to fly during my time with the *Jackalope*. I found exactly what I was looking for, and relatively quickly. It was a small ship, big enough to hold five people, but only requiring one operator. I bought it with my own money, and named it *Gnosis*.

Gnosis came with a small problem of its own. Like most ships of its size, it was for local jaunts only. It had hypersleep pods for emergency situations, but no FTL drive. That meant I'd need to book passage on a ship large enough to tow *Gnosis* close to DSJ-1020, and then let me loose.

I went to bars. I asked friends, who introduced me to friends, who introduced me to associates. At the end of all these introductions, I went to a dive bar on Welkin, where I was introduced to a man named Flavio, captain of a cargo hauler called *Fortune's Dawn*. He was a man just entering middle age, with thinning hair up top and a beard starting to gray. He had a firm handshake, and drank beer like it was water.

"I can get you where you want to go," he told me. "Though why you'd want to be dropped off out there is beyond me."

I said nothing. I wasn't offering to pay Flavio to ask questions.

"I have a tight schedule," Flavio said. "I'll only be in orbit for a day or two after we deliver our cargo, and then I have to head out for the next job. I might be persuaded to stick around longer if you want to pay a little more, though. The *Dawn* could suddenly develop engine problems. Need repairs. That sort of thing. Happens all the time and no one blinks an eye."

I'd been so focused on the trip to DSJ-1020 that I hadn't thought about how I was going to get back. If, that was, I survived my arrival. Encountered these 'Ovomorphs' and 'XX121s.' I could certainly afford to pay Flavio for more time. But something in me rebelled at the idea. Not the expense, but the assumption that I was going to take a nice little trip to a quarantined world, and then leave again. This wasn't a day-trip. This was a holy pilgrimage. I was going to DSJ-1020, but once I was there, I didn't want to make any assumptions about what would happen. The galaxy—and the dark forces that drive it—would determine what came next.

I know how it sounds. I sound like a madman, whose logic contorts to his own needs. After all, why go to so much trouble to get there, only to hand myself over to fate once I arrived?

But I guess that's the thing about belief. About religion. You put your faith in something. You proceed in the way that makes sense to you, regardless of what anyone else thinks.

So I shook my head. "Once you've dropped me off, Captain, I'm not your problem anymore."

Flavio peered at me over the rim of his stein as he drained the dregs of his beer. He seemed genuinely curious, and was probably hoping I'd explain myself. I didn't. He set his glass down on the table and nodded. We shook hands and went our separate ways.

The next thing I had to do was figure out a way past the quarantine on DSJ-1020. That meant I had to figure out what the quarantine conditions were. That was a little trickier. I couldn't just ask my friends to introduce me to their shady associates. I needed someone with corporate-level knowledge.

I knew I couldn't go to you, so I seduced one of your friends. A junior executive at Weyland-Yutani named Morton. You might remember him from our dinner parties, the nebbish man with beady eyes and thinning hair. I knew he had a crush on me. He always looked at me with those hungry, sad, little eyes, like a starving child at the window of a sweet shop. I'd always been friendly. Flirty, even. I was curious about him. He didn't seem like the Weyland-Yutani alpha-male type.

Morton was only too eager to receive my secret messages. He was overjoyed to have my attention. Happy to keep me company while you were out of town, since I admitted to being lonely. He seemed completely awed when I seduced him for the first time. Like he couldn't believe his good fortune.

Don't be too hard on Morton, Roman. I steam-rolled him. He's as much a victim here as anyone. Save your anger for me.

When I asked him for information for the first time, I could tell he was anxious. He's not the dissembling type. Likes to play by the rules. But on the other hand, he'd already fucked his friend's partner. He was in it now.

Still, he stalled. Asked me what I wanted the information for. I told him that if he got me what I asked for and stopped asking questions, I would sleep with him whenever he wanted.

That did the trick. He got me encrypted files about DSJ-1020. I got blueprints of the entire colony. I learned that the world was being guarded by a single Colonial Marine ship, the *Fratto*. I was given the roster. I did background checks. I found someone who could be bribed, and I bribed them.

And now we've come to the end of the things I can tell you. This is everything that's happened so far. As I type these words, I'm preparing to go to the berth where I've docked *Gnosis*. I'm about to take her into orbit, to rendezvous with the *Fortune's Dawn*. What happens next? I have hopes, but no guarantees. Here's what I hope: I hope I blow you and all your comfortable little friends out of the water. I hope I fuck things up so bad you can never go back to your secrets and shadows. I want it all in the light, Roman.

Take care, my love. While you can.

14

NEW PROVIDENCE

Goodwin looked up from her laptop and blinked. She'd finished Bloch's memoir/manifesto. It had ended on a cliffhanger. She'd known it must—after all, she and her crew were here to help finish the tale—but knowing did nothing to soften the pang she felt when she came to the end of the manuscript.

She felt the way she always did when she came to the end of a good book: slightly hungover. The world felt dimmer, rather than brighter, around her as she shut her laptop and put it away.

She looked across the tiny clearing at Harris and Sam. Both sat with their hands folded in their laps, staring at the ground. Harris, apparently feeling her gaze, looked back at her. He appeared exhausted, but that wasn't all. There was little light in his eyes. He looked defeated. A man on the edge of giving up.

He could only hold her gaze for a moment before he looked away again. Taking pity on her tech, Goodwin looked over at Sam instead. He didn't raise his head to look at her.

Whatever you two had, her mother's voice said, *it's over now.*

Goodwin caught herself nodding along to the little voice's assessment and stopped. Not because she disagreed, but because she was afraid of looking crazy. She and Sam were done. She'd had to show him too much of herself on this expedition. He couldn't take it.

She tried to figure out how she felt about this revelation. She found she didn't feel much of anything. She acknowledged it the way you might acknowledge the day of the week, or the date. It wasn't good or bad. It simply was.

She had a greater purpose here. She would find Bloch. She would see what he had seen. She would understand the darkness that had haunted her all her life.

And then?

She wasn't sure what would happen after that. Would she be free of the malaise that had always hung over her? Would she be subsumed by it? She didn't know. She only knew that she needed to *see*. Everything else would have to take care of itself.

She put the laptop back in her bag, and stood. "We've rested long enough. Time to get moving."

Sam and Harris said nothing in reply, but stood,

shouldering their packs. Harris led the way as they marched back into the woods, across the final klick between them and the signal.

"We're almost there," Goodwin said, as they squeezed between two trees. "Be prepared."

"For what?" Sam said.

"Anything," Goodwin said. "That dossier didn't give me much to go on."

"Sounds like a waste of time," Sam said. "All that reading, and we know fuck-all about what we're walking into."

She wanted to argue. To make him understand that she'd gotten more than a mere description of a strange lifeform from Bloch's words. But she held back.

Why? her mother asked. *Because you'd sound crazy?*

She ignored the voice and said instead, "Dragons."

"Excuse me?" Sam said. Goodwin looked back and saw he'd stopped walking.

"That's what the dossier mentioned. There was a book Bloch read. By a man named Morse, who lived on a planet where... something like this happened. Morse talked about a creature he called a dragon. He never described it, except that it ran on four legs, and it was fast."

"Oh," Sam said. "Terrific. And did he say anything about whether these dragons were afraid of guns?"

Goodwin shook her head. "They didn't have guns, where Morse lived. Apparently the creature was afraid of fire, though."

"Perfect," Sam said. "All we have to do is set this whole fucking forest ablaze, and we should be safe and sound, right?"

Harris grunted what sounded like an unwilling laugh.

Goodwin found herself smiling. "If it comes to that, we can try," she said.

She was about to sound the order to resume the march—surely they must be close by now—when Harris sucked air between his teeth. Goodwin turned, looking from Sam to Harris. Harris stared down at the motion tracker, his face lit a sickly pallor by its greenish glow.

"What's wrong?" Goodwin said.

He looked up at her, eyes wide, mouth slightly agape. That was when she finally noticed the sound. The tracker's chirp. It was usually singular and steady, as they approached the source of the electric signal—almost like a cheerful electronic metronome. But now the sound had changed. The chirp was coming more frequently.

Harris turned the tracker so that Goodwin could see the screen. Two-thirds of the display was covered in yellow dots—so many that it was impossible to tell where some began and others ended. They were approaching like an amber cloud.

"Dragons," he said simply.

"It doesn't make any sense," Sam said. "I don't hear anything moving out there."

"Stick around and figure it out if you want, kid," Harris said. He turned away from Goodwin and Sam, bolted off through the trees.

In the ensuing quiet, Goodwin finally heard telltale sounds: tree leaves rustling, as though in a strong wind. Only there was no wind in the forest. The air was still as the leaves shook. The sound grew louder.

"Run," Goodwin said. She took off after Harris, moving as fast as she could between the trees. They seemed to thin out a bit, making it easier to move. She thanked whatever deities might be listening as she pumped her arms and legs.

Her breath came in short, ragged gasps. Her heartbeat pounded in her ears. Her arms and legs, unused to the strain, started to ache and beg for mercy. She ignored these cries and pushed her body as hard as she could, trying to look all around her at once—ahead, at the ground, and up into the trees. The leaves above were still, but the sound of rustling continued behind her, growing louder, and louder.

She saw light ahead, coming from between the trees. She pushed herself even harder, running for the light, her only hope.

She burst between two trees and onto an open stretch of muddy earth that looked like it had been ground up by industrial vehicles. Overhead the sky was gray, filtering the sunlight, making everything dark. Ahead of her, Sam was sprinting toward a group of squat, prefab buildings, surrounded by a metal gate. This must be New Providence. They'd made it. The colony. And even better, the main gates were wide open. Only—where was Harris? The way he'd taken off, she would have expected him well in the lead here. But she only saw Sam.

She glanced back over one shoulder, to check for him. At first, all she saw was the tree line, and she stopped, unsure what to do. Had he fallen behind? The leaves shook as something in the branches moved toward them.

A second later, Harris emerged from the darkness, sprinting toward her, a look of abject terror on his face. He waved his arms at her.

"Go!" he shouted. "Fucking go!"

The words were scarcely out of his mouth when something exploded from the treetops behind him. Goodwin wasn't sure what she was seeing. At first it looked like a black mass, an amorphous blob like a living tumor— the yellow cloud from Harris's motion tracker, made real, solid, and glinting in the weak sunlight.

No. It wasn't a solid mass. It was dozens of individual bodies packed into a tight space that were now emerging, leaping into the free air. Her mind tried to make sense of it, to focus on an individual creature, but all she seemed able to process were tidbits. Pieces.

She saw sharp talons at the end of long-fingered hands.

Elongated skulls with no visible eyes.

Undulating plated tails that ended in sharp spikes.

Grinning mouthfuls of teeth that shone as though made of metal rather than bone.

The teeth woke up the animal part of her brain, the part concerned with survival. She got moving again. She turned and ran. She came to the end of a muddy plane and ran up a concrete ramp toward the closest buildings. Sam was now out of sight. Goodwin hoped he'd found a safe place to hide.

"Wait!" Harris cried. "Captain, wait for me!"

Have to keep moving, Goodwin thought. *If I stop now, I'm dead.*

She glanced back just in time to see the horde overtake Harris. He disappeared with a scream, subsumed in onyx. He continued to scream, but the sound was muffled by all the bodies around him.

Goodwin kept running. She glanced to her left and right. She was passing buildings now. There were doors, but most of them looked flimsy. And if the creatures saw her run into one of these places, wouldn't they just follow?

"You."

Goodwin stopped. The voice had come from above, booming down like a sign from God. It had come from a loudspeaker hooked to a nearby wall. Goodwin saw identical loudspeakers, spaced out at regular intervals down the colony street.

"If you want to live, turn left at the intersection," the voice said. Even distorted through the cheap loudspeaker, she could tell it was a man's voice.

There was no time to think. No time to decide whether or not to trust the voice. Goodwin did as she was directed. She turned left at the intersection and started running down an almost-identical-looking street. The only difference was a big metal door at the end of the block with the number "01" painted on it.

"Head for the 01 door," the voice said. *"And hurry. They're almost on you."*

He didn't have to tell Goodwin. She could hear the clatter of their claws, deafening against the concrete. She dropped her backpack. With the weight off her shoulders, she was able to put on a little extra burst of speed.

As she approached the metal door, it groaned and began to slide open. Goodwin leapt with all her remaining strength toward the narrow opening. She slid between the halves of the door, the fabric of her jacket catching and tearing, and then hit the ground with a cry. It was hard, and it hurt. Trying to ignore the pain, she rolled over and looked back at the horde in hot pursuit. They were almost on top of her. In another second, they would be through the door, which was already closing again.

The door groaned shut just in time, as the horde came within a few feet of the entrance. Goodwin sat up. She was in complete darkness. In this darkness, she listened to the creatures clawing at the door and screeching. It was a high sound, as metallic as their teeth. It reminded her of the sound she'd heard from White's tent right before they were killed. She wrapped her arms around her knees and focused on her breathing.

She nearly choked when something landed on her shoulder and squeezed. She let out a strangled scream.

"Relax," Sam said. "It's just me. You alright?"

She swallowed hard and nodded. "In one piece, anyway. They got Harris, though."

"I know," Sam said, and gave her shoulder another squeeze.

Lights kicked on above them, flooding the space with a harsh fluorescent glow. They were crouched in a square space between two sets of metal doors. Above them, a security camera and loudspeaker hung from one wall. The loudspeaker crackled to life now.

"Don't worry about the monsters at the door." It was the same voice that had directed Goodwin into this space. *"They can't get in. But now that I've saved your life, please tell me: who are you?"*

"I'm Captain Cynthia Goodwin of the *Chariot*," Goodwin said. She looked into the camera as she spoke. She pointed to Sam. "This is Sam Kurzel, my pilot."

"What are you doing here?"

"That depends," Goodwin said. "Am I speaking to Corinth Bloch?"

A brief silence from the loudspeaker, followed by a simple, *"Yes."*

"We've been hired to rescue you," Goodwin said.

"In that case," Bloch said, *"I suppose I'd better let you inside."*

15

CORINTH BLOCH

Bloch opened the inner doors, admitting Goodwin and Sam to the interior of the building. They walked down a long corridor with metal walls and steel grates beneath their feet, before turning a corner and coming to another camera and another door. This door wasn't nearly as strong as the two they'd already passed through. It looked like an ordinary door on any ship or space station, and it slid open for them as soon as they approached.

They passed through the door into a room full of computer banks. It looked like some sort of command center.

"What is this place?" Sam said.

"The emergency shelter for New Providence." The voice came from across the room, no longer distorted by transmission through a loudspeaker. A man walked toward them. He was average in his height and build, perhaps a bit on the lanky side, with long salt-and-pepper hair and intense dark eyes. He was handsome, in a narrow, intense sort of way. This was Corinth Bloch. He looked remarkably like the photo Goodwin had seen of him at the start of the expedition. His hair was long, and a tad unkempt, but he remained cleanshaven, lacking even a five-o'clock shadow. All this time on DSJ-1020 didn't seem to have left many physical marks upon him.

"A place for the colonists to retreat during the planet's more extreme weather hiccups," Bloch went on. "It has extensive food stores, a media library, and best of all, its own power and ventilation systems, separate from the main colony. Enough for sixty days at full capacity, but if you're more frugal, like me, you can make it last a bit longer."

He offered his hand to Goodwin, then Sam. They both shook with him.

"Sounds like a survivalist's dream," Sam said.

"So where are the colonists?" Goodwin said, with a pointed look around the command center. "This world is under quarantine. This place should be packed."

Bloch made a tight smile. "When I first arrived, I found the doors closed, but unlocked. Getting in was easy. I made sure to announce my presence via radio so I wouldn't be shot by an overeager colonist, but received no answers. I got in and found the place completely empty."

"You think the colonists were taken?" Sam said. "By those—" He gestured over his shoulder, back the way they'd come. "—things?"

"That was my first thought," Bloch said. "But then I accessed the colony logs and found a curious thing. When the outbreak started—when the creatures first appeared—the director of the colony ordered a retreat to the shelter, but when they arrived, the entrance was locked. They tried hacking. They tried forcing the doors manually. Nothing worked."

"They were locked out of their own shelter?" Sam asked. "By whom?"

"Who else?" Bloch said, and jerked a thumb at a nearby monitor, which displayed the company logo: WEYLAND-YUTANI: Building Better Worlds.

"The company did this?" Sam said.

"They must've had a program installed when the colony was built, so they could remotely control its functions, if they wanted."

"But why would they lock people out?" Sam said.

"They wanted to see what would happen," Goodwin said. "Right? This whole thing. It wasn't a colony. Not really. It was an experiment. They wanted to use it as a test case. To see how long it would take to wipe out a colony."

Bloch regarded Goodwin curiously. "That's quite a leap, Captain. But an astute one."

Goodwin shrugged. "Your... I hesitate to call him

your lover, after reading your dossier. Maybe better to call him your keeper? Roman Fade. As part of this mission, he gave me your memoir, or manifesto, or whatever you want to call it."

"Did he?" Bloch said. "Curious. I reveal some pretty classified information in that document. I'm surprised he would just give it to you."

Goodwin shrugged. "When I met Fade, he seemed genuinely concerned for your wellbeing. My crew and I—what's left of us—don't get paid unless we bring you back alive."

"Even more curious," Bloch said. "That could mean one of two things. Either, he wants me back to debrief—since I'll be able to provide more information to the company with my firsthand experience—and then kill me himself. Or—and this really stretches my credulity—he's genuinely concerned for my wellbeing and wants me home, safe and sound."

Goodwin reached into her shirt, and pulled out the data card Fade had given her—the one she'd been wearing on her person, to keep safe. She pulled the chain over her head and handed the card to Bloch now.

"He gave me this to give to you," she said.

Bloch turned over the disk in his hand now. "A message from Roman," he said. "I'd like some privacy, to look at this. I'm sure you two wouldn't mind some food and a shower?"

"No, we wouldn't mind one bit," Sam said.

***

Bloch showed them around the shelter, pointing them to the cafeteria, the showers, and a huge room full of bunks for sleeping.

Goodwin almost asked Sam if he wanted to shower together, but he headed for the room marked 'Men' before she could offer. So she headed for the women's room instead.

After days in the cold and wet of DSJ-1020, the hot water of the shower was a revelation. Goodwin braced herself against the wall of the stall with one arm, and let the spray soak her from the crown of her head down to her toes. She stayed that way, braced against the wall, and for the first time in days, gave herself permission not to think, or feel, anything aside from the physical sensation of her body warming, the pleasant tingle blooming in her flesh.

When she felt fully thawed, she reluctantly turned off the water, dried off, and pulled a fresh set of clothes and flip-flops from a nearby locker. It was all a little big on her, but good enough. She didn't have the energy to search for something that might fit better.

She found Sam in the cafeteria, bent over a tray of food already half-inhaled. She fixed her own tray of dry cereal and milk, and joined him. They ate in silence, stuffing their faces. The food was bland, almost entirely tasteless, but somehow the best Goodwin had ever tasted.

Neither of them spoke until their trays were empty. But as Sam went back for seconds, he said, "Amazing what a hot shower and a warm meal can do for your disposition. We're well and truly fucked, but right now I feel kind of okay."

Goodwin nodded, to be agreeable. She didn't feel much of anything, and wanted to keep it that way.

Sam grimaced. "I'm sorry, Cynthia," he said. "I know you and Harris went way back. That was thoughtless of me."

"It's fine," Goodwin said, with a sharp little hand gesture. "You didn't mean anything by it."

"Right," Sam said.

He didn't say anything else after that.

Eventually, Bloch joined them. He stopped to fix three cups of steaming liquid, which he set on the table in front of Sam, Goodwin, and himself.

"Tea," he said. "I thought it would be a nice way to finish warming up."

"Thank you," Goodwin said. She took a sip. It was surprisingly sweet—a welcome bit of flavor after the blandness of the food.

"Feeling better?"

"Starting to thaw out," Sam said. He took a sip of his own tea. "Oh, that's good."

"The secret is a drop of honey," Bloch said.

"You have honey?" Goodwin said, incredulous.

"A little," Bloch said. "One of the indulgences I brought with me."

They sat and sipped in silence for a moment.

"So you're here to rescue me," Bloch finally said.

"That's the idea," Goodwin said. "Unless that private message from Fade to you says something different."

Bloch looked as though he wanted to say something, but then decided not to. Instead, he said, "Where's your ship? It can't be close? I would've seen it on the sensors in the command center."

"We hit a storm on our way in," Goodwin said. "The ship tore itself apart. We had to march the rest of the way here."

"And the rest of your crew?" Bloch said.

"We lost our android in the crash," Goodwin said. "The rest were… taken or killed on the journey. By those creatures out there."

Bloch's eyes lit with a hungry glint. A warning klaxon sounded deep within her mind at that, but it was buried by a sense of recognition. He was eager for the darkness. Was she any different?

She and Sam took turns, telling the story of how they crashed. How Cardona was carried away in the night. The clearing full of empty eggs and bodies with holes in their chests. The dead crablike creatures. How White was killed by a creature that burst from a dog.

"And you saw what happened to my engineer," Goodwin said. "Right on your doorstep."

"I did," Bloch said. "That's... a lot of loss to process in just a few days. You have my sympathies."

"Thank you," Goodwin said. She wasn't sure she believed him. Not after what she'd seen on his face when she first mentioned her crew's deaths.

"Our friend who was taken," Sam said. "Is there any hope for her? That she might still be alive?"

Bloch sighed. "I'm afraid not. The creatures you fled from to get in here—what Weyland-Yutani has classified as the XX121 Xenomorph. They approach living creatures for only one of two reasons. First, for food. They eat us, if they're hungry. But second is a far worse fate. You saw the aftermath of it in that clearing."

"The bodies fastened to the trees?" Goodwin said.

"Precisely," Bloch said. "They use living creatures—human, cattle, dogs, whatever—as incubators. It's how they reproduce."

"How do you know all this?" Sam said.

"I've stolen a great deal of classified material from Weyland-Yutani," Bloch said. "So I know all about the creature's life cycle. But more than that, I've seen it, in my time here."

"How?" Goodwin said.

"Come with me," Bloch said. "I'll show you."

He led them back to the command center. In one corner, Bloch had a bank of monitors turned on. Goodwin looked down at them. Every few seconds, each monitor switched its image. She tried to take in what she was seeing: low-res images of long, black corridors; of eggs, both opened and shut; of bodies stuck to walls, with gaping wounds in their chests, their eyes wide with terror; of the Xenomorphs moving, black against a black background, almost impossible to make out. Here it was: the crystallization of images from a lifetime of Goodwin's nightmares. It was all here. Validation. It was real.

"All the colony camera feeds are still online," Bloch said. "I can see everything that's going on from here."

Goodwin reached for one of the screens as a form passed the camera—one of Bloch's Xenomorphs—its long, curved skull sliding past like a wave of darkness. The screen sparked with static electricity as she touched it. Then the camera feed switched to something else.

She looked up and tried not to show her frustration. She found Bloch giving her a curious look.

"Pretty low-res," she said. "Hard to get a really good look."

"It is," Bloch admitted. "Luckily it's not my only source of visuals."

He flipped open a laptop next to the monitors, and typed in a command. A crisp image appeared on the screen. It was one of the corridors with bodies along the walls. Goodwin could make out the texture of the walls, finally. It looked like some sort of resin, coating the walls, into which the bodies had been stuck.

"How are we seeing this?" Sam said.

Bloch picked up a headset, which was plugged into the laptop. "Ryder? Can you hear me?"

"Yes, Mr. Bloch," came a voice through the laptop's speakers.

"Look down for me," Bloch said.

The camera panned down to reveal what looked like a man's body.

"An android," Sam said, understanding. "You've got an android down there?"

"I have a few," Bloch said. "The Xenomorphs don't seem to take much notice of them. Watch. Ryder?"

"Yes, Mr. Bloch?" Ryder said.

"Do me a favor, will you? Walk down the hall. Approach the first full-grown Xenomorph that you find."

"Yes, Mr. Bloch," Ryder said. The view on the screen shifted as the android walked down the corridor. He passed through a tunnel of what looked like hardened black slime and came to a Xenomorph carrying one of those egg things. Ryder stopped in his approach, but the creature kept on moving. It walked past him, down the corridor. He stood still and watched it go.

"It's like the creatures don't even register androids as living things," Bloch said, turning to Sam and Goodwin. "They just walk right past, as long as the android doesn't get in their way or stop them from doing what they're trying to do. They'll attack, but only if the android really pisses them off."

"Hey," Sam said. "Can you tell Ryder to look for our friend? Danielle Cardona. Maybe they're still alive somewhere in here, if the creatures took them."

Bloch frowned. "I can do that, but you have to understand—even if your friends are still alive, they're already dead. If the creatures have impregnated them, it's only a matter of time."

"So once a host has been impregnated," Goodwin asked, "there's no way back? The parasite can't be removed?"

"I've read theories," Bloch said. "It might be possible to surgically remove the creature without killing the host, if you operate early. But I don't know if it's ever successfully been done."

"Tell your droid to look for our friends," Sam said. "I need to know."

"Of course," Bloch said. He pressed a button on his earpiece, and directed the three androids working for him to start a search for living humans in the hive. As he did this, another Xenomorph passed by one of the security cameras, holding an egg.

"Where do you think he's going?" Sam said, pointing at the image.

"They're building a repository down in storage," Bloch said. "Ryder's seen it. Enough eggs to infect a densely populated planet."

"So these things start as eggs," Goodwin said. "The crab-thing is what's inside the egg. It jumps out and infects a host. Then one of these creatures—these Xenomorphs—grows in the host. When it reaches maturity, it punches its way out of the host, and grows up into one of those big things?"

"That's right," Bloch said.

"And the eggs. Where do these eggs come from?" Goodwin asked.

Bloch smiled, and waggled a finger at her. "Very astute, Captain. The eggs come from the Queen."

"There's a Queen?" Sam said. "Something bigger than these guys?"

"Oh," Bloch said, with an almost dreamy sigh. "She's much, much bigger."

"Can we see her?" Goodwin said.

"She's in the power plant," Bloch said. "Down on a sub-level without any cameras. And the one time I tried to send an android down there? Well, let's say I discovered the exception to their 'leave androids alone' rule."

"A Queen," Goodwin marveled. Bloch gave her a shrewd look, as though understanding more than she'd intended him to. She met his gaze, and let him get his fill. She wanted him to see her eagerness. Her curiosity.

"That's right," he said at last. "I saved the footage that I did get. It's not much, but she's beautiful."

"Beautiful?" Sam said. He looked at Bloch as though the painter were insane. Then he turned to Goodwin, looking for validation of his incredulity. Goodwin tried to mask her own hunger. No reason to alarm Sam if she didn't have to. But whatever Sam saw, it didn't seem to put him at ease. He looked back at Bloch, uneasily.

"Relax," Bloch said. "I'm not crazy, Sam. Just a passionate observer."

"That's why you came here?" Sam said. "To observe these things?"

"To observe them," Bloch said. "And to paint them." He looked at Goodwin. "Would you like to see what I've been painting?"

"Very much, Mr. Bloch," Goodwin said.

Bloch led Goodwin and Sam out of the command center and down a hall to another, smaller room. A low cot stood in one corner, with a flat pillow and thick blanket neatly folded and stacked atop it. An easel sat in the opposite corner, cradling an unfinished painting. A palette sat on a stool in front of the easel, and on a table next to both stood a jar full of water and brushes. The room was crowded with portable lamps and stacked canvases.

"Pardon my mess," Bloch said, as they crowded into the small studio. "I wasn't expecting company."

Goodwin barely heard him. She approached the closest stack of canvases, leaning against a near wall, and glanced back at him.

"May I?" she said.

Bloch nodded. "Be gentle," he said. "These represent hours and hours of work."

Goodwin knelt next to the stack and looked at the first painting. It depicted a Xenomorph's face in extreme close-up, as though viewed head-on. The head filled most of the frame, black against a bright pink background. The creature's lips were parted and its mouth was open. Between the rows of razor-sharp silver teeth, there appeared to be another, smaller mouth, with its own set of sharp little teeth.

"Do they really have an inner mouth?" she said.

"Yes they do," Bloch said. "The company calls it the inner pharyngeal jaw. Capable of being extended at incredible speed and force. I've seen it punch a hole through bone."

Goodwin flipped to the next painting. This one depicted an egg—or, she supposed, an 'Ovomorph.' Like the ones she'd seen herself, it was a color somewhere between green and brown, with a rough, leathery-looking texture. Through some trick of the paints, Bloch had actually made the egg look almost translucent. Goodwin could almost see something inside, although she had no idea what it was. Like the previous painting, this one had a bright solid color background, although this one was orange rather than pink.

"What's with the backgrounds?" she asked.

"I was trying for a pop art thing. Like Andy Warhol, you know?"

Goodwin shook her head. "I don't know much about art."

"And yet, here I am, desperate for your opinions," Bloch said with a theatrical sigh.

She continued to flip through the stack of paintings. Each depicted some part of the Xenomorph life cycle. Some were close-ups. Some were full-figure studies. Sometimes the creature had a smooth, almost translucent skull. Sometimes its skull seemed to be opaque and ridged. Sometimes the creatures were lanky and tall. Other times they seemed bent forward, muscular.

She'd almost been killed by these creatures. And yes, looking at paintings of them now inspired a visceral memory of her experience running from that horde. But the paintings also inspired another feeling: awe. There was no other word for it. She stood in awe of these creatures, the perfect approximation of what had haunted her life of nightmares.

Goodwin came to the bottom of her stack of paintings and stood. She turned to the painting on the easel. The image—incomplete, but still visible—was different from the others that Goodwin had seen so far. It depicted a different sort of Xenomorph. It was mostly depicted in silhouette, without truly defined features. Instead of the curved, elongated skull, this one had a crest that extended backwards like a fan. The creature also appeared to have an extra set of arms.

"Is this the Queen?" she asked, pointing at the painting.

"What I've seen of her, anyway," Bloch said. "Just a few quick frames of footage before the android was torn apart."

"Incredible," she said. She found herself reaching for the painting, as though her hand could pass into the frame and touch the creature inside. She paused with her hand in midair, then smiled sheepishly, and drew it back.

"She is something, isn't she?" Bloch said.

"I know how this is going to sound," she said. "But I feel like—"

"—you've been dreaming of this, or something like it, all your life?" he finished for her.

She nodded, and as she did, she became aware of Sam giving her side-eye from the corner of the studio.

"These are the things you've seen in your nightmares?" he said.

"Them—or something like them," Goodwin said.

"How is that possible?" Sam said.

The question hung in the air, unanswered.

"You're not alone in this, Captain," Bloch said.

"I read the dossier," Goodwin reminded him. "Duncan Fields. The Earthsavers cult. He had visions."

"That's not all, though," Bloch said. "Even setting prophets aside, these creatures are tied up with dreams. According to the Weyland-Yutani intelligence I stole, the Queens can communicate with humans through dreams. No one is really sure *how* it happens. Just that it does happen. It's been documented. Scientists working at company facilities where a Queen is present report dreaming of her. They feel her touching their minds. Probing at them."

"How is that possible?" Sam said.

"There are theories," Bloch said. "No proven facts."

"But this Queen," Goodwin said. "She's only been here—what? A few months? I've been having these dreams all my life."

"Duncan Fields had his visions," Bloch said. "I'm relatively certain there were no Queen Xenomorphs in the vicinity when he had them. Perhaps he—and you—were in touch with something else? Something greater even than the Queen, capable of reaching across star systems? It's all part of the great mystery. The dark secret at the heart of all things. We don't understand why it touches some of us and not others. Only that it does happen, and some of us are called to explore these mysteries."

Goodwin found herself nodding along, but Sam scoffed.

"What are you?" he said. "Some kind of religious nut?"

"I guess you might call me that, yes," Bloch said. "No doubt my actions and ideas make me sound insane. It's the price of seeing what I've seen, and being what I am.

I know how it sounds. But it's all true."

Sam studied Bloch, his arms crossed. He clearly didn't like something here. Goodwin tried to see it from his point of view, how crazy this must seem. But she couldn't bring herself to sympathize. She found herself firmly on Bloch's side.

"So let me get this straight," Sam said. "You came here, all alone, to observe these monsters. To paint them. You somehow managed to survive your arrival here and get into the shelter, and you've been safe ever since."

"That's right," Bloch said.

"So you've been here for weeks," Sam said. "You've observed the creatures. Don't you think it's time to go home?"

Bloch considered. "That's a good question. As Captain Goodwin knows, I came here without an exit strategy. All my thoughts were bent on getting here, accomplishing the work, and getting answers. But I still haven't gotten my answers, or truly finished my work."

"What answers?" Sam said.

"I want to know where these things came from," Bloch said. "They scream 'intelligent design,' don't they? The perfect killing machine. The perfect weapon. The perfect expression of the central contradiction at the heart of all life: in order to live, life must consume other life. How do these creatures connect to the things I saw as a boy? The things that killed my parents and everyone I knew? I've been here weeks, but I still can't connect the dots."

Goodwin shrugged. "It may be beyond us."

"It might," Bloch acknowledged. "But even setting aside the answers, the work still isn't done." He gestured at the unfinished painting of the Queen.

"But you said it yourself," Sam said. "You can't get any closer to the Queen. That's a dead end."

"Sound logic," Bloch said, in a reasonable tone of voice. "I suppose it's time to leave New Providence."

"How?" Goodwin said. "Our ship is wrecked. We're stranded, remember? Even if we get an SOS signal out, that frigate in orbit will intercept and kill it."

"There are still a couple of ships in the colony's hangar bay," Bloch said. "Including one or two with working FTL drives. If those don't work, there's always the *Gnosis*. I landed it without an issue when I arrived. The only problem there is that it doesn't have an FTL drive, so even if we got off-planet, we'd be facing a whole new set of problems—not least of which is the Colonial Marine frigate in orbit."

"You bribed them, right?" Goodwin said. "So, they shouldn't be a problem."

"They didn't give me any trouble going in," Bloch said. "I'm not sure if they'll let me out without a fight. But I can try my contact onboard once we're up there. See if she'd be willing to look the other way, for some extra money."

"Okay, so that gets us past the frigate," Sam said. "Assuming we have to take *Gnosis*, can it get us to a habitable system? Some place where we could contact Roman Fade and get him to send for us?"

"It might," Bloch said. "There are cryo pods aboard, so we could sleep while we make the journey. Prolong the ship's power reserves."

"Okay, so it's settled," Sam said. "We go to the hangar bay, find a ship, and get out of here."

"I'll need to pack." Bloch said. "I can't leave all this behind." He gestured at his paintings.

"Okay, about that," Goodwin said. "Fade is only paying us if we return with you alive. But your dossier made it sound like he didn't want any of your discoveries to get out. Even if we make it back, won't he destroy all your work?"

Bloch held up the disc which Goodwin had worn on a chain around her neck through most of the journey. He smiled at it, and there was genuine warmth in the smile. "Roman's message does indicate that he'll forgive and forget. But you're right. Even if I consent to go back with you to the comfort of Roman's home, there's still the matter of his ties to Weyland-Yutani. His fortune is tied to supplying them with the Ovomorphs they use in their experiments. If he goes against them, they'll find a way to silence us both. If he and I are going to survive, I'll have to resume a life of lies." He looked at Goodwin. "I'm not sure I can do that. Could you?"

Goodwin considered. Part of her felt like she'd been living a lie her entire life, and that she was only now waking up to the truth of things. She tried to imagine, having seen this truth, being asked to go back into the dark. To live as though ignorant.

"It's no kind of life at all," she said.

"And this is?" Sam said, gesturing around the studio. "Alone on a monster-infested planet, making paintings that no one will ever see? I mean, you'll run out of food eventually."

"Not for a long time," Bloch said. "I have enough to feed dozens of colonists for months. Even taking you two into account, we could be safe for a good long while."

"Assuming the creatures—the Xenomorphs—don't find their way in here," Sam said.

"I'm not asking you to stay here with me," Bloch said. "I'm only asking you not to force me to come with you."

Sam looked plaintively at Goodwin. "We don't get *paid* if he's not with us. And we lost our ship on the way in. We need him."

Goodwin couldn't disagree with anything Sam said, but she also wasn't sure she could bring herself to coerce Bloch along. She and Sam had a gun, but Bloch seemed to have the run of the colony. He could make trouble for them, if he wanted.

"I'm not comfortable forcing anyone to do anything," Goodwin said.

"I understand you're being asked to make a hard decision," Bloch said, stepping between Goodwin and Sam. "You must be tired after your journey. Beyond exhausted. Why don't you get some sleep, and we can discuss what to do once you're a bit more rested?"

16

AWAKENING

Goodwin and Sam allowed Bloch to lead them from his studio, and back into the long, narrow, low-ceilinged room lined with bunk beds.

"Not the most intimate or luxurious quarters," Bloch said. "But a warm place to sleep, at least."

Goodwin was surprised to find herself longing for one of the bunks. She hadn't realized just how tired she was until she saw a bed, but now she felt an immediate, overwhelming need for sleep.

She collapsed onto the nearest bunk with a groan. Sam sat down on a bunk next to her, stifling a yawn. She had a passing impulse to invite him onto her cot, but suppressed it. The cots were small, and anyway, she was too tired for anything but sleep. Still. It would be nice to be held. To be close again.

"We should probably take it in shifts," Sam said. "Keep a watch?"

"If you wish," Bloch said. "But you're perfectly safe."

"Mm," Goodwin said. She stretched out on the bunk, pulling its blanket over herself. It was thin and scratchy, but better than her sleeping bag. The cot felt impossibly soft. "Sam, can you take the first watch? I don't think I can keep my eyes open for another second."

If Sam replied, she didn't hear it. She was already plunging deep into the waters of unconsciousness.

For a time, she was nowhere, and nothing. For a time, she didn't dream.

The dreams came, eventually. They crept in at the edges of sleep. Sensations. Images flickering in the dark. A feeling of wetness. Textures both slimy and leathery at the same time. And a yearning, a feeling of something calling out: *Come to me. Come to me.*

She drifted through all of this vague, confusing imagery and sensation and sound, and tried to make sense of it. She was close now, she could feel it—so close to understanding everything that had ever been at the edges of her mind.

In the middle of this dark, revelatory soup, she heard a voice. This one wasn't yearning, but commanding. It was her mother, and she was saying the same thing over and over again:

Kiddo, you need to wake up, right now.

Kiddo, you need to wake up, right now.

Wake up RIGHT NOW.

She tried to open her eyes. Her eyelids felt impossibly heavy. She groaned and tried to move, but found she couldn't. Also, she was no longer warm. The blanket she'd had was no longer draped across her.

She tried again to open her eyes. Her eyelids complied this time, but slowly. She blinked a few times, trying to understand what she was seeing. She was upright, and looking straight at Sam. Her pilot appeared to be strapped to a gurney, which had been stood upright. Straps stretched across his forehead, shoulders, stomach, and thighs to hold him fast. To her left, she saw Corinth Bloch, similarly fastened to an upright gurney, but wide awake. She tried to move, and realized that she was also strapped to a gurney.

In the middle of the three gurneys, placed on the ground, was a single, unopened Ovomorph.

Goodwin tried to understand. Her thoughts came slowly, like sludge. She looked at Bloch questioningly.

"Welcome back, Captain Goodwin," Bloch said.

"What's going on?" Goodwin said. Her voice sounded thick, slurred, a perfect match for her murky mind.

"I do apologize," he said. "But I knew you would never agree to this. So, I drugged your tea."

"Why?"

"Isn't it obvious?" Bloch said. "My work here isn't done. There are... pieces of the experience of these creatures that I'm missing. The first is incubation. By the time I arrived, all the colonists were dead. I never got to see an Ovomorph hatch. I never got to see it impregnate an incubator. I didn't know what it felt like to have one of those creatures growing inside you. And there's the second piece: the Queen. The androids can't get close. But I'm willing to bet that a human being, carrying a Xenomorph embryo, will be able to approach without interference. That the Queen won't risk damage to one of her children. So whichever of us is impregnated will go to the hive with a camera and get close to her. I can finish my work."

"Three of us," Goodwin said, trying to clear the brain fog. "One egg."

In the middle of the room, the Ovomorph's flaps rippled and twitched. Goodwin bit the inside of her cheek, trying desperately to wake all the way up.

"Very astute, Captain," Bloch said. "I've been afraid. I couldn't take the leap by myself. So I've made a bargain here. I've had my androids strap all three of us to the gurneys and place the egg. The egg will decide which of us to impregnate. You, me, or Sam."

"Androids aren't... allowed to hurt humans," Goodwin said. She had to close her eyes and concentrate to get the words out.

"Usually not," Bloch said. "But since these work for Weyland-Yutani, they seem to have a backdoor in their programming when it comes to Xenomorphs. They were only too happy to strap us in here."

"Don't do this," Goodwin said.

"It's alright to be afraid, Captain," Bloch said. "Terror is part of the experience. This is what you came all this way to see. This is the dark secret at the heart of all things. These creatures. These... perfect organisms. The purest expression of life, and its ruthless consumption, that the universe has ever known. Let fate, or God, take over now, and decide whether to make you a part of her machinations."

Across from Goodwin, Sam began to stir. He mumbled something Goodwin couldn't make out, and his eyelids twitched. He was still at the edge of unconsciousness.

Stay asleep, she willed. *Don't wake up.*

But his eyelids fluttered open. She watched him go through the same cycle of realizations she'd had a moment before. He began to make noises deep in his throat as he struggled against his restraints. Incoherent sounds of panic.

"Hey," she said. "Sam, it's alright. Look at me. It's alright."

He didn't look at her. His eyes were transfixed on the egg in front of him. It was difficult to tell in the room's dim light, but she thought she could see something stirring inside the egg, barely visible through the thin, leathery fabric.

"Sam, stay calm," she said. She worried that sound would speed the process along. She was suddenly desperate to prolong all three of their lives for as long as possible—even if that time could only be measured in seconds.

Sam wasn't listening. She wasn't getting through. He opened his mouth and began to scream. Mouth and eyes wide open, a straight yell from his gut, a sound of pure terror.

Goodwin did the only thing she could think of in that moment. She screamed even louder, trying to drown her lover out.

Between them, the egg flaps twitched. The thing inside jittered and stirred. Beside her, Bloch watched it all with wide eyes, as though trying to record every detail.

Sam ran out of breath before Goodwin did. He paused to inhale, and it happened: the Ovomorph's flaps flew apart at the seams, and something exploded up and out, too fast for her eyes to follow. It made a tiny screeching sound, and she had just enough time to realize it was heading for her before her face was covered and she couldn't see anything at all.

She felt its tail wrap in a chokehold around her neck. She was vaguely aware of her jaw being forced wide open as something was jammed into her mouth and down her throat, pushing past her gag reflex's attempts to expel the intruder and clear her airway. She could hear Sam screaming, his cries muffled, and then everything was gone, and she was alone in the dark.

17

THE NEST

She dreamt in the dark, the usual blend of strange textures and presences just out of reach, but combined this time with a sense of suffocating, of being smothered beneath some immense blanket. The dreams seemed to stretch on forever, and only came to a stop when she felt a hand on her shoulder.

"Cynthia?" It was Sam. "Are you still with us?"

She groaned and shook her head a little. The sensation of being smothered was gone.

"Captain," Sam said. "You've gotta wake up."

Her eyelids twitched and she licked her lips as she came all the way awake. She seemed to be lying down, in a different room than the one she'd been in before. Sam loomed over her, his face wan with worry.

"Where am I?" she said.

"You're in the medbay, in the shelter in New

Providence," Sam said. "Do you remember what happened?"

"I was dreaming," she said, blinking through a brain fog. "Strange nightmares." She shook her head a little, trying to clear it. "I remember. I woke up… We were all tied to gurneys in front of one of those egg things. The thing inside jumped on me. Then… nothing."

Sam caught her up on what had happened in the meantime. How the crab-creature from inside the egg—what Bloch called a 'facehugger'—had stayed on her face for hours, breathing for her. How Bloch's androids had taken her to the medbay to scan her body and watch the impregnation process. How he, Sam, sat with her and waited.

"I wanted to kill Bloch. I tried to think of something to do, some way to make it right," Sam said. "Some way to get back at Bloch for what he did to you. But there's nothing. I feel like even killing him wouldn't be enough."

She touched her chest. She had one of those things—a Xenomorph—growing inside her now. She touched her face, and her neck. Her throat and jaw ached, and she felt a vague burning in her chest, like the onset of heartburn.

"I'm a dead woman," she said. Her voice came out hoarse and flat. She was surprised to find that she didn't feel much at the pronouncement. She was glad it hadn't happened to Sam. He was good. He didn't deserve any of this.

He touched her cheek. "I know what you did," he said. "You screamed loudest, to call it over to you. You saved me."

She put a hand over the one on her cheek, and was surprised to feel a tear roll down over their entwined fingers. She'd done it without thinking. Without worrying at the consequences. She realized what this meant, and she said it now:

"I love you, Sam."

He nodded and smiled. "I love you too."

"Sorry I waited until it was too late to say it," she said.

"You didn't," he said. "Bloch is offering a little bit of hope, as long as we do what he wants."

"What's that?" Goodwin said.

"What else?" Sam said. "He wants you to go into the hive and get footage of the Xenomorph Queen. He says once we have that, we can leave, and a surgeon might be able to take that thing out of your chest."

Bloch and Sam fitted Goodwin with a helmet that had a camera and flashlight strapped atop it. They gave her a motion tracker and ration bars.

"It's a long walk from here to the hive," Bloch said. "You might get hungry."

"I don't know if I'll ever be hungry again," Goodwin said, but she tucked the bars into her pockets all the same.

"Remember," Bloch said, "all you have to do is walk down and observe. I don't think the creatures will interfere with you. We'll be on the radio with you the entire time, so you won't be alone. There's nothing to it."

"You're a coward," she said. "All your talk of the great mysteries, wanting to know the dark secrets. But you won't risk your own safety."

His calm quavered for the first time. "I was strapped in, the same as you."

"So you worked up the nerve to play Russian roulette instead of putting the gun to your own head," Goodwin said. "Does it cleanse your conscience?"

Bloch's face twisted. "You want to watch how you speak to me, Captain. I am currently your only hope of survival."

Goodwin turned to Sam.

"Go in, observe, get out," he said. "Easy as pie."

"You ever actually made a pie?" she said. "It's not that easy."

"We're wasting time," Bloch said.

"I'm going to waste a little more right now," Goodwin said. "I'd like a moment alone with my pilot."

Bloch crossed his arms and did not move, the suspicion plain on his face.

"You have nothing to worry about," she said. "I'm still caught in your snare. You're still getting what you want. What choice do I have? Give me my privacy."

Bloch looked from Goodwin to Sam and back again,

as if still trying to puzzle out what she intended. But he did eventually drop his arms and leave.

Goodwin waited until she could no longer hear his footsteps before she turned to Sam. She cupped his face in her palm.

"You're a good person," she said. "You didn't deserve any of this."

Sam put a hand over hers, and pressed her palm tight against his stubbled cheek. "Stop talking like this is goodbye. It's going to be fine."

"How?" Goodwin said.

"You tell me," he said, with a wan smile. "You're the captain."

Goodwin went to the metal doors of the shelter—the only way in or out—while Sam and Bloch went back to the command center. She waited in the dark until she heard her radio crackle to life.

"Captain, can you hear me?" Bloch's voice came over the headset.

"Loud and clear," Goodwin said.

The inner door to the shelter opened. Goodwin stepped through, into the entryway. There was a single door between her and the rest of the colony now.

"I'm going to open the outer door," Bloch said. "I don't see anything outside at the moment, but the noise might draw the creatures. Be ready."

Goodwin stood up a little straighter as the outer door rumbled open, revealing a wide driveway ahead, and beyond that, the open colony gates. Through those gates, she saw the muddy field she'd run across only the day before. Further back stood the edge of the forest she'd lost her crew traversing. Goodwin's gaze darted restlessly around, looking for any movement, any sign of the creatures. She saw nothing.

"Okay," Bloch said. "Looks like the way is clear. All you have to do is follow the map I gave you. It should lead you to the power plant, where the hive is located."

"Ten-four," Goodwin said. She began walking. "Just out of curiosity—how long do I have? Before this thing in my chest is birthed."

"Realistically?" Bloch said. "I don't know. For some people, it happens in as little as a few hours. For others, it can take nearly a day. Best-case scenario, you're carrying a Queen, which takes several days to gestate."

"And how long will it take me to get to the power plant?" she said.

"Assuming all systems are still online and the way is clear?" Bloch said. "About forty-five minutes."

"Sam, how long's it been since the facehugger let go of me?" she said.

Sam's voice piped up on the headset: "About ninety minutes."

Goodwin did some quick math in her head. At her current pace, she would reach the Queen about an hour and forty-five minutes into her gestation. Assuming she spent ten to twenty minutes photographing the Queen, it would take her another forty-five minutes to get back to the shelter. Then they still had to get to the hangar bay, and find the ship, and get her into cryo.

She bit the inside of her cheek. This shit was going to be incredibly close (assuming that she could even believe Bloch's timeline).

The driveway from the emergency shelter looped away from the forest and toward the colony itself, a wide expanse of squat, ugly buildings surrounded on all sides by a metal wall. She walked up a long expanse of the dirt road, looking to either side. It was eerily quiet. The skies remained gray and cloudy, but the winds and rain were done for the time being. It was so strange not to hear birds, or other kinds of life. She would have to ask Bloch about that, when she returned. Had the Xenomorphs wiped out all forms of life they couldn't incubate? Had they eaten their way through the bird population already?

She saw no Xenomorphs on her walk. She heard no sign of them. She could have been walking through an empty film set.

According to Bloch's map, the quickest path to the power plant was to cut through one of the residential buildings, which she found and entered quickly. The doors opened for her at the press of a button. Bloch and his androids had cleared the way for her.

She entered a long, claustrophobic corridor lined with flickering fluorescent lights. She could hear her own footsteps clomping on the grated metal floor.

It was this sound that finally drew the creatures. Two emerged from doors at the end of the corridor. Then she felt something hit her shoulder. She looked around, for the source of the sensation, saw nothing—and then looked up.

A third Xenomorph hung from the ceiling, less than a meter above her head. It had an opaque, ridged skull, and broad limbs. Clear fluid dripped from its opened jaws. Some of this drool had landed on her shoulder.

"Jesus Christ," Goodwin said.

"What's it like, being so close?" Bloch asked, over the headset.

Goodwin licked dry lips and tried to think coherent thoughts. It was difficult to get past the animal urge to run, to scream, to hide. It took all of her control to remain still.

"It's like nothing I've ever experienced," she said.

"You're in the presence of the sublime," Bloch said. "Greatness beyond measure. You've been given a great gift."

The creature held perfectly still, except for its mouth. The outer jaws opened, exposing the smaller jaw inside. The inner jaw slid forward, dripping more of that slimy fluid down onto Goodwin.

"Remember, Captain," Bloch said. "If it wanted

to attack you, it would've already done so. Just keep moving."

Slowly, Goodwin looked away from the Xenomorph on the ceiling, and back toward the end of the corridor, where the other two crouched, waiting and watching. As she drew close, one of the creatures hissed softly. The sound was barely audible.

"Steady," Bloch said. "They won't hurt you."

As Bloch promised, the two creatures allowed Goodwin to pass unmolested. Their heads turned as she walked past, seeming to watch even without eyes. She came to the end of the corridor, and turned down another.

"See?" Bloch said. "Nothing to fear."

"Except the monster inside me, waiting to be born," Goodwin said.

Remembering that she was on a tight schedule, she picked up the pace. New Providence wasn't large. It had been home to less than 200 souls at its peak, so it didn't take long to get out of the residential building, which put her on the doorstep of the power plant.

Entering the plant was like stepping into another world. She knew was still technically in the colony, but the walls were no longer bare metal. Instead, they were covered in a black resin that looked grown, rather than built. Like a natural rock formation.

"I think that resin is the same stuff you just had dripped on you," Bloch said. "I think the creatures secrete it, and this is what it turns into when it hardens. They use it to build their nests. Fascinating, isn't it?"

The resin structures grew thicker and more elaborate the deeper she moved into the nest. She soon saw the reason for this, as she came to a human body, embedded in the walls. The resin needed to be thicker, to hold the weight and restrain the incubated body from moving or escaping.

The first body was a man. He looked like he had been middle-aged, with a huge bald spot atop his hanging head, and a paunch that obscured his belt. There was no egg or facehugger before him, which seemed odd. In the forest, all the marks of the incubation process were still present. But not in here.

She moved forward. She found more bodies. Sometimes there were open eggs on the ground in front of them. Sometimes not. Goodwin wondered if the hive had a system for when the creatures placed or moved the eggs. What did they do with the empty Ovomorphs and dead facehuggers? And did they just leave the dead bodies until they decayed?

She studied the faces of the dead as she passed them. She was looking for Harris and Cardona. They might be down here. If they were still alive, she might be able to save them, too. But each face Goodwin passed was a stranger. Some looked like they were sleeping. Maybe they'd been unconscious when their chestbursters had emerged. That would have been a mercy. Others appeared to have been wide awake when they died, and that was hard to look at. The dead eyes, still somehow reflecting terror. The mouths open in silent, eternal screams.

And among the bodies, she passed more and more Xenomorphs. An army of onyx bodies, hard to distinguish from the black resin behind them. They crouched and shuffled and occasionally hissed, but all moved out of Goodwin's way, parting like a jagged sea before her.

"Getting hot down here," Goodwin said, wiping sweat from her brow.

"You must be getting close now," Bloch said.

"Am I in any danger from radiation?" Goodwin asked.

"That's what you're worried about right now?" Sam said, his voice crackling in her headset.

"Fair point," she said. She walked down a set of stairs, and then another, and another. At the bottom of all these stairs, she emerged into a low, dark chamber, containing a veritable sea of Ovomorphs. They stretched away from her in all directions, as far as she could see.

Granted, she couldn't see far, or very well. There was a strange haze in the room that made the edges of the chamber difficult to make out. She wondered if the haze was steam from the power plant, or something to do with the eggs.

"Huh boy," she said.

"It's alright," Bloch said. "I don't think the eggs will trigger, either."

"You really think the eggs can tell whether something is impregnated or not?" she asked.

"I'm guessing," Bloch said. "But if you don't continue to move forward, there's not much point here. You're *achingly* close, Captain."

Goodwin stepped gingerly between the eggs. Things within moved, and the seams twitched, but they remained closed, and nothing emerged. Bloch seemed correct.

She gingerly walked among the neat rows of eggs. The steam, or fog, or whatever it was, seemed to grow denser, slowing her progress even more. She was so busy watching the eggs and her step that she nearly screamed when she looked up and realized she was about to walk right into another figure—a figure so large it was difficult to make out in its entirety.

She stepped back, hands clapped over her mouth, heart pounding, and looked up at the fanned head, the extra arms. All the things she had noticed in Bloch's painting. He had done a good job capturing her basic shape, but the painting had failed to communicate the sheer scale of the creature.

"There she is," Bloch said, his voice hushed in a tone of religious reverence.

Goodwin waited until the urge to scream had passed, then lowered her hands. "She's... huge."

She was easily twice as tall as a regular Xenomorph, and three times as broad. Her body was attached to a large, slimy ovipositor, which was currently laying a fresh egg on the ground beside her. Behind the Queen curled her massive tail, which ended in a lethal-looking spike.

The Queen seemed cramped even in this large chamber, and Goodwin wondered how she would ever leave the hive, if she needed to move.

The creature's entire head seemed to be able to retract into that crested skull. It extended forward now, and down toward Goodwin. Bloch's painting hadn't captured this, either—the massive skull. It stopped about a meter and a half from Goodwin's face, and hissed.

Goodwin's breathing grew louder. She was hyperventilating now, her breath coming in sharp, ragged gasps. She was right on the edge of panic.

"You're okay, Cynthia," Sam said. "Just breathe. Listen to my voice. You've got to get control of yourself. Cynthia? Can you hear me?"

Goodwin held her breath for a moment, trying to calm herself. "I'm alright," she said, speaking both to herself and to Sam. "I'm alright. I'm alright." She made herself look up into the Queen's face. These things didn't seem to have eyes. How did they move through the world? Was it entirely by sense of sound and smell? She wondered if Bloch knew.

"Magnificent, isn't she?" Bloch said. "The most beautiful thing I've ever seen."

Goodwin and the Queen regarded one another, the Queen's breath hot and rancid in Goodwin's face. Goodwin waited for some sign of recognition, some moment of clarity. Surely, this was the moment all the dreams had been leading toward. The Queen had called her here. She was the one saying *Come to me*. She had wanted Goodwin, and now Goodwin was here.

Then the moment passed. The Queen's head retracted into its carapace, her curiosity apparently satisfied. Goodwin felt a strange sensation—almost like she could see herself from outside her body. Like she was looking down at herself, a tiny human, a supplicant to this dark god. Seeing herself, dwarfed by the Queen, Goodwin was fully aware, for the first time in her life, just how truly small she was, in the scheme of things. A seeker after truths who'd finally found the one truth at the center of the galaxy. The Xenomorph Queen felt like a true secret. Something no one was supposed to see. An expression of pure dark malice, but also thriving life itself, pared down to its most essential elements—live, consume, reproduce.

"She's the most beautiful thing I've ever seen," Goodwin said. And she did a strange thing, then. She knelt in front of the Queen, and bowed her head, in acknowledgement of the sublime.

"The fuck?" Sam said. But she removed her headset. She didn't want her communion interrupted.

The thing in her chest shifted. She put a hand to

the space between her breasts and grimaced, but the grimace became a smile. This was all part of it. Part of the communion. The holy moment. The dark secret at the heart of all things was almost distressingly simple.

"Thank you," she said.

18

GNOSIS

Eventually, Goodwin stood again. Holy moment or not, she was skirting death with the embryo growing in her chest.

She put her headset back on, to hear Sam and Bloch shouting at her.

"I'm here," she said. "Calm down."

"What is the matter with you?" Sam said. "We thought you were dead."

"Nope," she said. "Not yet."

Bloch gave her directions. He had Goodwin stand at different angles before the Queen, holding still for several seconds. The Queen seemed curious about this. She shifted her 'gaze' following Goodwin as she moved around the chamber.

"Okay," Bloch finally said. "I think I have what I need."

Goodwin turned her back on the Queen slowly, with reluctance. It wasn't just that she was afraid to expose her back to this apex predator, although that was definitely part of it. She was keenly aware of this moment as a split in her life. Everything leading up to this moment had been an exercise in confusion, and frustration. Here was the apotheosis, the thing she had been searching for, without knowing it. And now she would turn away from it, and go on with her life (whether that life be minutes, hours, days, or years) in the shadow of this revelation.

She re-traversed the sea of Ovomorphs, and the hive. Around her, the resin structures and the bodies on the walls thinned, and then disappeared entirely as she moved back through the colony and toward the shelter.

"See?" Bloch said. "It's all gone smoothly. Everyone gets what they want."

Goodwin said nothing in response, but touched her chest again.

"Sam's going to keep you company on the comm," Bloch said. "I'll go finish packing for our departure."

A moment later, Sam's voice came on the line. "Everyone gets what they want," he said, his voice sour. "Cardona is still missing, White and Harris are dead. Compton probably ripped in half by the storm when the *Chariot* crashed. You're infected with one of those goddamn monsters. This isn't what I want. Is it what you want, Cynthia?"

Goodwin's hand remained on her chest, which ached like she had the all-time worst case of acid reflux.

"Let's try to focus on the positive," she said, swallowing hard. "We have Bloch. We'll bring him back to Fade. We'll get paid. Fade will get this thing out of me. The money will be enough to cover my debts, and put down a payment on a new ship. And we're still alive."

"For now," Sam said. Then, "Is it enough? After everything we've been through, is this enough?"

As Goodwin approached the outer door of the shelter, Sam opened it for her. The sound was distressingly loud again, and she gritted her teeth, and looked over her shoulder to see several of the creatures crouched nearby. They must have followed her from the hive, and watched her now. Could she read curiosity in their postures? She thought perhaps she could.

"Sam, get this thing closed behind me as fast as you can," she said, stepping through the still-opening doors. "We have company."

"Shit," he said.

They didn't try to get in behind her. Instead, they remained several paces away, until the outer doors were shut.

Sam met her at the inner door. He looked pale, wan.

"How are you feeling?" he said.

"Not great," she admitted. "We need to hurry."

She squeezed his shoulder, then pulled him into a

hug. He hugged her back, squeezing her hard. She felt tears prickling at the edges of her eyes, and swallowed a sob.

"Hey, hey," he said. "It's okay. You're okay. No crying, okay?" He ended the hug but pulled back and kept his hands on her shoulders. "We're on a tight schedule. You can cry in cryo. Or after we get that monster out of you."

She wiped her cheeks with the backs of her hands, grateful for him. For his kindness. His goodness. She didn't deserve him. And yet here he was.

"Right," she said, wiping her hands on her pant legs. "Let's get moving."

Sam and Goodwin packed some supplies—changes of clothes, dry rations from the cafeteria—and met Bloch near the inner door of the shelter. He had a large hand cart stacked with finished art and unused supplies. He pointed out a truck nearby, which they would use to get to the hangar bay. Together, he, Sam, and Goodwin loaded the cart of paintings into the bed of a truck.

"This is going to make a lot of noise," Goodwin said. "Might draw the creatures."

"And it's not particularly armored," Sam said, running a hand along the truck's light metal frame. "Not meant for combat."

"True," Bloch said. "But it's better than trying to take

everything on the cart by itself. And if I can't bring my art with me, I'm not leaving."

"You really think Fade is going to let you keep all this?" Goodwin said. "It's a huge liability."

"That's why you're going to hide it for me, Captain," Bloch said. "We'll find some storage location and dump all of this before we head back. That way, when I come home, I seem empty-handed. You get paid, Roman gets me back, I get him back, everyone is happy. When the heat dies down, I'll go to the storage location and get the art. Then the truth will come out."

"This is the first I'm hearing of this plan," Goodwin said. "I haven't agreed to any of this."

"No, but I think you will," Bloch said. "Regardless of how you feel about me, you understand the import of what I've uncovered here. You won't let it go to waste, will you?"

Goodwin looked down at the stack of paintings. The one on top was the unfinished silhouette of the Queen. She felt the need to touch it, could feel herself growing lost in contemplation.

Sam broke the spell with a single, short sentence: "Fuck all of this."

"No," Goodwin said. "Bloch's right. People need to know about these creatures. They need to be warned what the corps are up to. We'll do what he asks."

Sam's sour expression deepened, and she squeezed his shoulder. "This is important to me."

He nodded once, sharply. "Fine. But we should get moving."

They climbed into the truck, which started with ease, and took it to the inner door. Bloch commanded Ryder, the android, to open the doors for them. Goodwin braced herself. Last time she'd passed through these doors, there had been Xenomorphs out front. Would they still be there? And if so, could the truck outpace them?

The doors opened on an apparently empty stretch of driveway, and Goodwin breathed a sigh of relief. She eased the truck out of the shelter, and down the driveway, then turning onto the wide dirt road that ran through the colony, heading for the hangar bay, following Bloch's directions. He sat in the middle seat, between Goodwin and Sam. Sam held Goodwin's mother's revolver in his lap.

There traversed several blocks of buildings, driving slowly to keep the noise at a minimum, and hopefully avoid the creatures.

But as they reached what Goodwin would call the halfway point, Sam glanced into the rearview and groaned.

"Here they come," he said.

Goodwin looked back. She'd been glancing at the rearview every few seconds. The last time she'd looked, the coast had been clear. In the time since, a wall of onyx carapaces and metallic teeth had assembled in the street behind them, and it was moving *fast*.

Goodwin slammed her foot down on the accelerator. The truck sped up, but reluctantly, slowly, spinning mud into the air around them.

"How fast can those things move?" she asked Bloch.

"I'm not sure anyone's measured them over long distances," Bloch said. "So we'd do well to go fast—but not too fast. If one of them gets in front of us, and we hit it—even assuming the vehicle can absorb the impact? If the creature bleeds, our journey comes to an end."

"What happens when they bleed?" Sam asked.

"They have acid for blood," Bloch said.

"Of course they do," Sam said dourly.

Goodwin kept the accelerator floored, slowly gaining speed and putting a little distance between herself and the horde. It was the journey of less than a minute, but it felt like a month passed, Goodwin, Sam, and Bloch trying to look everywhere at once.

A few creatures burst from the alleys, and one even leapt from a roof. Goodwin managed to weave around each without slamming into the creature or a lamp post or building, which she considered a miracle.

At last the hangar bay came into view, at the end of the street. They quickly approached the wide hangar bay doors, which sat closed against them. Goodwin glanced at Bloch, then at the swarm of aliens in the rearview, still in hot pursuit. She wasn't sure if she should brake or not.

"Ryder," Bloch said, into a headset. "Open the bay doors please."

She tapped the brake as the bay doors began to grind upward. She gripped the steering wheel and gritted her teeth. In the rearview, the horde continued at its own high speed, growing closer as she slowed down. Goddamn these things were fast. Their sounds grew pronounced as they approached, their hard bodies clacking, high-pitched screams coming from their bodies, stained brown as they ran through the mud.

As soon as the bay door looked high enough, Goodwin floored the accelerator again, and the truck lurched out of the daylight into the darkened building.

Startled by the sudden lack of visibility, she hit the brake. The wet, muddy tires screeched and the car skidded, fishtailing.

"Fuck fuck fuck fuck," she said, but her own voice sounded far away, like it was coming from someone else. The truck entered a spin, and the open door through which they had just passed spun into and out of view again and again. Each time, Goodwin expected to see a crowd of Xenomorphs crowding through.

"Close the door, Ryder," Bloch shouted, as Goodwin regained control of the truck, and flipped on the headlights.

The hangar was a huge, mostly empty space, the biggest building she'd been in since her arrival on DSJ-1020.

The door began to rumble shut behind them. She wanted to look back but stopped herself. Either the creatures would get inside or they wouldn't. She couldn't do anything about it now. She needed to drive, and not slam this truck into one of the parked ships dotting the space.

"Where am I headed, Bloch?" she shouted.

"There," Bloch said. He pointed to the right. Goodwin turned her head to see a small silver ship, shaped like an arrowhead. It looked like something from an old science fiction novel. The loading ramp was open.

Goodwin turned and reversed the truck so that its bed was directly in front of the loading ramp. She pulled a lever next to the steering wheel to lower the gate on the bed, then turned to Bloch.

"Did any of them get in?" she said. "The Xenomorphs."

"I didn't see any," Bloch said. "I think we got the door shut in time. But they probably know their way around the vents by now."

"Guess we'll just have to risk it," Goodwin said. She put the truck in park, killed the engine, and hopped out. She headed up the ramp.

"My art," Bloch called after her.

"You and Sam start unloading," Goodwin said. "I have to get into cryo."

She entered the ship proper. It was tiny—little more

than a shuttle. Most of the interior was a single cabin, with two cryo pods, and a control console.

Goodwin frowned at the two pods. "There won't be enough for all of us."

"Bloch and I can flip a coin or draw straws," Sam said. "You don't worry about it, okay?"

He looked at her for a long moment, and in that moment, she saw all that he'd been to her, and all that he might still be.

"If we get out of this," she said. "Will you—"

"Don't," he said. "Ask me again, if you mean it, once we're out of this. Okay?"

"Right," she said. She turned away from him and started flipping switches on the command console, powering up the ship. As she waited for the cryo pods to power up, she left the cabin and started down the ramp to the hangar bay. She stopped at the top of the ramp when she saw Bloch at the bottom. He stood with his back to her, facing the back of the truck. His arms were raised, as though he were surrendering to law enforcement.

"Bloch?" she said.

He didn't answer, didn't move. She took a step toward him, then stopped as she saw now what had captured Bloch's attention. A full-grown Xenomorph crouched atop the cabin of the truck. It was poised on all fours, its spiked tail high in the air over its back. It stood as still as Bloch. It could've been an image from one of his paintings. Only this was too real. This wasn't some academic argument or artistic expression. This was death, only a few meters away, ready to pounce.

Goodwin's mind raced, as she tried to figure out what to do. She glanced around the hangar bay. It was still dark out here, but her eyes had adjusted now, and she realized that the Xenomorph atop the truck was not the only one. There were several other Xenomorphs lurking in the shadows. Not a full horde, but several full-sized adults. All were poised and still, looking almost like one of Bloch's sculptures.

She heard Sam clomping toward her, and shouted, without looking away from Bloch.

"Sam, stay where you are!"

The clomping sounds stopped abruptly.

"What's going on?" Sam said, his voice slightly muffled from inside the ship.

"Bit of a situation out here. No need to panic. Bloch," she said. "Stay where you are, okay?"

Bloch wasn't listening. Instead, he extended his right arm up and toward the creature. It hissed and its mouth opened, revealing the slobbering inner jaw. It shifted ever so slightly, tensing. It was preparing to leap.

"Bloch, don't," Goodwin said. Her voice sounded far away, like a radio signal coming from a different room. "Don't."

She took another step down the ramp. The Xenomorphs in the shadows shifted. Bloch kept his raised arm toward the creature atop the truck.

The Xenomorph launched itself off the top of the truck just as Goodwin threw herself down the ramp. She hit Bloch's back and they hit the floor as the Xenomorph slammed into the ramp just above their heads.

Still on the ground, Goodwin scrambled to cover Bloch with her own body, then turned to face the creature. It lunged toward her, and she cringed back, one arm up above her face, as if that would protect her.

There came a horrible screech, almost deafening in her left ear. She opened her eyes. The Xenomorph was crouched on the ramp, between her and Sam. Its jaws were centimeters from her face. It was frustrated, but not attacking. Pain bloomed in her chest, like fire rushing up her throat. She put a hand to her neck and tried to swallow. It was difficult.

How long do I have? She wondered. *Minutes? If I'm lucky?*

"That was exceedingly foolish, Captain," Bloch said from beneath her. "Why did you save me?"

"I need you to get this thing out of me," she growled. "And get me fucking paid."

Keeping her eyes on the monster, she stood, keeping her body between him and the creature. She spread her arms wide, trying to corral Bloch behind her. "Don't you want to live?" she said.

"Not if God wants this for me instead," Bloch said.

She shuffled about, alongside the ramp. The Xenomorph turned to keep her in its sights (if it *had* sights).

She started to step onto the ramp, but grunted, leaning forward with her hand to her chest. Fuck, that hurt.

On her second try, she got onto the ramp. "Climb up behind me," she told Bloch. She glanced away from the Xenomorph to shove him. He clambered up behind her. Together, they backed up the ramp, followed step for step by the Xenomorph. Its footsteps were heavy thuds against the metal. Goodwin's chest ached worse than any pain she'd ever felt in her life.

Not yet, she begged the parasite inside her. *Please, just a few more minutes.*

Because she'd learned something, in the presence of the Queen. She had discovered the secret at the heart of all things, what Bloch had been looking for all his life and somehow missed. The point of life was no great mystery. The point of life was to live, as long as possible, or to give up your own life to ensure that others—people or creatures you cared about—could continue living.

It was distressingly simple, and Bloch seemed all the more fool for never realizing it. Yes, the universe was a dark place, sometimes an evil place, but it was also full of good things. Like Compton, her selfless android. And Cardona, who'd been like a little sister to Goodwin. And White, with his comforting irascibility. And Harris, who'd cared for her through the loss of her mother. And her mother, Alice Goodwin—yeah, the old woman had been tough, and a little cold, and had died too young, but she'd taken good care of Cynthia, had given her a better life than a lot of people in this galaxy got. And Sam. And Sam. Who loved her. Whom she loved. Who she wanted to make a real life with.

So no. Not yet.

She tried to back up another step up the ramp, but bumped into Bloch. He wasn't moving.

"We can't leave!" Bloch said. "My art!"

Goodwin looked back over her shoulder, at Bloch, who stood directly behind her, and Sam, just visible inside *Gnosis*. Both had panic on their faces. She looked back at the truck bed, full of canvases. She looked at the Xenomorph between her and the truck. She spared a glance at the others, lurking on the periphery.

Her mind raced, trying to form a plan where everyone got what they wanted. Maybe she could send Bloch aboard, and then retrieve the art herself? But no—even if she got Sam and Bloch safely inside, what would keep the creatures from just going into the ship while she was ferrying paintings back and forth?

Nothing, her mind supplied. *Nothing would keep them out. Sam and Bloch would die.*

She turned back to Bloch. "I'm sorry," she said. "We have to leave it all behind."

"What?" Bloch said, disbelieving. Then: "No. No." Shaking his head vehemently.

"Look at it like this," Goodwin said. "They won't destroy the work. It will be safe here. If you want to come back someday, after I've been paid? That's your business. But we are *leaving* right now."

"Captain, I'm not leaving without my work," Bloch said.

Goodwin gasped and clutched at her chest, as she was wracked by pain. How long did she have now? Minutes? Seconds?

"They will kill you," she said. "Do you understand? If you try to get those paintings, you'll die."

"Get out of my way," Bloch said.

"No!" Sam said. "We need him! Without him, we don't get paid!"

Goodwin doubled over, clutching her chest. She couldn't act, couldn't *think*. She felt Bloch shuffle past her, so that he now stood between her and the Xenomorph on the ramp.

Goodwin fell back on her ass and cried out. Fuck, this hurt so bad. She grimaced and flattened her hand on her chest.

Then the pain passed. As quickly as it came, it was gone again. She could breathe. She could think. She looked up, and saw Bloch standing before the Xenomorph, his arms spread apart as though in supplication.

"Bloch," she said. "Don't."

The Xenomorph regarded Bloch for a moment, seeming to think. It could've been one of Bloch's paintings—the religious supplicant before the otherworldly creature. An encounter with the true face of God.

Then the creature's right arm struck out, and its claws raked across Bloch's face, jerking his head to one side. His eyes were glazed, shocked, as though he couldn't quite believe this was actually happening to him.

Bloch's body rocked backward, as if he were going to fall from the force of the blow, but the creature grabbed him by the shoulders, arresting his descent. It yanked him forward until their faces were almost pressed together.

"Mother," Bloch murmured.

There was a great crunching sound, as the Xenomorph's inner jaw punched through the back of Bloch's skull. Blood and brain sprayed into the air in great gobs, splattering the ramp and docking bay floor.

Goodwin startled as something grabbed her beneath her armpits and yanked her to her feet. She nearly screamed, but a glance back revealed Sam as the grabber. She let him drag her into the ship, and slap the door control as soon as her feet were over the threshold.

As the door slid shut, Goodwin got a final glimpse of Bloch, cradled in the Xenomorph's arms as it devoured him. Its face was covered with his blood. Behind them stood the truck bed full of paintings.

"We just lost everything," Goodwin said, looking up at Sam.

"Not everything," Sam said. "Not yet." He was already running away from her and to the ship's console. It was fully powered up. She stood and staggered up behind him as he fired the thrusters and *Gnosis* lifted off the hangar floor. As they ascended, a *thump* sounded. A Xenomorph landed on the ship's front viewport, splayed out like a bug on a windshield.

"The docking bay doors are still shut," Goodwin said. "And our connection to Ryder was in Bloch's headset."

"Only way out is through," Sam said. He punched the throttle up and the ship rocked forward.

Goodwin had just enough time to grab a seat and strap in as the *Gnosis* sped toward the closed bay doors in front of them. She closed her eyes and gripped the armrests of her chair. She'd know in the next second or two whether this was the last mistake of her life.

The ship rattled around her and there was a great sound of grinding metal. Goodwin opened her eyes. She wasn't dead. The ship still seemed to be airborne. She could see the sky of DSJ-1020 through the viewport—sort of. The Xenomorph had managed to hang on through the crash, and clung to the viewport frame.

"We've gotta shake that thing!" she said.

"Hang on tight," Sam said. "You're not going to enjoy this."

He switched the ship to manual control, grabbed the yoke, and put the *Gnosis* through a barrel roll. Goodwin's insides lurched and she gritted her teeth against the g-force as the world spun around her. Everything went gray for a moment.

When the world faded back in, the alien was gone from the viewport. Sam had shaken it free.

The ship rose up, up, up through the storm clouds, rattling all the way. Warnings chirped and bleeped at Sam from the control console.

"What's wrong?" she said.

"Just ion interference," Sam said. "Hang on."

Gradually, the shaking stopped. The storm thinned and faded from view, revealing a sea of stars above—and, against the sun, the silhouette of the Colonial Marines frigate.

"The *Fratto*," Goodwin said.

"They're hailing us," Sam said.

"Open the comm channel," Goodwin said.

"Shouldn't we get you on ice?" Sam said. "Like right now?"

"Won't do us any good if they blast us out of the sky right now," Goodwin said.

Sam bobbed his head to show he'd heard and agreed, then opened the comm.

"*Gnosis*," came a voice on the channel. "This is the USS *Fratto*. You are attempting to leave a quarantined world. Please turn back at once, or we will open fire."

"Lieutenant Diaz, please," she said.

They went through the ritual. Diaz came on the line. Goodwin gave her the password. There was a long moment of silence, when Goodwin thought maybe it wasn't going to work out—that the password was only good for entering DSJ-1020, not allowing craft off a quarantined world. She could almost hear Diaz thinking it over on her end.

They really shouldn't let us out, Goodwin thought. *I'm carrying an alien parasite.*

"Move along," Diaz finally said. "But this is the last time, okay? No more."

"Understood," Goodwin said, closing the channel.

Sam set a course for the nearest inhabited system. It was a months-long journey without FTL, but they had the fuel, and the cryo chambers. They'd make it. The plan was to get there, and contact Roman Fade, tell him what happened. See if he was interested in getting the monster out of Goodwin's chest. Maybe even paying them for the specimen. And if that failed, maybe he could direct them to a doctor who could get the creature out without killing Goodwin.

As Goodwin undressed for cryo, she thought about Bloch's paintings. Probably his greatest work. It survived, but was trapped down there, on DSJ-1020. Lieutenant Diaz had made it clear no one was getting past the *Fratto* again. She had no proof of what she'd seen, the creatures she'd encountered, or even the great work Bloch had made at the end of his life. She'd lost her ship, and most of her crew. This adventure had cost her almost everything.

But she'd survived the experience. And she still had Sam. She looked up at him as she settled into the tube. She had no idea how long she would remain in cryo. He would likely keep her frozen until he could guarantee her safety.

"Will you marry me?" she asked him. "I mean it. I don't want you running off with someone else while I'm playing popsicle."

He licked his lips and blinked glassy eyes as he leaned down and kissed her on her forehead, both cheeks, and then her lips. "I'll give it some serious consideration. Rest now, okay? I'll take care of you until it's time to wake up."

"Okay," she said.

The cryo took her down into unconsciousness, and there in the cold dark she dreamt. But for the first time in her life, the dreams were sweet.

ACKNOWLEDGMENTS

When I was in middle school in the mid-1990s, I found a copy of A*liens vs. Predator: Prey* (by Steve and Stephani Perry) in my local bookshop, and the top of my head blew off. There were novels set in the worlds of *Alien* and *Predator*?

A two-pronged obsession was born that day: 1) to devour every piece of *Alien* media I could, and 2) to contribute a story of my own to this vast and mysterious cosmos.

This novel is me finally making good on the second part of that obsession, and there are a few people who deserve specific thanks for this novel: George Sandison, the editor of the UK versions of my original work, who put me in touch with the licensed team at Titan; Steve Saffel, now retired, who started the conversation about me writing an *Alien* novel; Daquan Cadogan, who picked up the conversation and pitched my ideas to Disney, securing me this job; Fenton Coulthurst, who edited this novel and sharpened it into something clearer and (hopefully) more fun than my original draft; and of course, my agent, Kent D. Wolf, who helped keep the ball in the air during the long series of conversations and false starts that led to the book you now hold.

More general thanks: the teams at Titan and Fox, who helped bring this book into being and put it into readers hand; all the other creators in the Alien franchise, past and present, who make films, comic books, novels, and games that continue to entertain, terrify and delight; and most of all, to Dan O'Bannon, who had an amazing idea and gave us the nightmare that just keeps giving.

It's been an honor to add my small embellishment to the tapestry, and I look forward to seeing what comes next.

ABOUT THE AUTHOR

Shaun Hamill received his MFA from the Iowa Writers' Workshop. He is the author of *A Cosmology of Monsters*, *The Dissonance*, *Alien: Perfect Organisms*, and the forthcoming *Solomon Kane: Suffer the Witch*. He is the host of *The 616 Files: An Unofficial History of the Marvel Comics Universe* and a frequent cohost on *The Dungeons & Dragons Lorecast*. He lives, works, writes, and games in North Texas.

For more fantastic fiction, author events,
exclusive excerpts, competitions, limited editions and more

VISIT OUR WEBSITE
titanbooks.com

LIKE US ON FACEBOOK
facebook.com/titanbooks

FOLLOW US ON TWITTER AND INSTAGRAM
@TitanBooks

EMAIL US
readerfeedback@titanemail.com